THE MARILYN TAPES

THE
MARILYN
TAPES

E. J. Gorman

A TOM DOHERTY ASSOCIATES BOOK

NEW YORK

THE MARILYN TAPES

This book is printed on acid-free paper.

A Forge Book
Published by Tom Doherty Associates, Inc.
175 Fifth Avenue
New York, N.Y. 10010

Design by Brian Mulligan

Library of Congress Cataloging-in-Publication Data

Gorman, Edward.
    The Marilyn tapes / E.J. Gorman.
        p.   cm.
    "A Tom Doherty Associates book."
    ISBN 0-312-85646-6
    1. Monroe, Marilyn, 1926–1962—Death and burial—Fiction.
    2. Hoover, J. Edgar (John Edgar), 1895–1972—Fiction.   I. Title.
    PS3557.O759M37   1995
    813'.54—dc20

                                                                94-38163
                                                                CIP

First edition: January 1995

Printed in the United States of America

0   9   8   7   6   5   4   3   2   1

A NOTE TO THE READER

This is a work of fiction. All of the characters and events portrayed in this novel are either products of the author's imagination or are used fictitiously.

To my friend and editor Robert Gleason—
for his faith, ingenuity and patience.

I couldn't have written this novel
without the considerable help of
Larry Segriff.

DRAMATIS PERSONAE

SARA DRURY, editor at *Insight*

DAVID LENIHAN, agent for the president

MICHAEL DRURY, estranged husband of Sara

JEFF WILLIAMS, employee at *Insight*

MELANIE BAINES, unofficial agent for the FBI

FRANK BELLAMY, associate publisher and partner at *Insight*

ERICA DANE, dancer and Frank Bellamy's mistress

DEL MAYHEW, studio head, Millennium Pictures

LAURA DRURY, daughter of Sara and Michael

SALVITORE ROSSETTI, the Mob's number-two man on the West Coast

TULLY, a private investigator

VANESSA, Tully's wife

MRS. HELEN GREGORY, Laura's babysitter

HISTORICAL FIGURES

JOE KENNEDY, patriarch of the Kennedy clan

JOHN F. KENNEDY, president of the United States

ROBERT KENNEDY, attorney general of the United States

J. EDGAR HOOVER, director of the FBI

CLYDE TOLSON, number-two man at the FBI

LOUELLA PARSONS, newspaper gossip columnist

Excuse the mess. Not the sort of room you expect to see a goddess living in, is it?

And yet, over the past four or five years, she's taken to her bedroom as if it were the last bastion of safety in the world.

Look at her now.

Hard to believe that this very pale, fleshy, middle-aged woman had just a few years ago been the leading box-office draw in the world. And had been called by no less a connoisseur than Pablo Picasso, "The most erotic girl of her generation."

If you listen closely, you can hear it all in the silence of this room: the shouts, the applause, the whistles, the excited laughter of the GIs when she toured with the USO during the Korean War . . . the scream-ing semi-hysterical fans when The Seven Year Itch *opened in New York . . . and the nervous whispers of the locals when she would appear with Clark Gable on the Nevada set of* The Misfits.

All the tumult; all the fuss; all the splendor . . . echoing here in the stillness of this room as the goddess lies unmoving on her mussed and sweaty bed, a small empty bottle that once contained twenty-five Nembutal tablets near her dangling, unmoving hand . . .

Out by her pool, if you wanted to go check right now, you would find two small, stuffed animals, symbolic of the sentimental little girl Marilyn always was . . . And in her diary, no more than six feet from the bed where she lies, you would find all sorts of references to men she felt had betrayed her. Though she was not unintelligent, and though

11

she was anything but the "simple" star of the tabloid press, she did yearn after one unreachable goal: to be the darling of myth, and yet be a quite normal wife and mother as well.

But all this is moot now, in the silence of this room, for a life has ended, all the different Marilyns from down all the years converging here on this bed . . . sweet and cruel, innocent and cunning, joyous and melancholy, hopeful and despairing . . .

Listen now a final time; a song is faintly playing, "Dancing in the Dark," a song she loved all her life, "my princess song," as she always called it, imagining herself a cool and poised Grace Kelly (a woman she greatly envied) instead of the hardscrabble working-class girl who never felt quite pretty, who never felt quite loved.

But the story does not end here tonight in this messy Hollywood bedroom . . .

For just as there were jackals in Marilyn's life, so too there will be jackals after Marilyn's death.

"Old Joe Kennedy was the most despicable sonofabitch I ever met."

—*Franklin Delano Roosevelt*

TRAGIC STAR DIES OF APPARENT DRUG ALCOHOL OVERDOSE

Early in the morning of August 5, police were summoned to Marilyn Monroe's Hollywood home.

Police found the star in bed. They estimated that she had been dead for several hours.

HOOVER J. Edgar Hoover said to his friend and associate Clyde Tolson, "I'll be upstairs in the den for a while." He smiled. "Just some last minute catching up."

The smile was in reference to Clyde's remark at dinner that Edgar was working too hard these days.

"I worry about you, Edgar," Clyde said from the comfort of the leather armchair in the living room. A handsome man with wavy hair combed straight back in the fashion of a forties movie star, Tolson, unlike Hoover, was an avid reader. Tonight he was finishing a best-selling adventure novel by Hank Searls.

"Well, I worry about you too," Hoover said. "All that reading you do is liable to make you blind." He chuckled.

Despite their friendship of several decades, there was a curious formality between the men. Sometimes it almost seemed as if they were strangers, which was odd indeed for two people who spent virtually every day and most evenings together. Clyde had an apartment, but he spent much more time at the house on Thirtieth Place NW, which was a retreat of sorts for both of them. Usually, anyway. For the past few evenings, Clyde had sensed something wrong with Edgar.

Clyde sounded nervous when he spoke now, as if afraid he might be prying. "Are you all right, Edgar? The past few days—well, you've seemed kind of distant."

Hoover smiled. "You and those darned magazines you read, Clyde. You psychoanalyze everybody."

Hoover glanced about the house, the large Georgian-style home

17

having recently been redecorated. The living room walls were wiped wood to blend with the Adam mantel and the mixture of contemporary sofas and a few Oriental *objets d'art*. Hoover took abiding pride in his home.

Clyde smiled back. "There's no need to psychoanalyze you. I already know you're crazy."

The director laughed and went upstairs, passing a portrait of himself of the first floor landing, and then along a hallway that was a photo gallery of the rich and famous and powerful standing next to Mr. Hoover. Only the president, and perhaps the Pope, could boast such a gallery of friends and admirers. The hallway floor was covered with Oriental rugs. Hoover had a passion for them. Like most of the house, this wing had the feel of a museum that had been entombed in well-polished mahogany.

He closed the den door and went directly to the phone. It was a "safe" phone. Hoover had it checked for bugs every seven days.

As he lifted the receiver, he wondered if dear trusted Clyde had figured out what indeed had made Hoover so distant lately, so fixated to the exclusion of everything else.

If he could just find them, possess them . . . he'd show those snickering bastards just who was in control here. No more implications about him being past his prime; no more smirks about his friendship with Clyde. There had been a time when he'd enjoyed visiting the White House—back in the days when presidents had cooperated with him—but with the new president things were different. All the president's friends treated Hoover either coldly or with smug superiority.

But that would change, and damned soon.

As he was opening the center drawer in the desk, his eyes fell on the framed photograph of his beloved mother Annie, who had been taken from him in 1934. Not long before her death, a second-rate gossip columnist for one of the New York newspapers had hinted of an unnatural attachment between Hoover and his mother.

What fierce G-man calls his Mommy every single night and squires her around like a shiny new beau to the best restaurants and theaters? If we didn't know better, we'd say they were lovebirds.

Well, the man's laugh had been short-lived. Six days after his column appeared, he was accused by a fourteen-year-old girl of statutory rape. Ultimately the charges were dropped, but not before more than one hundred newspapers around the country had dropped the reporter's column.

As for the girl, the press didn't report that the charges against her were also dropped. A friend of the director had discreetly hired her to file the complaint against the columnist, in return for which her criminal record as a prostitute would be expunged from the files of the local police.

Hoover stared at his mother again and recalled, as if she were here in the room with him, the sweet soft scent of her cologne, the deep, exciting blue of her eyes. . . .

He put the photograph back, his eyes falling on a few of the other items in the drawer. The lucky rabbit's foot he'd had since he was a boy, to which he ascribed mystical powers; the stack of UFO paperbacks, a few of which had confirmed his suspicions that the Russians had made a secret deal with alien beings; and an autographed glossy of Olympic diving star and now movie star Buster Crabbe in skimpy bathing trunks.

"To Mr. Hoover, The Most Respected Man in America, Yours Sincerely, Buster."

From the middle drawer, he took out a sheet of paper with a telephone number written on it in pencil, and dialed.

On the other end, in Los Angeles, there were six rings before somebody answered.

"Hello?" Melanie said.

"It's me," Hoover said.

"I was hoping it would be. Things are going very well."

Hoover did not hide his excitement. "You mean you've got them?"

"Not yet. But pretty soon now. There's a private investigator named Tully. He doesn't know it yet, but he's going to give them to me."

"I was hoping you'd be a little further along."

"It won't be long. You'll see."

Sometimes he wondered if it was wise to work with a woman at all, even a smart, ruthless, beautiful one like Melanie. Of course, she had certainly served him well in the past.

"I think we're looking at twenty-four hours for this thing to be wrapped up," Melanie said.

"I didn't mean to sound cross, Melanie. You're doing a very good job. Keep at it." He paused. "It's just that, well, you know how important this is. The whole government could—"

"I know how important it is. It's all I think about, believe me. So why don't you go relax?"

"I think I'll do that. I'll check in with you tomorrow."

"Night."

"Good-night, Melanie."

He sat back in his chair and closed his eyes for a time. Sometimes he felt so old, so weary. He had to constantly defend himself against a variety of enemies—and sometimes one tired of the defense.

He remained in this glum revery for a few minutes. Then he remembered the photographs in the bottom left drawer of the desk.

The movie star Rock Hudson and his latest young man. Hoover had assigned an agent in the Los Angeles branch to do nothing but follow Hudson around and snap secret photos of his various trysts. A new batch had come in today.

Hoover spent the next twenty minutes going over each of the ten black-and-white shots carefully. Hudson was truly insatiable.

Then he went downstairs to say good-night to Clyde.

LOUELLA At the same time J. Edgar Hoover was saying good-bye to his friend Clyde, the world-famous Holly-wood gossip columnist Louella Parsons was just stepping from the limousine that was returning her from Joan Crawford's birthday party. Louella and Joan had been friends for many years, ever since Louella had obtained some pornographic photographs of the young Crawford. Louella had shown them to Joan.

"If you promise me the exclusive on anything that happens to you in the future, I'll burn these photos."

The Great Crawford agreed. Louella burned the photos.

But friendship aside, Louella hadn't felt like staying late tonight. Her bladder problems—she'd already seen three specialists—forced her to wear rubber panties when she went out these days, and of course by now virtually everyone in Hollywood knew about her blad-der, gossip being the coin of the realm in executive suites and fashion-able restaurants. So they snickered at her behind her back; she'd finally given them a weapon—albeit unwillingly—with which they could club her. Louella and her rubber panties.

At this point in her life, Louella Parsons, the gossip columnist, was not unlike Norma Desmond, the faded silent screen star portrayed in *Sunset Boulevard*. At the height of her prominence, Parsons' column had appeared in more than one thousand newspapers, not to mention the radio or the TV show.

But William Randolph Hearst, her benefactor and the man com-monly believed to be the model for *Citizen Kane*, had died not long ago, and Hearst's replacement, Gibbons, had started shaking things up by offering a variety of new columns. It was his stated belief that, with the rise and fall of magazines such as *Confidential*, gossip was becoming a cheap commodity.

Gone were the radio show, the TV show. Miss Parsons, as she liked to be called, was down to fewer than four hundred papers.

Gibbons said, "To be blunt, Miss Parsons, you haven't had a scoop that amounted to anything in ten years."

At this point, most industry people had pretty much written Louella off. Oh, there were award ceremonies and retrospective honors, and when she went to a nightclub (which was frequently, Louella being notorious for her love of night life), the singer, whether it was Patti Page or Frank Sinatra or Johnny Mathis, always saw to it that Louella had a ringside table, and always dedicated at least one song to her in the course of the evening.

But people weren't afraid of her anymore. And that was what Louella mourned most of all.

In the decades of the thirties and forties and the early fifties, Louella had enjoyed a power surpassed only by Walter Winchell. If Louella went after you in her column, you or your project was very likely dead. For this reason, most stars and all studios had devised elaborate methods of appeasing Louella—to the point that one studio paid $75,000 for screen rights to Louella's one and only (and very bad) romance novel.

The money was there and the mansion and the chauffeur were also there and so were all the "A"-list party invitations—but the power to scare the living shit out of people seemed gone forever.

And so Miss Parsons had her Norma Desmond days, times when she came downstairs angry and bitter at her loss of eminence, and God forbid that your name got drawn in her little lottery—because she would not only flay the hell out of you, she would do it with great relish.

Now, she fled to the privacy of her expensive new home, one of those sweeping, Moorish-like houses so fashionable in Los Angeles these days, pool, tennis court and greenhouse tucked discreetly behind palm trees, while inside the vast white rooms were filled with English furnishings and expensive art.

She needed some rest anyway. She had recently started writing a book about Marilyn Monroe called *American Goddess*, after Marilyn had made some tapes about her background for Louella's exclusive use.

Louella stood in her kitchen, pouring a 7UP over six ice cubes and then tapping two aspirin into her palm. She felt a head cold coming on.

The phone rang. The maid was not always good about picking up.

Rather than track down the maid and yell at her, Louella decided to pick up. A few moments later, she was very glad she did.

A suave man's voice said, "This is Salvitore Rossetti."

Louella thought what she always thought about him. Why would a man so cultured and polished want to be a mobster? He was the number-two man in the entire West Coast organization. Louella had dined with him many times and found him "enchanting," as she'd mentioned once in her column.

"I may have something for you you're going to like very much," Rossetti said.

"Oh?"

And then he told her.

At first, she thought he might be playing with her. He could be a terrible tease. But after a few more words, she realized he was quite serious.

"And you think you can get them?"

"Yes. Get them and give them to you, Louella."

"I'm very, very flattered."

"Let's face it, Louella. I owe you."

"Any idea about how much time it will take?"

"Not long. That's why I called tonight. To give you a little warning."

She was—quite uncharacteristically—speechless.

This wasn't gossip column piffle. This story could bring down a government.

"I'll call you soon," Rossetti said. And then hung up.

Louella stood there, stunned, the receiver still in her hand, a dial tone *burr*ing belligerently.

With one phone call, her life had changed.

If Rossetti could deliver what he had promised. . . .

She found a quart of good bourbon and mixed a little in with her 7UP.

She was doing a little celebrating. In advance.

JOE KENNEDY

Several of the staff had noted that old Joe Kennedy, the man who had bought the White House for his second-born son, was even more formidable following his stroke.

He would slump in his wheelchair and you would think he was dozing.

But he wasn't.

He'd sense you—the way a bat senses things—and then he'd start shouting at you in a frightening rush of incoherent syllables that were all he could muster after his stroke.

But the rage was coherent.

The rage was very coherent, sending his nurses running from him in tears.

He had a lot to be angry about these days, Joe Kennedy thought, as he sat at the window staring out at the Atlantic Ocean. A writing tablet lay in his lap. With a fountain pen, he had written some lines on the linen paper.

Palm fronds clacked eerily in the moonlit night, around a home many of the locals found eerie enough already—an old-world hacienda with white walls and red roof-tiles, fronted by an enormous hedge. But this was what old Joe wanted—to say to the world, I've got my fortune, shanty Irish sonofabitch that I am, and fuck you if you don't like it.

And one local wag, a relative of the DuPonte family, had been shrewd enough to say just that: "Darling, you're looking at the phrase 'fuck you' put into architecture." Imposing. Impregnable. Secretive. That was the compound, and that was the way old Joe liked it.

The fronds rattled again, bringing him back to his previous thoughts.

He hadn't planned on dying in Florida—too many rednecks for his taste—but he could no longer face the winters in Hyannisport.

Now, as he looked at the moonlight on the water, he felt a familiar tremor move through him, knot his stomach, clench his bowels, freeze his spine.

Jack and Bobby were going to blow it.

Three weeks before the Inauguration, Joe Kennedy had invited a friend of his sons' to the compound and had plied him first with liquor and then with promises of cash.

I want to know what goes on in that fucking place, Joe had grunted. You understand me?

The nice young man had nodded. He seemed nervous but interested. He didn't come from particularly good stock, Joe Kennedy noted, so of course the money interested him immediately.

But he played it coy, the little prick, self-righteously turning down three offers before the money got green enough.

And that was how Joe Kennedy learned that both of his sons, within the past six months, had spent time with Marilyn Monroe.

Some fucking dope-fiend Hollywood chippie.

Were those two boys of his out of their minds?

Even worse than that, his spy had told him that Bobby seemed to have serious feelings toward Marilyn.

Joe Kennedy shook his head.

Bobby had always been the smallest of the boys and the most vulnerable. While Jack just screwed Marilyn for a couple of months and then forgot all about her, Bobby had fallen in love. His spy told him that during the month before Marilyn's death, Bobby flew to L.A. five times just to see her.

Futhermore, the word was now out on Bobby's indiscretions.

Not that Joe was particularly worried about him. Edgar had kept a file on his boys for over fifteen years now. Occasionally he'd shown it to Joe. After the Inauguration, he'd presented Joe with photos of the whores Jack had banged during the 1960 Democratic convention.

That episode had been upsetting but still Edgar's files did not bother Joe in and of themselves. He accepted them as a fact of life. Hoover had a file on everyone, including Joe himself. The only people Edgar had consistently laid off of were members of the Mob, the reason for which Joe was well aware of.

Back in '38, two Mob-sponsored agents infiltrated the Bureau all the way to the top. One night Hoover received a call from a Mob boss who told him about the infiltration. The boss said that unless Hoover laid off the Mob, they would make the infiltration public and simultaneously ruin his personal reputation. So Hoover went easy on the Mob until the 1950s when—in order to get back at them—he aggressively wiretapped certain key Mob players.

Still, the boys had to quit playing around. They had to.

Well, this short note he was sending them would shake them up.

Nobody scared them the way their old man did. The same old man who'd killed any mobster who tried to take over his Prohibition whiskey business; who'd framed legitimate business rivals on trumped-up criminal charges and railroaded them into prison; who'd developed a profound respect and personal fondness for Adolf Hitler. This old man would have no trouble disciplining two snot-nosed kids.

If he'd only had someone around when he was their age to keep him in line and watch his back.

If the Jews in FDR's administration hadn't stopped him, he would have formed an alliance with Hitler, become the next president, and ruled half the world.

But the Jews, as always, had whispered and pushed and undermined. . . .

He tried not to think of how he'd been destroyed by a 1939 newspaper interview in which he expressed some admiration for Hitler.

The Jews had never forgiven him.

They had driven him out of Washington and into a kind of exile. He was rarely seen with his sons because he knew the press would spend most of its time writing not about the boys but about what an anti-Semite their old man was.

FDR, Hitler, his longtime mistress Gloria Swanson . . . some nights when he sat before this silent starry window he heard their voices, saw their faces. He even saw the face and heard the voice of his disturbed daughter Rose . . . all the shit he'd had to endure for lobotomizing her.

His doctor friend at the clinic where they took Rose told him about lobotomies. "You won't have any more problems with her. I promise you." Joe hadn't consulted anybody else in the family. He simply went ahead and did it. He tried not to think of a knife being pushed down into the front section of her brain. His family would always hate him just a little bit for that.

He looked down at his writing tablet.

The boys would not be happy when they saw this note:

I know about the phone call from that publisher. This could bring down your administration. Show some balls, boy, and do what you have to do.

After a time, Joe Kennedy slumped in his chair again and began to snore softly.

But then he jerked awake.

He had had a dream where young Rose was on an operating table and a maniac in a white surgeon's outfit was holding a knife directly over her forehead.

The surgeon was old Joe Kennedy himself.

Then there were just the night sounds, surf and wind and lonely distant dogs.

And somewhere out there—beyond the sky, in some other dimension perhaps—there was death, its dark arms spreading wide to envelop him.

Why couldn't he be eleven years old again with the golden sunlight on the blue bay of Boston . . . and the cute little Irish-Catholic girls watching him as he fished off the banks. . . .

We shouldn't have to die.

It made no sense.

It was so cruel.

Sunlight and laughter and innocence all lost to darkness . . . to utter extinction.

MELANIE Surveillance was boring. The worst part of her whole job. Surveillance was even more boring than all those "dates" her mother had fixed her up with back in Texas.

Two hours after she talked to Edgar, she was back at it.

She was sitting in an alley in North Hollywood looking up at a second-floor apartment window. There was light in the window, but no people. Off and on for a couple of days, she had been following a man named Tully—and a few other people.

She spent a few moments looking at herself in the moonlit rearview mirror. She tried not to dote on her fiery red hair and her beautiful looks. As her mother always said, God gave her those looks. Melanie hadn't earned them and therefore shouldn't be congratulated for having them. Of course, her mother was always the first to point out how gorgeous her daughter was.

Melanie put on fresh lipstick and smoothed the jacket of her fashionable aqua-colored summer suit.

The cop car came five minutes later.

It came from the opposite end of the alley, crawling past the orderly garages and neat garbage cans.

Melanie knew that, being LAPD, they'd have questions for her. *What're you doing out here, miss? It's after ten o'clock. May I see your license?*

She sure didn't want to answer any questions.

30

She moved automatically, wheeling the brand-new Pontiac Bonneville into a parking space to turn around.

She did all this with no headlights.

When Melanie floored her Pontiac, hurling gravel back at the squad car, the cops turned on their searchlight and their cherry.

Not that Melanie worried. By the time she reached the mouth of the alley, she was going forty miles per hour. Halfway down the block, she was going seventy. At eighty, she ran a stop sign, a red light, a flashing yellow light. At ninety, she took three different corners on two wheels, causing pedestrians to flee in panic.

But she still hadn't reached the freeway, and the cops were gaining on her. In fact, they were now pulling up so close she could glimpse their faces in her rearview. They looked real mad.

Darn it all. She had to get away.

Turning onto Sunset, she gave it the gas—only to have a woman with a baby carriage cross the street directly in front of her. Swerving to miss them, she jumped the curb and roared up the sidewalk like an express train. Plowing through two advertising sandwich signs, she finally broke free of the cop car and made the hard screeching turn onto La Cienega, burning rubber all the way.

In her rearview she watched the cop car hit a hydrant, flip twice, then skid on its top all the way down Sunset. Hydrant water spouted high above the boulevard.

Her laughter rang through the night. The night returned her howls with the echoing scream of sirens. She was high, heedless, free; the speedometer topped 100. She loved this kind of danger; it nourished her.

Glancing at the speedometer, she was now clocking 112.

Everything else was a blur—faces gawking, people shrieking, store windows flashing, cars pulling over, pedestrians running for cover. All they did was make her laugh.

Up ahead, just north of Melrose, something did get her attention: the roadblock.

These guys were fast.

The roadblock was two blocks away. She could have tried to turn left but it was too tight a corner.

Laughing, she put the pedal to the metal.

She laughed even harder when she saw the faces of the cops, diving for cover as the Pontiac bore down on them.

She hit the roadblock at 114 miles per hour, crashing through with no trouble, concerned only with keeping the car from rolling when she turned the next corner—the one heading away from the freeway.

Disappointing as it was, Melanie couldn't afford to push this any further.

Lord, if Edgar ever found out that she'd led the LAPD on a chase like this—

She roared away from the freeway, bringing the car gradually down to fifty miles per hour over the next four blocks.

The night was oppressive with sirens now. It sounded like the aftermath of an earthquake, that kind of panic, that kind of craziness.

She had to ditch the car fast. She stayed on the residential street until she found an alley.

A cop car was a few blocks behind her.

She turned in the alley, cut her headlights, raced down the gravel until she found a large garage.

She pulled in along the far side of it so the cops wouldn't be able to find it at first, and then got out, already fumbling with her purse.

She was sweaty and shaky and loving every minute of it.

A few minutes later, she was walking down the street when a squad car pulled over.

"Good evening, officers."

"Good evening, Sister."

She could see how tense and angry they were. How they ached to get their hands on the person who'd been driving.

"Sister, have you seen anybody running down the street in the last few minutes?"

"I'm afraid I haven't, Officer. I was just out walking and saying a few prayers and—"

"Thank you, Sister."

The cops raced away.

Melanie kept on walking.

Thank the Lord for that nun's habit she always carried in the large and stylish leather bag that doubled as her purse. The habit was so quick and easy to pull on. So blinding to others.

All they saw was the habit. They responded only with deference.

Humming a tune, Melanie started the long walk back to her hotel, losing the habit in a DX ladies' room a half hour later.

BOBBY Just as Melanie was leaving the service station, Robert Kennedy looked across the shadows of the Oval Office and said, "I don't have to tell you what would happen if that pansy Hoover ever got his hands on them."

Jack Kennedy said nothing. Just rubbed his eyes. There was a melancholy aspect to the Oval Office this late at night—the room largely in shadows, the blue and silver seal that had been ingeniously woven into the carpet; the two naval pictures of Jack's days in World War II flanking the fireplace; the small model of the USS *Constitution* on the mantel; and the rocking chair in the corner, a sad symbol of the president's dubious health.

"Maybe Lenihan's wrong," Jack said.

"I don't think so."

"Some guy just calls up the White House and tells David Lenihan that—"

"Goddammit. Can we establish once and for all that the fucking phone call David got was legitimate? It happened."

"Then you really believe this guy has what he says he has?"

"Absolutely."

"Fuck."

"You got a little wild there, brother. A little out of control. I mean, you're the president of the United States. You just can't take these kinds of chances."

Jack smirked. "No, you can only run around and fuck all the

girls when you're attorney general. Nobody ever notices the attorney general, do they?"

Bobby crossed the floor and dropped into a chair facing his brother's desk.

"This isn't exactly helping the situation, the two of us going at it this way," Bobby said.

"Then figure it out for me."

Bobby sighed. "We have to send somebody out there."

"And?"

"We'll have to find the goddamn things."

"And?"

"And destroy them. What else would we do with them?"

Jack Kennedy didn't respond for a long time. Then he said, in not much more than a whisper, "This isn't going to be protected by any national-security cover."

"I know that."

"If we kill anybody, it's just plain murder."

"Jack, for God's sake, you think I don't fucking know that?" He paused. "You know what the old man said the other night."

They both knew. Joe was enraged, telling them that this kind of gossip could destroy them. He used himself as an example, reminding them how he'd once made a few statements that people felt were sympathetic to Hitler and how once the statements had reached the press, his public career was over.

"This is spooky shit, Bobby."

"Tell me about it."

They stayed in the Oval Office six more hours, until the sky became a dusty blue and the cry of the morning birds intruded.

HOOVER

"Edgar?"

"Yes."

"Lyndon."

Oh, great. Just what he needed—starting the day with Lyndon Johnson.

Everything else up till now had pointed to a smooth-running day for Hoover. The walk with Clyde from the Justice Department to FBI headquarters; the ride up in an elevator that his staff always made sure was empty before the director stepped on; his greeting of Sam Noisette, the lone Negro to serve in the Bureau home office. Sam was a receptionist. Then into his own office, his true inner sanctum, walls filled with landscape paintings and a mounted sixty-pound sailfish he'd caught. The desk was essentially bare at the moment, but soon the mail would be delivered and Hoover could get to work.

As soon as he took care of Lyndon. The guy could wear you down in ten minutes with his whining and scheming and pushing.

But Hoover had found him useful.

In fact, two years ago, when Jack Kennedy had been looking for a vice president, Hoover had offered Lyndon's name, despite the objections of eastern liberals who had found Lyndon too crude, too corny, too unlike themselves.

But Hoover knew a different Lyndon—one who would play ball. Lyndon had always made that clear. From the beginning. From his first days on the floor.

And his hunger for gossip was inexhaustible.

36

After Jack was nominated, Hoover recommended that Kennedy put Lyndon on the ticket. Then Hoover had added:

"You know, Jack, I've never seen any reason to do anything with those photos of you and that young lady. I just want you to know that they're safe with me and that you don't have a darned thing to worry about."

So now, here was Hoover talking to the man he'd made vice president.

"Yes, Lyndon."

"Edgar, those Kennedy bastards are up to something. There're a lot of secret meetings going on over there. With Lenihan."

"Ah, yes, Mr. Lenihan. Their troubleshooter extraordinaire." He smiled, knowing how much Lyndon hated polysyllabic words.

"You think you can find out what's going on?"

"I can try, Lyndon."

"Do more than try. I smell dick trouble."

"Dick trouble?"

"Them Kennedy boys'd stick their dicks in a woodpile on the chance there was a snake in it, and now that snake's reached back and bit 'em."

"You may be right." God, he hated the way Lyndon talked.

"Edgar, the time's *now*."

"Time for what?"

"I want their balls. I want them two gelded. Edgar, you're gonna cut their dicks off for me."

"That may not be as farfetched as it sounds."

"Then let's make it happen, boy. I'm tired of eatin' Kennedy shit."

"That's the president of the United States and his brother we're talking about."

"And we're gonna *own* them."

"I've known their old man for forty years. They're his kids. They play rough."

"And I'm gonna have their balls. I'm gonna know when they eat, when they sleep, when they shit, how many times they make it with their old ladies. I'm gonna have their peckers in my pocket."

"How do I do that?"

"You stick it to 'em. You break it off. And I mean all the way, Edgar, right up to the balls. Right up their rich-boy assholes."

Excerpt from
Marilyn Monroe's
personal tapes

Maybe now would be a good time to talk about my psychiatrists. One day I asked my secretary to put together all the psychiatric bills I'd paid over the last five years and I couldn't believe it. Absolutely couldn't believe it. Louella, I'd paid more money to psychiatrists than I'd made on The Seven Year Itch *and* Some Like It Hot *put together.*

I find this really funny in light of the fact that I ended up sleeping with every one of them. It was almost like I was paying them to sleep with me.

That always meant the end of my relationship with them; once I started sleeping with them, I mean. Here were these men I was really depending on and every one of them would eventually tell me the same thing . . . that to make our psychiatric relationship "complete," we needed to sleep together so that I'd understand that I should find joy in giving myself to a man.

One of them couldn't get an erection the first couple of times he tried to make love to me. I thought of telling him that maybe he should see a psychiatrist but I guessed he probably wouldn't see the humor in that.

I tried to help him. I did him with my hand and then I put him in my mouth but it didn't seem to matter. He couldn't do anything. Then he got this idea that if I dressed up like a man, maybe that would help him. So the next time I came to his office, I brought this old Charlie Chaplin costume I had and he really loved it. He undid my zipper and put his hand inside to touch

38

me and I could feel him getting real hard, he didn't have any trouble at all as long as I had on that man's suit.

One of the other ones liked me to bite him until I drew blood. It really scared me. Ever since I was a little girl, the sight of blood has really frightened me, Louella. And to bite somebody so hard that you draw blood. . . . Well, it was scary, and I broke off with him the second time he asked me to do it.

Sometimes I wonder if I should have spent all that time and money on psychiatrists.

Some of them seemed a lot more screwed up than I was. I know that's not a nice thing to say but it's true.

One of them even knelt down in front of me one day and started crying and said he'd fallen in love with me and said he'd leave his wife and two little daughters and that he wanted to run away with me and live in Europe.

But all I could think of was his little girls—they were only two and three years old—and how he was willing to desert them just the way my father had deserted me . . . and I lost control. . . . I saw him down there on his knees and I started shrieking and slapping him.

Fathers shouldn't desert little girls. They should be loving and faithful and honorable.

From the Desk of
Dr. Sidney S. Wellborn

Notes on patient: Marilyn Monroe
1-23-61

    After four visits, Marilyn seems more open and trusting. The more she talks, the more my initial impressions seem correct.

    Given her childhood, she seems to have an inability to transcend her relationship conflicts with both her father and mother.

    She demonstrates low ego strength as well as pronounced depressive reactions to things. I'm guessing that she's a cyclothymic personality, her mood swings having more to do with internal rather than external factors.

    She is a very unstable woman emotionally and needs not only psychotherapy but some very practical guidance in her life. She makes a lot of money but is relatively broke. She shows definite exhibitionistic traits but is also painfully shy. These are only two of the many seeming contradictions in Marilyn's personality.

PART ONE

September 5, 1962

"Power is like a woman
you want to stay in
bed with forever."

—*Patrick Anderson*

SARA Sara Drury had never gotten over her midwestern fascination with Hollywood. During her lunch break she sometimes walked over to Mann's Chinese Theater, that famous haunt of silent-era movie stars, and frequently spotted Tony Curtis wheeling around in his silver Bentley or Jack Lemmon out for a brisk walk or, one afternoon, Sandra Dee kissing Bobby Darin on a street corner. Sara sensed that they'd had an argument and were making up.

As editor of a magazine devoted to the history of Hollywood, Sara felt blessed with the assignments she sometimes pulled. Just last week she'd spent an entire enchanting afternoon with Ida Lupino, who was just now getting credit for being one of the first female movie directors. A month earlier, she'd spent an entire day with Myrna Loy. And before that had been John Wayne and Ray Milland and Fred Astaire and Barbara Stanwyck.

While interviewing these people, she always had a stray impulse to rush to a phone and call one of her old friends back in Omaha and say "You'll never guess who I'm spending the day with!" Not that she meant to brag, but saying it aloud would reassure her that she was actually interviewing Ginger Rogers (not an easy woman to get along with) or Gary Cooper (who had not looked well when she'd interviewed him last year, and who had died just a few months later).

Of course, none of the stars would have granted her such lengthy interviews if they hadn't had faith in her talent. On first glimpse, Sara was a pretty, quiet blonde woman given to earnest eyeglasses and shy smiles. But to those in the movie industry, she was one of the best interviewers of her era. She put stars at ease because she never asked for dirt or gossip; rather she wanted to know what Hollywood had been like in the thirties and forties, back when both James Cagney and George Raft had been chorus boys. Her interviews were widely quoted and were the most popular part of *Insight*, a slick magazine devoted entirely to the subject of Hollywood.

Most days she liked her work, but more and more, it seemed, she was away from her ten-year-old daughter, and the separations depressed her.

Especially when Laura was ill. During these crises, Sara—a single mother—experienced genuine desperation. Today, for instance, when Laura complained of not feeling well, Sara had felt real panic. She wanted to quit her job on the spot and take care of her personally. But instead she'd called the sitter, Mrs. Gregory, and asked her to serve as "mommy." So Mrs. Gregory had taken Laura to the doctor to check out the scratchy throat.

Of course, it was only a sore throat, and Sara knew it was ridiculous to panic, but still she was frightfully anxious all day. And now it was after 7:00 P.M. and Laura and Mrs. Gregory were still not home from their three o'clock appointment.

Sara sighed, focusing again on the sheet of paper in her Royal typewriter.

The subject was Val Lewton, a distinguished director of low-budget but effective horror films in the early forties. Lewton was dead but Sara had been able to find several of the actors who'd formed Lewton's informal ensemble. She hoped that her article, illustrated with several startling black-and-white studio photos from *I Walked with a Zombie*, would convince serious students of film to check Lewton out. She was now typing some of the interview she'd conducted with DeWitt Bodeen, who had written *Curse of the Cat People* for Lewton. She tried hard to concentrate, to stop looking at the clock, stop staring at the telephone on her desk as if she could will it to ring, stop conjuring up images of all the health perils a young girl could encounter.

"Any word yet?"

She looked up at Jeff Williams, who was leaning in the doorway of her office.

Jeff had come to Hollywood right after World War II because a talent scout had told him that he had the same boyish quality as Van Johnson and other boys-next-door. Fifteen years had passed and the "boy" had hair that was turning gray, wrinkles around the eyes that were definitely not boyish, and a faint air of bookishness that never quite left him. Like Sara, Jeff had had the bad luck to draw a faithless mate. The disintegration of his marriage had been prolonged and aggrieved, and even now, two years after it had officially been put to rest, one still saw occasional flashes of sorrow in the quick dark eyes.

She shook her head. "No word yet. But you know me. I'm imagining the worst. God save us from over-protective parents."

"You're not being over-protective, Sara. You want to know where Laura and Mrs. Gregory are. That's a natural reaction for a parent. For a good, responsible parent, anyway."

Sara smiled. Jeff had never made any secret of his dislike for Michael, Sara's estranged husband. Michael was also a failed actor but one who still, despite a lot of evidence to the contrary, believed he would someday be as big as Newman or McQueen.

"Meaning Michael isn't?" she said.

"Meaning Michael isn't."

"You don't give him any credit at all." Sometimes she bristled at the way Jeff attacked her husband.

"And you give him too much credit. Maybe we should split the difference. How does that sound?"

She grinned. While she wasn't in love with Jeff—not in the way he was with her, anyway—he had become her best friend during her long ordeal with Michael.

"And now you need some food," Jeff said. "In fact, we both do. Cheeseburger sound good? I'll go."

She shrugged. Until she heard from Mrs. Gregory—

"Force yourself," Jeff said.

"I guess you're right."

"I'll be back in fifteen minutes. So please catch the phone."

Sara went into the front office to the water cooler. *Insight* had been founded by the wealthy son of a banking magnate. Thomas Sylver was rich and quite bored. In addition to scandalously young girls, he had only two interests: yachting and the motion-picture business. Five years ago, he published the first issue of *Insight* to worldwide acclaim from students of movie history. He had personally hired Sara, obviously with the thought that they would one day sleep together. The fact that she was married didn't deter him at all—indeed, he seemed to have been merrily challenged by this fact. Sara had no such intention. After a few passes, one of which was an invitation to accompany him for a weekend at his mansion in Mexico, she managed to end his ardor by threatening to quit if he didn't leave her alone. Gonad-crazed as he was, Thomas Sylver was also a businessman. Sara was valuable to the magazine. He never bothered her again. Last year, however, several of Sylver's biggest investments had taken some bad hits and suddenly he was left cash-poor. In order to keep the magazine up and running, he had to take on an investor: a crude, middle-aged man named Bellamy, who had spent thirty years publishing trashy Hollywood tabloids. It was an even trade—as half-owner, Bellamy got the prestige associated with *Insight* and Thomas Sylver got much-needed cash.

Sara had tried hard to like Bellamy. Sylver spent most of his time abroad these days, which meant that Bellamy ran the magazine on a day-to-day basis. His impact on editorial policy had been immediate. He always compared *Insight* sales figures to those of *Confidential*, and found *Insight* wanting. He instantly tried to give the magazine "sex appeal" by having Sara write articles about some of the sleazier scandals of Old Hollywood, including the woman who had allegedly been raped in Fatty Arbuckle's hotel room; the decapitated Black Dahlia; Charlie Chaplin's various flings with underage girls. Her inclination, after four issues of this, was to quit and find another job, but the country was in a recession; the studios were laying off, not hiring. There wouldn't be any publicity jobs open. She couldn't quit. She was Laura's sole support. Even though Michael got an occasional TV part—he'd even done a "Studio One" a while back—he only rarely gave her any financial help. The maddening part of it all was that she still loved him.

Bellamy didn't even look right in the magazine's handsome offices. His cheap, wrinkled suits did not belong in the same room as the framed Modigliani prints on the wall; his "fuck you" to half the people he talked with on the phone clashed with the quiet, friendly conversations Sara had with Jeff; and he was forever flicking cigarette ashes on the gold carpet and the beautiful plum-colored fabric couch in the waiting area. Jeff even told her that Bellamy had blackmailed stars when he was starting out. For a certain amount, Bellamy would turn over photos of the star being weak and foolish.

Sara phoned home again. Still no answer. She tried the doctor's office. An answering-service woman said that the doctor's office was closed for the day. Great.

She went back to the typewriter and forced herself to plod through three more sentences about Val Lewton, about how Lewton's movies weren't really "horror" at all but rather elegant suspense tales driven by strange and often neurotic stories of romantic love.

She heard the outer office door open almost hesitantly, and then a harsh cough grate on the air.

Bellamy and his Chesterfield cough. She groaned at the thought. She could still hear those Arthur Godfrey radio commercials: "Chester-field—good for your health!" The same brand of cigarettes that had killed Humphrey Bogart was now killing Bellamy.

The way the door had opened, Sara knew for sure that something was wrong. Bellamy always burst through doors, shouting orders; to-night he came in silent and limping. His white shirt, gray trousers, and hair were dark with sweat.

He was just inside when he collapsed.

Sara rushed to kneel beside him. Bellamy was still alive, but his breath came in ragged gasps.

She dragged him to his office couch, then went to the cooler and filled a clean coffee cup with water.

Incredibly, during her brief absence, Bellamy had dragged himself to his desk and poured himself a shot of whiskey from his familiar silver flask.

"Appreciate the help, kid," he told her, coughing on a cigarette.

"Maybe you should lay off that stuff?"

"You're really a fucking Girl Scout, you know that?"

Not until now, in this light, did Sara see that Bellamy had been in some kind of fight. His left eye was discolored, his lower lip swollen. And the way Bellamy rubbed his gut probably meant that somebody had hit him in the stomach.

"You better get out of here, kid."

"Will you be all right?"

The knowing stare. "You're classy. You know that? Classy and trustworthy. That's a nice combination."

"Thank you."

"That's why I'm going to tell you where you can find the combination to my safe. I may have to kind of disappear. You'll have to open the safe and bring me something. It's right here—taped beneath the top right desk drawer. The combination."

"All right."

"Now get out. I got some calls to make."

"Are you going to be all right?"

"Don't worry about me. I been kicked around harder'n this." Another hack. "You remember where the combination is?"

She nodded.

TOLSON Clyde hadn't thought about Melanie in several months, the bitch, and he wouldn't have thought of her now if Edgar hadn't been hinting about what a mess Clyde's office was these days.

Clyde was a saver, and hadn't cleaned out his desk drawers in more than three years. Among many other things, he saved matchbooks from posh restaurants, ticket stubs from sporting events, foreign cigarette packages, and cocktail napkins with bawdy jokes on them.

He used to have what he called his junk drawer, but that in time became two junk drawers, then three. Now five of the six drawers were junk drawers.

He began throwing stuff away, all the useless paper in his drawers. In no time he had only two junk drawers remaining.

He was just about to start on those when he found the photograph of Melanie Baines, a young, beautiful, red-headed woman in a red bikini standing on the stern of a yacht with her arm around another young woman of equal beauty.

Melanie Baines. He'd had one of the Los Angeles field ops tail her for a few days. This was the picture the op sent back. With no comment. Spoke volumes for itself.

Tolson looked at the photograph and shook his head. Edgar could be such a foolish bastard sometimes. God, for a time, Tolson had even worried that Edgar had developed a sexual interest in this young lady.

He took great pleasure in ripping the photograph into small pieces and letting them fall, like so much confetti, into the wastebasket.

Thank God that episode with Melanie Baines was over and behind them now. Edgar had nearly lost everything. Everything.

Clyde went on cleaning out the final two drawers.

HOOVER

"Hold my calls."

"Yes, sir. Even from Mr. Tolson?"

"Even from Mr. Tolson."

"Very well."

Hoover's secretary clicked off, leaving Hoover alone in his office to put his head down on his desk and nap. He didn't want anybody to know he did this, of course. There was enough gossip about him, especially these days, that he was getting too old for the job.

Bastards.

Didn't they have anything better to do than whisper all those lies about him to anybody who'd listen?

He put his head down. Closed his eyes. Tried to drift off. It was amazing how much better you felt after even a fifteen minute nap.

Drifting off . . .

And then the movie started.

Technicolor. Symphonic sound. Cast of thousands. Lord, it was the biggest, loudest, most violent movie ever made and right at the center of it, the star of the whole shebang, was not Hoover himself but—

Melanie.

Yes, Melanie.

Shooting at bad guys. Kicking in doors. Going 125 miles per hour on the freeway while chasing somebody. . . .

Hoover couldn't help but admire her. If he'd been a woman, he

51

would have wanted to be exactly like Melanie. Sometimes he even thought of her as his little sister.

Where both Hoover and Clyde were proper bureaucrats, careful not to violate laws and offend sensitive groups, Melanie had no such scruples.

Once, just to make a point, she had impaled a man's penis to a kitchen chair with a staple gun. He told her what she wanted to know.

The man turned out to be a bottomless fount of invaluable information.

She'd once baited a trawl line with a particularly uncooperative congressional staffer and spent a long, languid hour trolling the shark-infested waters off Key West. The man soon saw his patriotic duty and identified six highly placed congressional informants.

Melanie had once dissuaded a young reporter—fresh from Iowa's School of Journalism—from writing a story alleging homosexual conduct on the part of Hoover and Clyde Tolson. After Melanie's explanation of the ethical implications of such journalism, the young man admitted his mistake, withdrew the story, and handed the disputed negative over to her.

All this had occurred after Melanie had branded the young man's buttocks with a steam iron.

Looking back on the incident, Hoover could not help but remember her fondly. Her gift to him afterward had been so thoughtful, so typical of his little Melanie. Knowing Hoover's passion for photography, she had provided him with snapshots of the particular operation.

Head down on his desk, eyes closed, Hoover recalled once again those extraordinary photos of the young man's scorched derriere.

Even now, he smiled to himself.

Who could not help but smile at Melanie?

My God, the woman had more balls than any man the director had ever met, especially those swaggering cowboys the CIA was always coming up with.

If only Clyde understood.

Clyde loathed Melanie. Loathed her.

Sometimes Hoover even wondered if Clyde weren't just jealous of the relationship Hoover had with Melanie.

Poor Clyde.

Hoover yawned.

He remembered being no more than five years old, putting his head down on his blanket in Miss Kenyon's kindergarten class, and the luxurious drifting off into the world of sleep. . . .

And that's sort of how he felt now . . . still Miss Kenyon's favorite because he was such a good boy . . . and so sleepy. . . .

He luxuriously drifted off.

TULLY Weird that Tully would fall in love with a girl who had an artificial leg.

He had met her the previous fall, at an outdoor restaurant by the La Brea tar pits, where he was having a few drinks and watching the sunset.

As she drew near his little table, he saw how she kept her eyes downcast, as if shy or ashamed. She was really quite attractive, with big dark eyes and full, erotic lips.

She glanced up briefly and their eyes met, and everything he felt thereafter was as corny as a bad jukebox song.

Then she hurried on her way, her limp obvious beneath the autumn coat.

"I'd like to buy you a drink," Tully said when he caught up with her, nodding to his table.

"No, thank you."

"You have a husband?"

"No."

"A boyfriend?"

"I, uh, guess not. But I don't know you."

Still, he felt that she was intrigued.

"Come on. I'll buy as long as you promise not to get drunk."

And she smiled and agreed.

It took him three months to get her into bed and another two months to make love to her.

Tully wasn't used to this. He'd once seduced a coffee heiress—admittedly on VJ day when everybody went a little crazy in the posher watering holes of Gotham—and he'd once slept with a frisky lesbian who confessed that she'd never done it with a man before.

But Vanessa was different.

He was in love with her and she was, at twenty-four, a virgin.

After they first made love, she sat on the edge of his double bed in her sensible white underpants and sensible white bra and said, "I guess we might as well get it over with."

"Get what over with, hon?"

"My leg."

"Aw, hell, I don't even think about that."

"Sure you do."

So she showed him. Around her waist was an elastic band that extended down to the artificial leg, affixed just below her knee, where it hooked to a buckle. The leg was made of wood painted a flesh tone.

It was the result of being hit by a truck when she was four years old.

He wanted to take her in his arms and hold her tight forever; this was more intimate than making love.

Four months later they were married.

On their wedding night, she unhitched her leg and then performed oral sex on him for the first time. "You know, hon, you really don't have to do this," he said. She was almost superstitiously afraid of his cock, not liking to see it or touch it, and certainly not liking to put it in her mouth. But that was exactly where she put it and he feigned great groaning bliss with her performance, even though her gnashing little teeth were tearing the shit out of his poor little pecker.

And afterward, after she went into the bathroom and brushed her teeth and used Listerine—afterward, she came back and sat in the nook of his arm, in the darkness of the hotel room, and he said, "You don't have to do that anymore, hon."

"But you like it, don't you?"

"I like what you like, hon."

"I'm so lucky to have you," she said. "So darn lucky."

*   *   *

When he came in the apartment door, she knew something was wrong.

He kept clenching and unclenching his hands. The knuckles were bloody. There was dirt on the sleeves of his blue blazer.

"You all right, hon? Did you get in a fight?"

He wouldn't look at her. "Little scrape. Nothing serious," he said, going straight for their bedroom.

She heard him open the top drawer of their bureau, the one that squeaked.

She could hear him hiding something under his socks and underwear. That's where he always put secret stuff related to whatever case he was working on.

Tully worked as an operative for International Investigations. His specialty was electronic surveillance, mostly planting "bugs" in offices. He was a master of infrared and high-powered telephoto lenses.

He came out of the bedroom and went straight into the kitchen. He still hadn't given her a kiss. He had changed clothes.

The clank of bottle to glass meant he was pouring himself Scotch.

Then he came back in and said, "I need to go out, hon. Just a couple of hours."

"We're having spaghetti."

He leaned over and kissed her tenderly on the mouth. "Just a couple more hours, hon."

"Something big?"

"Very big. It could make us a lot of money."

"You promise?"

He crossed his heart. She liked it when he did that. This big Irish guy was cute.

"There's a Jimmy Stewart picture on the late show," she said.

"Great," he said. "We'll have that spaghetti and watch the Jimmy Stewart picture."

Then he was gone.

She didn't know why, but she was scared.

Back in the old days, when I was just getting started in the movies, I always ate the same thing over and over because it was all I could afford. There was this little diner down by the railroad tracks a couple of blocks from my apartment—this would've been back in 1948, I think—and I'd order grapefruit and coffee for breakfast, and cottage cheese for lunch, and for dinner I'd have a cheeseburger and a small salad and a glass of milk. The old woman who ran the place said I looked just like her daughter who'd been killed in an automobile accident a few years earlier. Sometimes—and she was real shy about this at first—she'd ask me if I'd mind wearing one of her daughter's scarves or hats or bracelets while I sat at the lunch counter. I felt kind of strange at first, with the old woman watching me and all, but one day when I was wearing this little white pillbox hat of her daughter's I saw the old woman start crying and I realized that what I was doing was a good thing after all. I was helping this woman deal with her daughter's death. And that was when I realized that I really was an actress. I could convince people that I was somebody other than me—and I could convince myself of that, too.

S A R A It was pleasant walking through the mild Los Angeles evening, the sky filled with opening-night search lights and the bright glimpses of airplanes on the way to LAX. And, it was comfortable to talk with Jeff. It took her mind off Laura.

He chuckled. "Bellamy is pretty tough to deal with, isn't he? I keep trying to find something decent about the guy, but I can't."

"After I heard that he might be involved in blackmail. . . ." She shook her head. "No wonder those movie stars show up every once in a while. When they're so mad, I mean."

"Would you like to come over?" Jeff said. "After you find Laura, I mean."

"Think I need some sleep, Jeff. Maybe tomorrow night."

He nodded and smiled but she could see the disappointment in his eyes. She wished that she no longer loved Michael, had all those awful, idle daydreams about getting back together. . . .

They reached the smart, new office building where they worked. Their cars were in a parking lot behind the building, Jeff's near the entrance. Hers was at the opposite end. "You want me to walk you over to your car?"

"I'll be fine. But thanks."

He kissed her, a quick chaste kiss. "Night," he said, and climbed into his five-year-old DeSoto.

When she reached her car, she saw Bellamy walking toward his new red Caddy convertible.

"Are you feeling any better, Mr. Bellamy?"

Bellamy nodded and stuck a cigarette in his mouth. "I'm all right, kid. Don't worry about me. Just remember about the safe."

Bellamy wore a sports jacket, but it didn't cover his considerable belly. Sara saw a pistol tucked in his belt.

Since when had Bellamy started carrying a gun?

Bellamy strolled over to his Caddy, and drove quickly from the parking lot.

Something more serious and scary was going on. And too close for comfort.

MELANIE Hospitals spooked Melanie. When she was ten, her dear uncle Mike had come to a hospital to get well, and had died hemorrhaging as she watched at his bedside.

Melanie stopped at the nurse's station and asked for Jean Stephens. The nurse directed Melanie to wait in the lounge down the hall.

In the lounge were two orange plastic tables with matching chairs, a stack of well-thumbed *Saturday Evening Posts* and a noisy Pepsi machine. Next to it was a small table with two half-filled coffee pots on heating grids.

Melanie sat down, cold and trembling. She blamed the air-conditioning.

"Hi, stranger," Jean said, strolling briskly in.

"Hi."

Jean got coffee for them and they sat. "How're you doing?"

"Fine. Just thought I'd stop in and say hi."

"Bullshit." Jean smiled. She was thirty-six, petite and graceful, with dark hair cut fashionably short and faint eyeliner flattering her green eyes. "You're starting a new job?"

"Edgar's lined something up." She told her about the car chase.

"I'm happy you're alive," Jean said.

"C'mon, don't you think it's funny?"

Jean shook her head. "I worry about you. Just because you moved out doesn't mean I don't still care."

They had lived together six months, but finally Melanie's life-style brought them down. Though they were still friends, Melanie had

60

taken an apartment in San Francisco. Whenever she came back to
L.A. she got a hotel room.

"You could have been killed. Or the cop could have been killed.
He probably has a wife and children." Jean touched Melanie's hand.
"If you ever learn to accept yourself, then you won't need to do all
this. You can settle down."

"And be bored."

Jean smiled, withdrew her hand. "Still, you don't need to constantly
put your life in danger and . . ." She sighed. "I'm on my soapbox.
Sorry."

"You still on the hospice wing?"

Jean nodded.

"You're a saint, Jean. You really are."

Jean laughed, embarrassed. "Oh, yes, in fact the Vatican's talking
about canonizing me right now. First saint to ever be canonized before
she dies." Tenderness was in her eyes and voice. "I hope I can convince
you someday that the world is filled with decent people, Melanie.
You see that up here on the hospice wing, how people love and care
for each other." She smiled sadly. "Even people like us, Melanie.
We're decent, too. We don't have to be—" She stopped herself. We
don't have to be crazy and violent and hateful, she always said at this
point in the argument. But now she stopped herself.

"Maybe this is one you shouldn't get involved in, Melanie. This
job."

"You don't even know what it is."

"I can tell you're anxious. I've never seen you like this. Maybe it
should tell you something."

"I'll be all right." Melanie shrugged. "I guess I shouldn't have come
here. I . . . just had some time on my hands."

"We're friends, Melanie. Always. Any time I can help you, all
right?"

Melanie stood up.

"Go easy on yourself, Melanie," Jean said.

Melanie nodded and left, suddenly frantic to get out of the hospital,
out of the burning whiteness and the tart antiseptic smells, and the
proximity to death.

TULLY He skimmed the L.A. *Times*, had a couple of neat Scotches and then went to the phone booth in the back.

He put his handkerchief over the speaking end of the receiver to muffle his voice. Double-crossing clients was a treacherous business.

A cool voice answered. "This is the Mayhews."

"Mr. Mayhew please. This is Charlton Heston's office."

A half minute later, a rich male voice said, "Hello?"

"I've got some tapes you'll want to hear."

"Who is this?"

"I want a quarter of a million dollars in cash for these tapes. And if you don't buy them, I know somebody who will."

"Who are you?"

"I'll call you tomorrow. At the studio. But in the meantime, I'd start getting that money lined up."

Mayhew said, "You sonofabitch."

Tully went back to the bar, had another Scotch, and thought about going back home. He'd always been true-blue, but tonight he needed to get out. Go to some dance clubs and check out all the nookie that came in from the Midwest, all those fine young women with their perfect ankles and perfect breasts and perfect smiles. Looking wouldn't hurt anybody.

Especially when a fella was about to come into a quarter of a million dollars in hard currency.

SARA Laura was fine.

They'd been late getting home because Mrs. Gregory's car had stalled several blocks from the doctor's office, and she'd had to call a service station.

By the time Sara got home, Mrs. Gregory had already put the young girl in bed for the night and straightened up the apartment.

Sara eased open the door to Laura's room and saw that she was sleeping.

When she bent over to kiss her daughter, her lips touched a forehead and streamers of blonde hair that were damp with sweat. Laura smelled of warmth and sleep.

Sara looked at the array of Laura's friends neatly lined along the wall. When she wasn't sleeping, these friends filled the bed: two teddy bears, a doll in a Scottish kilt, a Sandra Dee dress-up doll, and smiling Bullwinkle.

When Sara returned to the living room, Mrs. Gregory was watching "The Garry Moore Show" and packing up her familiar Thermos, plastic sandwich container and various rosaries and prayer pamphlets and missals. Mrs. Gregory was a relentless Catholic. She'd once inquired, cautiously, trying to be inoffensive, about Sara's religion. When Sara had made the mistake of saying "I used to be Catholic," she'd had no idea of the fervor in Mrs. Gregory. Ever since then, Mrs. Gregory discreetly left holy cards and prayer pamphlets throughout the four-room apartment. She had obviously taken upon herself the burden of saving Sara's soul. But despite her missionary zeal, she was a doggedly reliable woman who loved Laura with maternal passion. Mrs. Helen Gregory was in her sixties, all three of her own children long gone, and so she spent herself on young Laura.

Mrs. Gregory apologized again for worrying Sara.

Then she said, "Your husband called."

Three simple words.

These days, Sara told herself that the worst of it was over. In the eleven months Michael had been gone, she had regained her equilibrium.

She also told herself that when he called, as he occasionally did, wanting to come over and see Laura, she would no longer feel her stomach tightening, or sweat breaking in her palms, or her heartbeat increase uncomfortably. But she felt all of these things now, along with bitterness.

She tried to act composed. "Did he say what he wanted?"

Stout Mrs. Gregory shook her graying head. "He never does. Said he'd call back." Her disapproval of Michael was tart in her voice. The Drurys had lived in this apartment house for the past five years. Nice as these apartments were, with large rooms and shining hardwood floors and back windows that looked out on a wooded area, they had not been built to keep secrets. When you argued as frequently and angrily as Sara and Michael Drury had, everybody else in the apartment house knew your business. So Mrs. Gregory knew a great deal about Michael's various dissatisfactions.

"Thanks, Mrs. Gregory."

"If you want my advice, Sara, I wouldn't let Michael see that little girl anymore. He's not a good influence—living the way he does."

Sara edged closer to her so that Mrs. Gregory would get the hint and leave.

Mrs. Gregory put a white meaty hand on the doorknob and gave it a sharp twist. "He's a bad influence. You mark my words."

"Good night," Sara said. "I'll have your money for you tomorrow."

From the other side of the threshold Mrs. Gregory said, in a quiet voice lest her neighbors hear, "I know you think I'm a busybody, Sara, but I love that little girl and I just want the best for her."

Sara smiled. "I know you do, Mrs. Gregory. And I'll think it over. Good night, Mrs. Gregory."

And then she was gone and the door was closed and Sara was left alone with her thoughts.

TOLSON Ever since he'd seen the snapshot of Melanie Baines, Tolson had been able to think of nothing else.

Edgar had promised to sever all ties with the woman.

Tolson closed his office door.

He dialed the number of an agent in the Los Angeles office, a man named Rollins. Tolson had used Rollins twice before to check on Melanie's activities.

"Why, hello, Clyde."

Rollins was a tall, fleshy man, not brilliant, but one hell of a good tail. He was also slick at getting records of phone conversations from the phone company.

"I'm nervous again, Hal."

"Our old friend the beautiful redhead?"

"Yes. Check Edgar's home phone number. And the office number here. See if they've talked."

"I'll be back to you as soon as I can. It's probably nothing."

"I hope you're right."

MELANIE West Hollywood was changing. You saw more and more clubs like The Icon now. Long fancy cars in the parking lot. Even a chauffeur or two. And carefully disguised movie stars rushing inside before anybody got a good look at them. The Icon was a lesbian bar, and while there was a lesbian underground in Hollywood, few people knew about it and even fewer talked about it. Sleaze magazines such as *Confidential* had hinted at it but not even they had dared run any substantive stories. The old-time studio heads had allowed them their dirty little mentions because the magazines hadn't hurt box office grosses. But a serious investigation into the underground, with the naming of names. . . . The studio heads were not above hiring killers. And keeping this in mind, the magazine publishers knew just how far they could go. They left places like The Icon alone.

Melanie came here looking for something. She wasn't sure what.

It was early so the place was quiet. On the dance floor a pair of young women danced slowly to a moody saxophone on the jukebox. Along the bar, several couples talked and joked among themselves, giving Melanie the sense of apartness she had felt all her life. She didn't belong anywhere.

The walls were painted with large gold Oscar statues. Every few feet along the bar a huge bowl contained an imposing blue gardenia.

Melanie sipped her spring water and lime. Should come back later when the craziness started. Maybe that's what she was looking for: craziness.

67

"Hi."

When she turned, she found an attractive young woman standing to her left at the bar. Strictly Kansas City. Staid blue suit and white pillbox hat. Little white gloves. White plastic purse.

"Hi," Melanie said, trying not to smirk at the hayseed getup.

"They keep it pretty dark in here, don't they?"

The girl's voice was uncertain. Melanie recognized her as a first-timer. Tourist. Come to this den of lesbians to find out if this was where she fit. Always something wrong with her relationships with men, so maybe women were the answer.

"They like it dark."

"Oh," the girl said, nervously biting her lower lip.

"Where're you from?"

"Springfield. Illinois, not Missouri."

"Ah."

"I lived there all my life. Till last year. When I turned twenty-one. Then I said good-bye to Roger and my mom and dad and just sort of . . . well, moved out here."

"Roger being . . ."

"My boyfriend. Or ex-boyfriend. He told me two months ago that he met somebody else, a secretary who likes to water-ski."

"You ever been here before?" Melanie said.

"No—well, yes. I snuck in here one night and just kind of looked around."

"And then you—"

"Ran right back out. So anyway, I decided to give it another try tonight."

"Well, I'm glad you did."

The girl put forth a gloved hand. "My name's Myrna."

"Tracy," Melanie said. "Tracy Deeds."

"What an interesting name."

"Yes," Melanie said, "isn't it, though?"

HOOVER He ordered up several special files and now he sat, door locked, poring over them in his orderly, efficient, but sterile inner office. Even the proud colors of the American flag seemed cold in this room.

People had no idea what Hoover knew about them.

Take this file. Martin Luther King, or Martin Nigger Coon, as some of the southern agents referred to him. A dozen secret snapshots of the high and mighty Reverend escorting various white ladies into and out of motels. Hoover had managed to bug a few of those rooms and he knew the kind of filthy things the holy Reverend went in for.

Then the file on Roy Cohn. Roy was always good file material. Stuff about Bobby Kennedy going after mobsters and Roy defending them. But the best parts were Roy's boyfriends. He liked them big and blond. A little queer, hiding behind the American flag.

Or the file on Louella Parsons. Dear old Louella. While the FBI director and she ostensibly were friends, he knew that she'd been writing a book about Marilyn Monroe. He'd asked her to share with him names of the men—and women, if rumor were true—that Monroe had been sleeping with. He was especially interested in Marilyn's relationship with the Kennedys. But Louella had amiably refused to tell him anything. And so, three months ago, he'd put her under surveillance. As yet, he didn't have anything especially interesting.

And then there were the Kennedys, the whole tribe, right down to those still in high school. They all had the same randy sexual tastes, if not the skills. "Selfish," as one woman said, not knowing that her phone conversation was being taped. "Jack slid his cock in me and started whaling away and a minute or so later, it was all over. And Bobby isn't much better. And they seem to hate doing you, like it's really dirty or disgusting or something. I mean, frankly, if they weren't so good-looking, I'd just as soon do myself. It's more fun."

The president of the United States a bum lay.

This was just the sort of fact that made the director of the FBI smile.

Then there were files on Mayhew, the head of a Hollywood studio; and Rossetti, a mob man who had called Louella last night and hinted that he might have something for her; and Tully, a corrupt private investigator. He'd gotten these names from Melanie on her call earlier today. They all seemed to be involved in what she was looking for. And Hoover already had files on each of them because in some way their pasts had proved interesting to the agents.

But now the whole project rested in Melanie's hands.

He wondered how Melanie was doing.

Excerpt from Marilyn Monroe's personal tapes

I went into church one night and knelt down and said a prayer and realized that there was no God. I was just saying words and nobody was listening. I'd never felt that before. It reminded me of when they took my mother to the asylum then. All I could think of was, My life is over. I'll just kind of exist from now on but I won't really have a life. And that's how I feel now, after realizing that there isn't really a God, Louella, that we just invented him the way some of those smart New York intellectuals say we did. Later that night I got pretty drunk and I was with Lawford and I told him about not believing in God and he got real mad and said I was drunk and stupid and I should shut up. I felt real bad about making Peter mad. He's actually a very decent guy, despite what the press prints about him.

BELLAMY The apartment house was old, the faded wallpaper in the hall stained with moisture, the carpet bald in spots. He could smell spaghetti sauce. As soon as Bellamy said he was a police detective, she came to the door.

When she opened the door, Bellamy saw that she was pretty enough, but beneath the right hem of her housecoat was empty air. She didn't have a right leg. She walked with a crutch.

"Do you have a badge I could see?" she asked pleasantly.

He lunged forward, shoving her into the apartment. She went over backwards, sprawling on the floor.

He closed the door and took the gun from his waistband.

"You know what I'm after, lady. Don't waste my time. Where are they?"

He had the gun pointed right at her face, no more than three feet from the tip of her nose to the snout of the .45.

She propped herself up on her elbows and tried to struggle to her feet.

He put his foot on her stomach.

"Stay where you are."

Her blue housecoat had pulled up around her left thigh, and he got a pleasant little glimpse of her dark pubic hair behind the white fabric of her panties.

But he wasn't here for sex.

"Where are they?"

"I don't know what you're talking about. Honest, I don't."

72

"I saw your husband leave. Where did he go?"

"I'm not sure."

"Bullshit. He'd tell you where he was going."

"Sometimes he doesn't. Honest."

He looked around the apartment. Nobody would ever accuse them of living beyond their means. The furnishings were from the thirties and forties, big and heavy, everything claw-footed, the lamp shades soiled and all the arms of the couch and chairs covered with old-lady doilies. This was the kind of place his mean Irish grandmother lived in.

"What happened to your leg?"

"Car accident. When I was little."

"You always use a crutch?"

She shook her head. She really was attractive in a sad, worn way. "I have an artificial one."

He looked at her face and then at the stump of her right leg, cleaved off just below the knee.

"Too bad. You're a good looking girl."

"I'm really scared, mister. I don't want to wet my pants but I'm afraid I'm going to."

"I don't have any reason to hurt you if you tell me the truth." Sometimes that was the best approach with women, the soft, understanding approach.

"I don't know what you're looking for."

"Something that old man of yours brought home with him in the last twenty-four hours."

He saw the sudden recognition in her eyes.

He knelt next to her. He put the .45 right up to her crotch.

"Anybody ever fuck you with a gun before?"

"Oh, God. Please. Please, don't."

One minute and thirty-five seconds later, she told him what he wanted to know.

ROSSETTI

Salvitore Rossetti was a killer who got his break by saving the lives of killers.

At the end of World War II, the United States became the site of many bloody Mob wars. The generation of mobsters that had gone off to fight in Europe and the South Pacific returned wanting a much bigger piece of the action.

Prior to 1946, Rossetti was a Mob soldier who had pulled only small-time duties in the New York organization.

Then one night, he had been leaving a "carpet joint"—a Mob creation that combined the speakeasy with the gambling casino—when he saw a black car sweeping toward the entrance, the rear end fishtailing. Rossetti instantly grasped the scene. The car was filled with men and tommy guns. They were about to kill two of Rossetti's bosses, men who'd just stepped out ahead of him and were walking to their car.

Rossetti dove for the men and knocked them down behind a parked car.

The men in the black car opened fire, but it was too late.

The bosses were grateful to young Salvitore Rossetti.

They asked Meyer Lansky of Miami and Cuba if he had a spot in his organization for a nice-looking young man, because otherwise the men in the black car would certainly hunt Rossetti down and kill him.

Lansky, who owed the two bosses a favor, quickly dispatched Rossetti to Havana, where Rossetti became a kind of glorified floor walker in one of Lansky's lavish casinos.

It was like being in a movie, spending each night in a fresh tuxedo, wandering around the vast gaming floor while the full orchestra performed erotic rumbas or melancholy sambas, watching American movie stars and industrial magnates and champion boxers play blackjack or baccarat. They came to Havana to play.

He was the fixer. If a well-heeled customer was having trouble, it was up to Mr. Rossetti to make sure that both customer and casino were ultimately satisfied. With his easy-going charm, Rossetti found his duties rewarding in every sense—with one exception. He had seen men, and a few women, shot, stabbed, drowned, beaten, and pushed into beds of lime, and he had never developed a taste for it.

But he fell in love with the movie industry. Movie people were his favorite dinner guests in Havana—stars, directors, producers, and studio executives. The entire business dazzled him.

And the movie people liked him, a handsome (even dashing) and somewhat mysterious man whose charm brought him the favors of beautiful ladies from a dozen different nations.

Then came Castro and everything changed. Fidel, pledging to rid the country of parasites and immorality, burned the casino to the ground.

There were rumors that Fidel planned to execute some mafiosi. Mobsters fled the island.

Six months later, Rossetti found a niche as a fixer for the West Coast mob. The organization was infiltrating major businesses throughout the United States, and the movie industry looked ripe, especially to some of the Vegas kingpins who skimmed huge profits from their gaming tables.

Rossetti was the ideal man to serve as a bridge between the organization and Hollywood studios.

Sometimes when Rossetti sat in his light, spacious office—surrounded by Danish-modern furnishings and imposing black-and-white blow-ups of silent stars such as Buster Keaton and Mary Pickford and Charlie Chaplin—he felt comfortable, at ease, as if this were the very spot fate had had in mind for him.

Usually, anyway.

But not today. Today he was anxious. Mayhew was the key. If Mayhew did his job properly, Rossetti could bring down the entire government of the United States. He would know a power beyond imagining.

He dialed Mayhew's private number.

There was no answer.

Rossetti mumbled obscenities and hung up.

TOLSON Clyde saw gossip as an effeminate habit, and hated it. Of course, he would never dare say this to Edgar.

Now, over a late meal at Edgar's house, the director said to him, "Did I tell you about Anthony Perkins?"

"No."

Edgar stopped cutting his roast beef. "What's the matter?"

"Why?"

"The way you looked just then."

"I'm a little tired is all."

"I thought you'd want to hear about Anthony Perkins."

"Of course."

"I mean, if we didn't have our agents looking in on these people we never would have been in a position to—well, we could get rid of the Kennedys."

"With Anthony Perkins?"

"Of course not with Anthony Perkins. But with our friends in Los Angeles."

"Ah."

"Now let me tell you about Anthony Perkins."

"Fine."

"And don't get that look on your face again."

"All right."

"You know how I hate that look."

"Right."

Then Edgar told him about Anthony Perkins.

77

MELANIE So Myrna said, "I don't know."

"You don't know what?" Melanie asked.

"If I'm a—well, you, know."

"Ah. You don't know if you're a you-know."

"Did that make you mad? You seem like you're mad."

After The Icon, Melanie and Myrna went to Myrna's two-room apartment where, after a couple of drinks, Myrna let Melanie pull down the Murphy bed, and they lay down on it with their clothes on.

"Can I ask you a question, Tracy?"

"Why not?" Melanie said.

"You sure you're not mad?"

"Not mad. Honest."

"You seem mad."

"If you keep saying I'm mad, I'll probably *get* mad."

"That's a good point."

"You were going to ask me a question," Melanie said.

"Oh. Right." Giggling. Drinks apparent in her voice now. "It's personal." She giggled. "Have you ever done it? You know. With another girl?"

"Ah."

"See. The way your jaw is all clenched up. You are mad."

"Myrna, I'd like to kiss you."

"Well."

"Then we could do a couple of other things, too."

"I guess you're answering my question, aren't you?" Myrna giggled.

"Yes," Melanie said. "I guess I am." She took the sweet, addled girl in her arms and kissed her.

Myrna was not responsive. "You don't have a beard."

"What?" Melanie said.

"I've never kissed anybody who didn't need a shave before. I mean, kissed passionately."

"Oh, Lord." Melanie sat up and swung her feet to the floor.

"Now you're really mad, aren't you?"

"Just shut up, Myrna."

"I want you to like me. I want you to help me find out if I'm, you know."

Melanie stood and slapped Myrna's face.

Myrna fell in a sobbing heap on the Murphy bed. Her skirt was hiked up to her hips. Garter belt and panties clear to see. Pubic hair dark behind the tan panties.

Melanie dropped to her knees and put her face between the sobbing girl's legs and began to partake.

Myrna flinched. "Oh, no. This isn't right."

But she yielded. Melanie undid the garters, slid the panties off, and the girl began to gasp and moan.

In the low animal noises of the sweet midwestern girl, Melanie heard what she had been so frantically searching for today.

Afterward, as Melanie held her tenderly, Myrna said, "Who's Jessica? You kept whispering her name."

"Jessica was the best friend I've ever had," Melanie said.

She was up and out the door before Myrna could see the tears in her eyes.

MICHAEL The first time Michael Drury ever sold himself to a woman, he was twenty-nine years old. An ample Beverly Hills matron had intimated to Michael that she would just *love* company this weekend on her trip to the Racquet Club in Palm Springs. . . .

He had the matron pick him up in front of the Hollywood Hotel, where he said he was staying. She seemed amused with his little fiction.

He got in the back seat of her chauffeured silver Bentley. She took him shopping and bought him a new Beverly Hills wardrobe.

For a boy who'd grown up behind the Omaha stockyards, Rodeo Drive was paradise.

His only fear—which haunted him all the way to Palm Springs— was: What if I get in bed with this fat old woman and I can't get it up? What kind of gigolo can't get a hard-on?

He performed beautifully and often during those two long days, and she showed him off to her friends.

The affair ran five months. By the time she dumped him for another struggling actor, Michael had acquired a string of other rich playmates.

His marriage, of course, was now a joke. He came home at most two nights a week, always afraid that he would pass on a venereal disease to Sara. But after a time, Sara and he no longer made love, and his fear went away.

The pattern remained the same. The matrons he squired around showered him with gifts and passed him on to others. Kathryn Wilson was such a referral.

She was different. She paid for dinners, and tickets, and introduced him to sailing and skiing. But she did not give him lavish gifts, his customary allowance, or access to any of her credit cards or charge accounts.

Yes, she was different. After spending a few evenings at her weathered redwood frame house on the edge of a bluff overlooking the Pacific Ocean, he found himself able to talk to her as with none of the others about his life.

He told her how one day he'd gone to the slaughterhouse and watched as his father took a huge machete-like knife and slashed open the gut of the cow that was hanging upside down. All the blood, all the innards . . . The nightmares lasted into early manhood. And he told her about how his mother spurned his affection, how even when he shipped off to the Army, she wouldn't let him kiss her, only giving him a small peck on the cheek. And of Sara, how he'd let Sara and his daughter Laura down so many times. . . .

The way she listened, he knew that she was in love with him. She was twenty years older, and the product of a most respectable upperclass California family (oil accounting for the bulk of their fortune), and she should not have been able to understand him at all. But she did. And after they made love, she was always tender, and told him how sorry she was for his past life, and how things would be different now—that she had never believed that she would love again after being widowed at thirty . . . but with Michael she was once more happy and whole . . . and she would make Michael happy and whole, too.

He even got used to saying "I love you" after their lovemaking. It made him feel less like a toy.

After six months, she began taking him to formal sit-down dinners with friends of hers, including James Stewart and Gregory Peck and Gloria Swanson. He saw Pickfair, and attended Buster Keaton's birthday party, and was invited to play golf with a threesome that included William Holden and James Cagney.

Now he felt a part of Kathryn's Old Hollywood, an accepted member. Going back home to Sara and Laura was increasingly difficult. Though he loved them, he could barely get through a night at the small apartment.

Then Kathryn asked him to marry her.

He was still trying to give her an answer.

"We should really try and stop."

"God, it would be hard."

"So would lung cancer," Kathryn said.

She had read a *Time* story about the Surgeon General's new report on smoking.

Now when they lay abed in the evening shadows, smoking their cigarettes after making love, Kathryn was inclined to give little speeches.

He laughed. "Can't I enjoy my cigarette in peace?"

She leaned over and kissed him. "Are you still going to call Laura?"

"I already did."

"Oh."

"It'll be nice to see her."

"Yes, it will."

Kathryn lay back. She always kept herself covered. She was self-conscious about her fifty-two-year-old body. Actually, she was an erotic woman.

"I know you're scared about it, Kathryn."

"I guess I am."

"Just because I'm going to see my daughter doesn't mean I'm going back to my wife."

"You aren't ever tempted?"

He wanted to be honest. "Sometimes. In some ways, I still love Sara."

"I know you do."

"But that doesn't mean I'll ever go back. It really doesn't."

"I hope not," she said. "We have a nice life together. I don't want it to end."

He leaned over and kissed her gently on the mouth. "Neither do I, Kathryn. Neither do I."

SARA After watching Jack Paar for a while, Sara went into Laura's room and gave her another good-night kiss, then went to bed.

She tried hard to forget how Michael, celebrating his first role in an "A" picture, had swept her up and carried her into this bedroom. Their lovemaking was tender that night, much as it had been back in Omaha when he was the class rebel and she was the earnest upper-middle-class girl from the area known as Happy Hollow.

How handsome he'd been, dark hair, menacing eyes—and how bright.

She remembered how they met. He surprised her one warm September afternoon of junior year when he strolled into her journalism class. Each was cautious around the other, but when Michael won the lead in the production of *Our Town* in which Sara had a small part, they found themselves sharing a common interest.

The rest was history.

The phone rang.

She snatched it up quickly. It was Bellamy.

"I'm gonna have to vanish for a little while but expect to hear from me."

When she put down the phone, she was shaken. She'd never heard Bellamy this frantic.

Maybe this time he'd really done it.

Maybe he'd finally bitten off more than he could chew.

BOBBY It was 2:43 A.M. and Bobby still couldn't sleep. He sat in his study at his desk, still in his shirt sleeves. He stared at a photo album he'd taken from a locked desk drawer.

He'd been crazy to take such a risk, all these photographs of himself and Marilyn, but . . .

He closed his eyes and remembered her. How sweet-natured she'd been. And how ineffably sad.

She'd had one of those terrible childhoods you read about in the sob-sister magazines, and it had left her scarred. She was all need, all feeling, inexpressibly lonely.

Tell me I'm pretty. Tell me I'm sexy. Do you like this new dress? Do you like my hair? Do you like me?

She wasn't a star at all when you got to know her. She was this naive girl, intimidated by all the people who wanted something from her.

She was also the girl who took his virginity—not physically, but emotionally and spiritually.

He put his head back now and thought of all the ways she'd changed him.

She had taught him the beauty to be found in sunsets, in animals, in music, in holding each other. She had taken him away from a brutal world of dog-eat-dog and winner-take-all.

They had been so erotically attuned to each other, sometimes making love three or four times a night.

And she had taught him how to love.

And now, instead of loving her and venerating her memory, he had to think of his career, had to be the old Bobby: hard, controlled, insular.

He wanted the taste and scent of her. He wanted the soft-eyed little-girl tenderness. He wanted another job, another world, another life.

He wanted *her*.

And he wanted Lenihan to find the tapes and save his brother.

Most of all, he wanted to close his eyes and remember the waves crashing at Big Sur, remember how they'd swum in the moonlit ocean and then made love on the beach beneath a wool blanket, and how sometimes when Marilyn's tiny cat sat on her lap in her bedroom they pretended that this was the child they would have someday.

Most of all he wanted *her*.

He wanted Marilyn.

HOOVER J. Edgar Hoover lay in his bed saying his nightly prayers. He used to kneel, but now the damned arthritis in his knees was killing him.

He prayed for himself and his good health, for Clyde and his good health, for the good health of his dogs, and for Melanie's success.

Please God. This country needs a leader who is pure in both mind and heart and who will run it the way the Founding Fathers intended. And punish those who do not behave properly.

Please help Melanie succeed, Lord. She's just like you and me. A real patriot, Lord; a real patriot.

PART TWO

"Nothing is more dangerous than
the influence of private interests
on public affairs."

—*Jean Jacques Rousseau*

I'm going to tell you about Rob because I saw his picture on the society page the other day.

When I was in ninth grade, there was this handsome, wealthy boy named Rob (I won't say his last name) and he started giving me rides home from school. He was a senior. His parents had given him this really nice new Chrysler convertible.

But pretty soon I noticed that Rob never picked me up right at school . . . he waited until I'd walked several blocks.

I lived kind of out of the way, so I didn't see many other kids on my way home.

He'd always drive out along the ocean to where you could find private little groves of trees in the hills. And we'd . . . Well, we didn't go all the way, but everything else.

Then one day I asked him why he didn't ever let me get in his car at school, but of course I knew why.

He said his parents wanted him to go out with "nice" girls and that meant girls with money. He told me he loved me. I could see that he was sincere, that he really did care about me. But I also could see how afraid he was of his parents.

Things went on the same way for another month and then the prom came along and I knew he wouldn't ask me. And he didn't. He asked this beautiful, prominent senior girl to go with him. She was a diving champion. People said she'd probably go to the next Olympics.

The night of the prom, I let this other boy, this kind of mean

89

kid named Mitch who lived down the street from me—I let Mitch get me drunk on some wine he'd swiped from his parents.

And I let him put his hand inside my bra. And I let him put his hand inside my panties and then I went all the way with him. My first time.

I didn't enjoy it. I just wanted to be able to tell Rob that it had happened . . . that now, no matter what he did, he'd never be the first boy who had me.

Well, when I got home, I was really drunk and really wasn't paying much attention to what time it was, and I called Rob and told him what had happened, with Mitch and all, and then his mother got on the extension and said, "Rob, I don't know who this tramp is, but I never want you to talk to her again."

And you know what? Rob never did. Ever. He'd see me in the hall or in the cafeteria at lunchtime and it was like I was invisible.

I hadn't thought of him in years, and then the other day I opened up the L.A. Times and there Rob was in the society section, getting some kind of humanitarian award.

You know what I wonder now, Louella?

If I ran into Rob today, do you think he'd speak to me, now that I'm a movie star?

MELANIE One day, when she could help herself no longer, Melanie confessed her real feelings to Jessica, and Jessica fled the mansion in which beautiful twelve-year-old Melanie lived.

A few weeks later, Jessica came down with rheumatic fever and died.

The years bore on. Melanie Baines was presented to Dallas society, looking like the teenage Grace Kelly. She went east to Vassar, where her mother herself had gone, and on some weekends flew down to Washington, D.C., where J. Edgar Hoover, a good family friend, showed her around the FBI building and told her all about the Bureau.

In her junior year, she told Mr. Hoover that over the past two years she'd become a black belt in Tae Kwon Do, a champion marksman, and an expert with electronic bugging devices, and now she wanted to become the first female FBI agent.

The director was stunned. He gave her all the reasons why women weren't suited to be agents.

She listened patiently and said, "I'd be an ideal agent, Mr. Hoover. I don't drink, smoke, or even use bad language. I was raised to be a lady and I'm still a lady." She smiled at him. "I could really be a help to you if nobody knew about me. I could do jobs that some of your official agents couldn't."

The director smiled. He'd long had the same notion himself: an unofficial troubleshooter he could use for the most delicate jobs. And who better than a pretty young woman? What a perfect cover.

In her first six months, she seduced a congressman, long an opponent of the FBI, and taped the proceedings. Suddenly the man became a big supporter of Mr. Hoover. A few weeks after that, she broke into the offices of a Georgetown shrink and photographed some of his files. He had several congressmen as patients. A month after that, she bugged the room in which a strategy session for a Democratic congressman was being held. The congressman lost badly.

As her professional life prospered, her personal life grew grim. She still thought about her childhood friend Jessica and a particularly troubling incident that had happened years ago.

While other girls her age were discovering boys, Melanie had no interest in boys at all. She just wanted Jessica.

One day at a class picnic, she saw Jessica kissing a boy. Melanie was sick, angry, and disgusted.

How could Jessica betray her this way?

The next day, Melanie invited Jessica to the mansion, and they went out to the gazebo in the back. Melanie told her how much she loved her and how she wanted to spend her life with Jessica and how she lay awake nights longing for Jessica to be next to her in bed.

Jessica said, "But, Melanie, I want to be with boys now. I want to be a nice, normal teenager. And you should too."

Melanie slapped her until her nose bled, until Jessica got up and ran far away. Melanie collapsed on the gazebo floor and stayed there until sundown.

And then two weeks later, Jessica died.

Melanie too, "discovered" boys. She didn't like them much, and so the summer of her high-school sophomore year, she had another lesbian affair, this one with an energetic girl visiting from Milwaukee. Everything went fine until the girl began to regard Melanie as highly unstable.

She didn't share any of this with Mr. Hoover. He wouldn't understand.

Melanie drove around the grade school several times in the blue Chevrolet sedan, rented from Hertz.

Neither the nuns nor the lay teachers were aware of the car. They were too busy scooting kids inside the wide double doors of the two-story red-brick building.

Then she pulled up in the shade of a dusty oak tree.

Melanie wore a white silk blouse, a dark blue fitted skirt, and red two-inch pumps that emphasized her delectable legs. She checked her rearview mirror for the bronze Pontiac that had been following her since last night. The tail's name was Tully, a private investigator. She'd already checked him out.

Melanie glanced at her Longines wristwatch. The school bell would ring in two minutes. Maybe she'd missed the woman she was looking for.

The red 1959 Plymouth two-door suddenly appeared at the west corner of the playground, near the jungle gym.

She picked up her binoculars to get a better look at the woman driving. She recognized her immediately from the photograph she'd been given. Sara Drury.

The passenger door of the Plymouth opened and a delicate little blonde girl in a blue jumper and white blouse got out.

Laura Drury. Age ten. Melanie had spent the past two days familiarizing herself with all of them—Bellamy and Sara Drury and Mayhew and Tully.

Laura leaned back into the car to give her mother a kiss. Then she was off, carrying a lunch bucket in one hand and a book in the other. She went straight into school.

Melanie watched Sara for a few moments. She was a nice-looking blonde, slightly prim and bookish. Definite possibilities there. Melanie speculated on many women as possible lovers. Most of them failed to meet her standards.

This trip hadn't been strictly necessary, but Melanie had wanted to check out the routine of Sara and her daughter. If she couldn't find Sara's boss, Bellamy, then Melanie would have to compromise Sara. And her little girl.

Take the kid and Sara would find those tapes. Somehow. Some way. Melanie was sure of it.

Melanie had just reached the corner when she saw the bronze Pontiac sedan in the rearview mirror. Tully was still hanging in there.

Melanie would settle with him right now.

TULLY Vanessa had suffered all night, reliving the nightmare over and over: Bellamy putting the gun barrel next to her sex. As for Tully, he had a full night trying to find Bellamy. He'd promised Vanessa he wouldn't kill him. But that still left him a lot of leeway.

Finally, on one of his cruises by Bellamy's house, he'd spotted Melanie Baines' car. She was obviously looking for Bellamy, too. Tully decided to follow her.

Suddenly, the redhead's car squealed away from the school curb.

Before Tully could even get his car in gear, she was rounding the far corner. He floored the accelerator.

He was going to stay on Melanie's tail, find Bellamy, and take care of business.

S A R A She spent all morning working on a piece about the forgotten Hollywood beauties of the forties. For Sara, their stars still shone.

Jean Peters . . . Jennifer Jones . . . Arlene Dahl . . . Ann Sheridan . . . Wanda Hendrix . . . Mona Freeman . . . these were the young women Sara idolized when she was growing up. In the theater darkness, they'd made her laugh, cry, and shudder as they worked their way through unlikely scripts.

Though most of them continued working well into the fifties, they had reached their zenith a decade earlier. Now, a few of them were on TV occasionally, but the movies had changed and there was little room for the quiet beauty and dignified sexiness of these women.

She was just finishing the sixth page, thinking that she might have slighted Arlene Dahl early in the article, when she heard the shouting in the outer office.

She hurried to the door and peered out.

A distinguished-looking gent—gray hair, ascot, natty sports coat and slacks—was trying to push his way past Jeff to get into Bellamy's office.

"I'll kill the sonofabitch with my own hands!" he shouted.

The line didn't fit the man's persona. Back when Curtis Simmons had been a star at MGM, he'd always played paternal doctors and professors and elder statesmen. He would never have taken a part like the one he was playing now.

Jeff held him off like a football lineman. Sara scurried over to them.

"This is really a coincidence!" she spouted. She got a whiff of the actor's breath and realized that he was drunk.

"Do you know that I had you on my list of actors to call tomorrow morning?" Sara said.

Curtis Simmons suddenly gave up his struggling, and looked at her. "What are you babbling about, dear lady?" He slipped into the familiar ersatz British diction.

"I'm writing a piece on movie stars who are also great Shakespearean actors."

It was easy to see that his vanity was overcoming his wrath.

"Why don't we go into my office and talk? You can even have a drink if you like." She nodded at Jeff. Bellamy kept a fifth of bourbon in his desk drawer.

She led Simmons into her office, helped him into a chair, took the bottle and glass that Jeff handed through the door, and seated herself on the other side of the desk. "You looked pretty angry out there, Mr. Simmons. Would you care to tell me what's bothering you?"

He was not yet drunk. He poured himself a stiff drink. He took a gulp, gasped a little as the bourbon burned its way down, and said, "I keep trying to put a good face on this, but I guess it's impossible." She thought of all the times she'd seen his face on movie screens in Omaha.

"My wife is dying of cancer—hasn't got more than a month or two—and during the last six months of her illness, I've been having an affair with a young actress I met on the set of a TV show. I've been lonely—my wife basically shut me out over a year ago, preferring, I guess, to die alone. Anyway, your boss Bellamy took some pictures of the young actress and me . . . in a most indelicate position. I got a phone call from him recently demanding $20,000—or else he would send the photos to my wife."

Sara felt sickened. Bellamy was scum.

"I'm sorry," she said.

"I want those photos," he said. And, with quick and certain grace, he took from inside his suit jacket a silver gun and pointed it at Sara. "And you're going to help me get them. Right now."

TOLSON Director Hoover had two offices in the FBI building. One was the large, flag-bedecked room with the long table and soft leather chairs where Hoover officially greeted important visitors and held senior staff meetings. On the far wall of this office was a door leading to the inner office where he did most of his work.

Clyde Tolson returned from a United Way luncheon. Clyde had always agreed to participate in charities since Edgar despised glad-handing events. Clyde, on the other hand, enjoyed them.

Tolson opened the door of the large office. Empty. Edgar loved the majesty of the room—the two large American flags and the emblem of the FBI between them—this kind of ceremonial intimidation. Tolson was uncomfortable around it.

Tolson walked to the smaller door on the far wall and knocked.

No answer.

Though Edgar didn't like to admit it, he was starting to lose his hearing. For a man of Edgar's vanity, a hearing aid was out of the question. So one spoke to him a little louder. And knocked a little more forcefully.

Tolson knocked a little more forcefully.

He would go in and leave Edgar a note, asking for a brief meeting about the cars in the next year's budget.

Tolson went inside, closing the door behind him. The small office was as dark and personal as the official office was bright and formal.

He went behind the desk, looking for a note pad.

The desk, as usual, was clean of everything save for standard black telephone and intercom, lone gold Cross pen and gold-framed photograph of Edgar's mother, a woman Tolson had always considered to be something of a cold and hostile authoritarian. Tolson's own mother had been sweet and silent, a beauty who had spent her life being pushed around by a selfish husband and selfish in-laws. Tolson could not think of his mother without an enormous melancholy overtaking him.

The drawers were as neat as the desk top. He found a small note pad in the middle drawer on the left row and took it out. And then he saw the name and numbers that Edgar had written at the bottom of the page.

MELANIE, ROOM 408, SYCAMORE 6-5358

Tolson recognized the prefix as the Los Angeles area. Pasadena, if he wasn't mistaken.

He stood there angry and frightened as he realized the implications. After the last episode, Edgar had given his solemn pledge that he would never again have anything to do with Melanie. Yet here it was, less than two years later, and Edgar was dealing with her again.

Clyde Tolson felt like a betrayed lover.

He thought back to last night. They always watched the late news together, then had a nightcap before Tolson went back to his own apartment. But last night Edgar had excused himself and disappeared upstairs for a time, and now Tolson knew why.

So he could contact Melanie.

This was the dark side of Edgar, the reckless side. It scared Tolson because someday it would bring Edgar down. And with him would come Clyde Tolson.

He had no idea why Edgar had contacted Melanie again but he was damned well going to find out—by confronting Edgar directly, damn the consequences.

The confrontation would best be left for dinner, where he would say: Edgar, we have a partnership. A bond. Based on our affection for each other and our mutual desire to see the Bureau get the respect it deserves. Working with Melanie could destroy everything we've built up over the years. I want to retire with you and spend our last years fishing in the mountains and seeing the new shows in New York and eating fresh shark in Miami Beach.

Melanie could destroy everything.

The really funny thing, Louella, is that I can pretty much talk about everything that happened to me—sexually, I mean—except for the very first thing when I was six years old. There was this man that my family called "Uncle," and one day he babysat with me and he kept having me get up in his lap. I knew something was wrong with it. I'm not sure how I knew, I just— knew. That's when it happened. He asked me if I'd give my "Uncle" a kiss and I did but it was just a quick little one and then he said, "No, give Uncle a better kiss than that," so I gave him a longer kiss—I think I was still kissing him on the cheek— and while I was doing that, he put his hand up my dress and touched me down there. I tried getting away from him but he was very strong. He just held me there, wouldn't let me move at all except for how I was squirming, and then he slid his finger inside me and up me and I can remember how much it hurt and how hard I started crying and how I just kept begging him to let me go. But he didn't, he just kept his finger up there, and he was breathing real hard now and I could smell onions and beer on his breath, and he started moving his groin against my backside and breathing even harder. After a while he took me in and laid me down on my bed and he said that if I ever told anybody, we'd both be in a lot of trouble and that we'd both be put in prison. I wasn't real sure what prison was exactly but I knew it was a terrible place where terrible things would happen to little girls. So I promised I'd never tell. And I didn't, not until now, Louella, because you said you wanted the truth and that's what I want to give you, the truth. For the first time in my life.

MELANIE

As a tail, Tully wasn't much.

He lost Melanie twice, in fact, and she had to do everything except send up flares so he could find her again. She loved toying with people, but enough was enough. Tully was pathetic.

Melanie led him into the heart of Los Angeles, to a decayed area with an entire block of empty warehouses. She found a warehouse with a door that would open up. She drove in and parked in the center of the vast, shadowy space that smelled of dust and oil. The floor was littered with crunchy dried rat droppings.

She left her car and hid in a dark corner behind a large, rusted barrel.

Would Tully be so dumb as to fall for this setup?

Sure enough. A few seconds later, Tully came in. On foot. With his gun out. He was dressed well, a nice-looking guy. He crept into the big empty echoing warehouse, looking around cautiously.

He looked inside Melanie's car, then opened the door and leaned in to check out the glove compartment.

Melanie came up and put her gun with the silencer right at the bottom of Tully's back.

"Stand up."

"Hey, shit, no need for guns."

"Right. Give me yours."

Tully stood up. And gave her his gun.

"Hands over your head."

"What the hell're you doing?"

"Do it."

"Like in the movies, huh?" Tully tried to smile but Melanie could see he was scared.

"Yeah, like in the movies," Melanie said.

She patted Tully down and got his wallet. She looked Tully's investigator's license over carefully and handed back his wallet. "Who's your client?"

"They never tell me."

"Right. Who is it?"

She put the end of the silencer against Tully's right eye.

"Jesus, the name is Mayhew. He's a studio executive."

That was enough for Melanie. She hated pathetic assholes.

"Jesus, listen—"

She put the bullet right into his eye. The exit wound sprayed blood and tissue and bone chips into the air. A little got on the windshield. She could take care of it with a handkerchief.

She dragged Tully by one arm over to the corner with the barrel. She took the lid off, tipped the barrel down on its side and stuffed Tully in, stood the barrel back up, and put the lid back on.

She wiped the windshield. There was blood all over the floor, but there wasn't much she could do about that.

TOLSON
Tolson called a friend on a lower-order movie magazine who might have heard something about Melanie.

"Mel?"

"Yeah?"

"I call you at a bad time? This is Clyde Tolson."

"Shit."

"Well, nice to talk to you, too."

"Got fuckin' coffee all over my fuckin' crotch."

"How's the wife, Mel?"

"Bitch left me. Took the kid, too."

"I am sorry, Mel."

"Said I was too hard to live with. Fuckin' cunt."

"Yeah, Mel, pretty hard to imagine you being hard to live with. Say, Mel, do you remember a gal named Melanie Baines?"

"Sure I do. A lesbo. Used to go out with dyke movie stars. Face and bod like that and she likes broads. A fuckin' waste."

"You heard anything about her lately?"

Mel laughed. "Oh, yeah, I heard about her all right. Crazy fuckin' bitch."

"So she's still out there?"

"Oh, yeah. Helped demolish this lesbo bar one night. Threw a dyke through a window."

"My, my."

"No charges filed, though. This dyke had pulled a shiv on her. Seems Melanie had tried to pick up the dyke's girlfriend."

"Hey, Mel? Thanks a lot for your help."

"Any fuckin' time," Mel said.

Tolson hadn't wanted to call his informant at the LAPD until he knew for sure that Melanie was still out there. Even a single call would alert a few ears that the FBI was interested in Melanie, and Tolson didn't want her name associated with the Bureau in any way.

Now he'd call the LAPD and see if her rap sheet had any new material. He wanted to have his argument with Edgar laid out in advance.

S A R A All her life Sara had seen people pull out guns and point them at other people. But Curtis Simmons' gun was real, not celluloid, and it was pointing right at Sara.

"My wife deserves to die with some dignity," Simmons said. "If she ever saw those—" The words caught in his throat. For a moment, she thought he might cry. "He even made some audiotapes of us somehow, bugged the room we were in, I guess."

"I wish you'd put the gun away."

"When I have the photos."

"You don't think I have anything to do with this, do you?"

"I don't care. Getting the photos is all that counts." He leaned closer to the desk and stuck the gun in her face. "Let me into Bellamy's private office."

"Put your gun away, and I'll take you into his office. I'll help you look."

"What kind of trick is that?"

"No trick. I'll help you look for the photos."

A knock sounded on her door. Jeff called, "Are you all right in there, Sara?"

"I'm fine."

Curtis Simmons allowed himself a small smile. He clicked on the safety and put the gun away. "I believe we have a deal."

They searched for twenty minutes—desk drawers, filing cabinets, closets, even the linings of two worn topcoats—and found nothing.

"What makes you sure they're here?" Sara asked.

"He's blackmailed other people. I'm not the first. He keeps the photos here. I've been told all about it."

Sara could tell by his sighs that Simmons was sliding back into anxiety.

"He's quite the bastard," Simmons said after starting a second search through the filing cabinets. "He wanted cash. My God, I don't have twenty thousand dollars. My wife's medical bills have wiped us out."

She wished Bellamy were here so she could confront him with this.

"I told him that my wife had terminal cancer and he said, 'That's your problem.' "

She said, "I'm going to open the safe for you."

"The safe?"

"Yes. Behind that landscape print over there."

She opened the top drawer, found the combination taped to the bottom.

She swung the hinged landscape back and set to work on the numbers, discreetly shielding them from Simmons.

"I'm indebted to you," he said.

"The photos may not be in here, Mr. Simmons. Don't get your hopes up."

She turned the dial right, then left again. A faint click.

"That should do it," she said.

She reached in, felt two manilla envelopes, and pulled them out. One had "CS" on it. The other was unmarked.

"Here we are," Sara said.

Inside the first were several black-and-white prints showing Simmons and a fetching young woman, and a roll of film.

"You said there were some tapes?"

"Yes."

In the second she found two Scotch audio reels. "Here." She handed him the envelopes.

"You're just giving them to me?"

"I am."

"But why?"

"Mr. Simmons, just go home and see your wife."

He took her slight shoulders in his large hands and kissed her on the forehead. "Thank you."

She closed the wall safe, swung the painting shut, and escorted Simmons to the reception area door and showed him out.

The incident was over.

TOLSON

"Captain Miller? This is Clyde Tolson."

"Yes, Mr. Tolson."

"I don't know if you remember meeting me at that charity benefit for the Rams last year."

"Of course I do. It was a pleasure meeting both you and Mr. Hoover. How can I help you, Mr. Tolson?"

"Clyde, please."

"Clyde, then."

"I'm calling to ask you a favor."

"The LAPD is always glad to help the FBI."

Tolson paused. "Actually, this isn't strictly for the FBI. It's more personal."

"I see."

"A favor for a friend, actually. He wants some background information on a young woman."

"And she has a record?"

"Well, frankly, he doesn't know much about her. He would like to have some sense of her background. Ordinarily, I'd go through channels."

"No problem, Clyde. Just give me the lady's name."

"Melanie Baines." He spelled it.

"Got it."

He returned Tolson's call forty-seven minutes later.

"Well, she definitely has a record," Captain Miller said. He seemed hesitant. "I don't mean to pry here, Clyde, but I hope your friend is not involved with this lady."

"Serious?"

"Assault and battery in a lesbian bar in North Hollywood, among other things. She destroyed most of the place herself."

"Jail?"

"Not according to this. Charges were dropped."

"What else?"

"Attempted murder. She put two bullets in the windshield of a female friend. The friend called the department but then decided to drop charges."

"Anything else?" Tolson could feel his heart sinking.

"Then there's two counts of reckless driving and one of resisting arrest. The second reckless got her another assault-and-battery charge."

"Oh?"

"She blamed the driver of the parked car she hit. He was an older man and she beat him up pretty good."

"Any jail time on that one?"

"Not on any of them. This one has friends in high places, somebody who can put the heat on the boys downtown. The worst she's ever done was six hours in a holding cell."

Yes, and Tolson knew just who that "somebody" was.

"Oh, wait a minute," the officer said. "On her second reckless driving she was ordered to see a psychiatrist. Judge made her go to twenty weekly sessions. A Dr. Nessmith. Oswald Nessmith."

"In L.A.?"

"Yeah, and the D.A.'s office was really pissed. Her file is full of their memos wondering why they've never been able to put this one away."

"Friends in high places you said."

"Federal friends, you want my guess. Big time friends."

"I hope you're wrong."

"I do too, Clyde. I do too."

SARA

"Some guy, huh? That Eichmann."

Sara nodded. Manny, who ran the outdoor hot dog stand, was looking at the cover of the three-month-old *Time* magazine someone had left behind. The cover subject was Adolf Eichmann. Manny's left arm still bore the tiny blue numbers he had been given in the concentration camp where his wife and two sons had been killed.

Manny gave Sara her chili dog. While she ate, and drank her usual Pepsi, Sara read the *Los Angeles Times*. She tried to forget the scene in the office with Curtis Simmons.

Meanwhile the world was going to hell. Russia had agreed to send arms to Cuba. Three more deformed Thalidomide babies had been born. The U.S. was establishing a military council in South Vietnam—some experts worried that we might be headed into a war there.

"How's the screenwriting business?" Manny said, wiping off the counter with a clean cloth.

Good old Manny. He took an interest in his customers. L.A. needed two million more like him.

"My agent's shopping my latest to Warner Brothers," Sara said. She held up crossed fingers. "Here's hoping."

"You're due to score," Manny said.

Several years ago, a beautiful young midwestern couple had left Omaha, he to be an actor, she a writer. In Los Angeles, they pursued their dreams. A little girl came along unexpectedly and changed their plans some—six months after giving birth to Laura, Sara freelanced

111

a few articles to movie magazines. There was little time to write the screenplays she was fashioning after her idol, Billy Wilder.

Sara began to notice frustration in Michael. He was a skillful and engaging actor. But so were several thousand other young men around Los Angeles. He started working with a small, experimental theater group that soon became his whole life. He got a good notice in the L.A. *Times* for one of his theater plays, and as a result became convinced that this small theater could bring him to the notice of major picture executives if he just hung in there. Sara saw less and less of him.

They began to argue viciously, and after such fights, he'd stay away even longer. He began showing up in very nice clothes, and driving a very nice car. When she asked where he got them, he slammed out of the house, shouting that it was none of her damned business. She feared that he was in trouble with the law. How else to explain handtailored suits and white convertibles? But one day, on Wilshire Boulevard, she saw him stepping out of a shiny new Cadillac sedan. A liveried chauffeur had opened the door for him. Behind Michael came a glittering older lady a bit overdressed for the middle of the afternoon. She sparkled as only a Beverly Hills matron can, Zsa-Zsa Gabor being the patron saint of all these women. The woman took hold of Michael's arm possessively, and they swept into a photography studio. Now Sara knew where Michael got his suits and convertibles. The polite word for it was gigolo.

It ended without much drama. She came home after work one day to find all his possessions gone. That night he called her and said, "Maybe we should try it apart for a while."

"Michael, we've been apart for a long time already. You're never here."

"You know what I mean."

"Please, Michael," she heard herself pleading. "Let's give it another try."

"Not right now, Sara. I've got a lot of things I need to think through."

In a week, she had lost six pounds and developed a fever. She had Laura and her job at *Insight*. She had to hold all this together. And somehow she did.

"Another Pepsi, Sara?"

Sara raised her head. "No, thanks. I'd better get back to the office."

She walked back to work, unaware of the red-haired woman following her.

In the office, Sara asked Jeff, "Any sign of Bellamy yet?"

Jeff shook his head.

"Did you try his house again?" Sara said.

"Uh-huh. Mrs. Bellamy is of the opinion that he's probably in Vegas, quote, sticking it in some hooker who'll give him a disease, unquote."

"Nice to know there are still a few happy marriages left, anyway."

Jeff laughed as Sara went into her office. "They're sneak-previewing that William Holden picture in Pasadena tonight. I've got tickets."

She stuck her head back out the door. "I'll talk to Mrs. Gregory. I could use a movie tonight."

For the next twenty minutes, she forgot all about Bellamy—she was going to confront him with the Curtis Simmons episode—and about Michael and about her own unsold screenplays, and instead worked with great concentration on a piece about the "Hollywood Canteen" pictures used as American propaganda during the darkest days of World War II. Propaganda or not, some of them had been very entertaining pictures.

Her phone rang. "For you," Jeff said on the intercom.

"Take a number."

"It's your ex-husband."

Even though Sara was not actually divorced, Jeff insisted on calling Michael her "ex." She picked up the phone.

"Sara," he said, "something's come up we should talk about."

There was this older girl in high school. She was the prettiest girl I'd ever seen and I had kind of a crush on her. I don't know what else to call it. Every time she'd even look at me I'd break out in a smile and feel giddy. I started fixing my hair like hers and wearing the same shade of lipstick and the same bobby sox and brown-and-white saddle shoes. And sometimes at night, I'd have dreams about us, and we'd be embracing. In the dream, you couldn't tell who was who because we were so much alike. Then all of a sudden, at school the girl started avoiding me, like there was something wrong with me. And when I'd see her talking to somebody in the halls, she'd always lean in and whisper and smirk at me. Then I started avoiding her, too, because that really hurt. I imagined all the terrible things she might be whispering to the other girls. And I couldn't get it out of my mind, how bad and cheap and freaky I felt. Like down inside I was this freak that didn't belong with good, decent people. Not with the kind of thoughts and dreams I had sometimes. Then I couldn't wait to get home—to whatever foster home I was living in—so I could go down to the basement and hide the way I used to. When I was down in the basement and nobody was around, I didn't feel like such a freak. I felt safe. I still wonder about that girl. I wonder what she thinks when she sees one of my movies. Or sees me on TV. She probably tells all sorts of lies about me and her whole family believes them.

MELANIE Where was she most likely to find the tapes? After killing Tully, Melanie decided to give Bellamy's girlfriend, a dancer named Erica Dane, another try.

For the past two days, Erica's duplex had been empty. Melanie assumed she was hiding out with Bellamy somewhere. But she had to be back soon because she had a chorus job at Twentieth tomorrow, a Shirley MacLaine musical. Now was a good time to sit and wait for her.

As Melanie sat waiting in her car, she thought about some of the bars she'd been touring lately. There were times when she just wanted to have fun. L.A. was a labyrinth of bars, gay and straight alike, and she promised herself a major tour of all the new "in" spots when this gig for Mr. Hoover was over.

In her rearview mirror, she saw a Yellow cab approach and stop, and a woman get out.

Erica Dane looked just like her photograph, except her tits were even bigger.

She was carrying an overnight bag. She wore a frilly pink blouse and her knockers made Melanie's mouth water. She was tall with bleached hair and a hard face. Melanie had found out that she'd left home when she was fourteen and worked the midwestern striptease circuit of the early fifties. Now twenty-seven, she'd lived several lifetimes already.

She went up the walk to her duplex.

Melanie was within three feet of her by the time she opened the front door.

Melanie pushed her through the doorway, stepped inside, slammed the door shut, and then proceeded to slap her four times across the face.

Blood started running from Erica's nose and mouth.

"I'm nobody to mess with, Erica. And I just wanted to make sure you understood that. All right?"

Erica dropped her overnight case on the floor. She started sobbing, standing there in the middle of the room with those luscious tits heaving inside that pink blouse.

"Who the fuck are you?" she sobbed. "Who the fuck are you?"

TOLSON

'Dr. Nessmith, please."
"May I say who's calling?"
"My name is Tolson."

He hated checking up on Edgar this way, but he had to. He had worked too long, too hard to let Edgar ruin it. In the past six months, John Kennedy had seemed less afraid of Edgar—feeling his oats as President. Edgar needed something even more destructive on the Kennedys, and Clyde was going to get it for him.

The brothers' affairs with Marilyn Monroe—which had driven Edgar to enlist Melanie—was what he needed.

"Dr. Nessmith here."

"Hello, Doctor. I'm Clyde Tolson of the FBI. You were contacted by Special Agent Rollins, who confirmed that I would be calling, and that I'm who I say I am?"

"Yes, sir. Nice meeting you, Mr. Tolson. How can I help you?"

"I just need a little information on a former patient of yours. A young woman named Melanie Baines."

"What information, Mr. Tolson?"

"I know that the court ordered her to see you."

"Yes. But I'm afraid any information I have is confidential."

"Even where national security is concerned?"

"National security?"

"Dr. Nessmith, I'm not making this call frivolously."

"I'm sure you're not."

"I don't need specifics. Just some general conclusions."

117

"All right."

"Is she dangerous?"

Hesitation. "She's what we call chronically antisocial, Mr. Tolson, meaning that she's a person likely to be in trouble, who doesn't seem to learn from experience. People like this are typically callous and without firm loyalties."

"That's interesting," Tolson said. "About loyalties." He wondered how Edgar would like hearing that.

"People of this type are emotionally immature and hedonistic. She also tends to rationalize and justify anything she does."

"Meaning what?"

"Some of my colleagues would call her sociopathic. By that they mean someone who commits heinous acts without any guilt."

"In other words, she would never be effective as, say, a law enforcement officer?"

"Oh, no. She doesn't even share what most people would call common reality let alone a conscience. She acts on impulses that the rest of us couldn't possibly relate to." He paused. "Among other things, she's obsessed with this dead friend from her girlhood. To Melanie, her friend is far more real than the people around her."

Tolson had written down the words "antisocial," "callous," "sociopathic" and "impulses."

Dr. Nessmith said, "I'm very uncomfortable talking about one of my patients."

"I appreciate that, Doctor. We're done. Thank you."

He hung up.

He couldn't wait to confront Edgar with his findings.

MAYHEW In 1896, Thomas Edison invented and marketed the Vitascope, a machine that projected images from film onto a screen. The unveiling was on April 23, at Koster & Bial's Music Hall in New York. Not until 1906, when famed director D.W. Griffith began taking his Biograph actors to Los Angeles for the winter months, did Hollywood begin to play a role in the emergence of film as the universal language. Studios began to give the world that most special of all human animals, the movie star. There were Famous Players and Paramount, Universal and Fox, Warner Brothers and General Film.

The glamour stars came from the studios, seldom the independents: Pickford, Fairbanks, Garbo, Gable, Bogart, Arbuckle, Chaplin, Keaton, Hope, Crosby—all creations and creatures of the studios.

And while these stars were shining over Hollywood, on a Pennsylvania farm a handsome kid named Del Mayhew was growing up. Even when he was ten years old and just one more farm kid in a crowded Saturday matinee, he knew that he could be one of those men up on the screen. . . . Randolph Scott or Robert Ryan or Gary Cooper.

When he graduated from high school, when most of his friends were going to work on their family farm or at the beef plant in town, he set off hitchhiking to the West Coast. His mother was convinced that an axe murderer would pick him up, his father that he would fall into the familiar Hollywood traps of drinking and drugs and gambling and women who gave you diseases.

They didn't need to worry. Del Mayhew was smart. When he got to Hollywood, he spent his first two weeks taking all the tours. He took a cold, hard look around and realized that he was only one of thousands of good-looking would-be actors in Hollywood. On his second Friday in town, he got a job in the mailroom at the prominent talent agency William Morris and a sleeping room in the valley.

A few short years later, he was a major Hollywood agent, thanks mainly to the fact that he'd saved the life of the agency's most major of major female stars. She liked to drink and to swim. One midnight at her beach house, she left sixty guests, waded out into the moonlit ocean, and didn't return.

Mayhew dove in and went after her. He swam her back to shore, performed mouth-to-mouth, and got her to the hospital.

This major female star was not one to forget a kindness and so she went to the agency and said, I want Del Mayhew as my agent.

Thus was born the Del Mayhew of the gossip columns, of the *Variety* front page, the Del Mayhew who was always seen with the most glittering starlet of the season on Oscar night.

He never told anybody that on the night he'd saved the star from drowning, he'd also put knockout drops in her drink so that if she took her customary dip he'd get to rescue her.

A few years later, Mayhew let himself be talked into dinner with Ross Finestein, a grumpy old bastard who'd run Millennium Pictures for the past thirty years—during which time, the studio had won Oscars for best picture. Millennium was considered the only small studio with real power.

At dinner that night—while Basil Rathbone and Greer Garson (both members of the British exile community in Hollywood) dined together and Ty Power hustled his starlet-of-the-week at the bar— Ross Finestein told Del Mayhew all about the cancer that was eating him up inside.

"I can't do it any more, kiddo. I can't run that fuckin' studio. I just ain't got the stamina. I'm losin' two pounds a week. Some friggin' diet this is, huh?"

Mayhew liked and admired Finestein. Let Louis B. Mayer and David O. Selznick have their pretensions and their huge empty block-busters. Mayhew preferred Finestein and Harry Cohn, men without polish, perhaps, but men who made good, honest, powerful smaller pictures.

"You're maybe too ambitious," Finestein continued, "but you've got good taste and you give a shit about pictures. That's why I'm talkin' to you tonight, understand? Because you give a shit about making good pictures."

Finestein died three months later. By that time all the legalities had been settled. Del Mayhew was president of Millennium Pictures.

In the first three years of his tenure, Mayhew bought and produced scripts from such writers as Clifford Odets, Ernest Lehman, Waldo Salt and Dalton Trumbo. They made fine commercial pictures, too, much to the surprise of many other studio heads. Mayhew was able to get a good alliance with a distributor so everything was fine. Except for one thing. Finestein had neglected to tell him about the massive studio debt that he had been forced to take on to keep afloat all those years—debt that was now eating up the studio.

Mayhew could see failure threatening within a year or two unless he came up with something. After lunch one rainy Tuesday, he walked into his office, and his secretary (whom he'd seduced on her third day here, just to get it out of the way) said that a man named Rossetti was waiting to see him.

Three weeks after he opened the door and got his first glimpse of Mr. Salvitore Rossetti, the entire studio debt was taken care of and several long-needed improvements were made at Millennium studios.

Everybody in Hollywood knew what was going on. The Mob was buying up Hollywood, and Rossetti was a mobster with a real yen to be a player in the glamorous film business. He had ready access to millions of dollars in cash from the Las Vegas skim. He bought fifty-one percent of Millennium. He kept his word to Mayhew about leaving the pictures alone. Mayhew made the pictures he wanted, exactly the way he wanted to make them. Rossetti became a part of the Hollywood scene.

It was because of Rossetti that Marilyn Monroe, the gorgeous but troubled superstar, agreed to do a picture at Millennium. Rossetti had gotten to know her years ago, when she was still number one at the box office, and after a brief affair, became the father she'd never had.

He told her to make a picture at Millennium, and so she made a picture at Millennium.

But two years ago, Rossetti made himself another friend, a man who happened to be a candidate for president of the United States.

All these years later, Del Mayhew, twenty pounds heavier, hair thinner, disposition grumpier, sat in his office and stared at the blinking button on his phone, the call he had to take.

"Hello, Mr. Rossetti," he said, trying to sound relaxed.

"I screened *Love on a Dark Street* for some friends last night, Del. They loved it."

"Good. Great."

"And I read that issue of *Film Comment* you sent me. I liked the piece on Hitchcock."

"Look, I know why you called."

"You haven't heard from Mr. Tully?"

"Not yet. He was trying to locate a woman named Melanie."

A pause. "I'm not happy about this, Del. I've never asked much of you. I want it resolved within twenty-four hours."

He had never given Del Mayhew a direct order before.

"It will be," Mayhew said. "You have my word on that."

"I want to pay the sonofabitch back. I'm not some piece of garbage he can throw away, even if he is president of the United States. Take care of it for me. Do the right thing."

"Consider it done."

Rossetti broke the connection.

Del Mayhew sat there a long time, rubbing his face.

Direct order. No excuses.

Twenty-four hours.

Five minutes later, Del Mayhew was wheeling his new red Corvette through the studio gates. He had to find Tully, the gumshoe that International Investigators had put on the job—the sleazeball who by now had probably been offering the tapes to the highest bidder. The tapes that Mayhew had fucking paid for and wasn't about to die for.

SARA "Actually," Michael said, "I've been meaning to call you for a couple of weeks. To, uh, tell you."

"Why don't you just say it, Michael," Sara said, "and get it over with?"

"I'm getting married."

She had to say something, couldn't sound as shocked as she felt. "Nice of you to tell me."

"I mean, I know we need to get a divorce, but we can actually do that pretty fast if—well, you know, if you don't contest it."

"Congratulations."

"Should I tell Laura?" Michael asked.

"All right."

"I know you're pissed."

"No. I've been expecting this."

"Sara, I'm really sorry."

"Michael, I have to go. I'll see you tonight."

After quietly hanging up, she had a good cry, hoping it would make her feel better. It didn't make her feel better at all.

TOLSON

The note was on Tolson's desk when he got back from lunch.

Re: Sullivan. Limp handshake; sweaty palms. Don't know if he's our sort. Maybe better off in Far West Office somewhere. Edgar.

Tolson sipped his coffee. Hard to tell how committed Edgar was to getting rid of an agent. Many times Edgar fired off a note in a moment of pique and then forgot about it. But other times he got very angry with Clyde for not carrying out his orders.

So Tolson had to interpret the notes.

Sullivan had a strike against him by virtue of his name. Edgar was not fond of the Irish—whom he still thought of as Socialist heathens—and he was even less fond of Catholics.

Edgar did not call for Sullivan's firing, merely for his banishment to the West, where Edgar wouldn't ever have to see him again.

Edgar tended to fire people on whims: bad breath, bad suit, bad haircut, bad posture, bad shoes and—Edgar's catchall category—"bad attitude."

Tolson, on the other hand, hated to fire people.

He spent the next half hour securing Sullivan a transfer to the Denver office, which was in fact a nice area for a man with three growing sons and a wife who liked the outdoors.

He found his mind wandering back to Melanie.

Tolson sat at his desk and shook his head. By rights, he shouldn't even wait till tonight. He should march right in to Edgar's office and demand that Edgar get rid of Melanie at once.

But Edgar would never forgive him if he started a scene at work.

No, Tolson thought, better wait.

His friend J. Edgar Hoover could be one mean sonofabitch.

MELANIE
Melanie said, "I'm going to give you a choice. You can take those clothes off yourself. Or I will rip them off."

They were in Erica Dane's living room. Melanie had her Luger out. She'd closed all the venetian blinds, and the living room was dim and stuffy. The only air conditioner was a small asthmatic window-unit that dripped onto the gray rug, making a dark spot like dog piss.

She wasn't impressed with anything she'd seen in this duplex. Couldn't Bellamy afford better than this for his mistress? Discount furniture and cheap knickknacks?

Melanie sat on the edge of an overstuffed armchair.

"So what's it going to be?"

"How come you have a gun?"

Melanie laid the gun on the arm of the chair. "I can handle this without it. Take your clothes off."

Erica smirked. "I done it with a girlfriend a few times. But I like a cock better."

"Maybe you had the wrong girl."

Erica quickly removed her blouse. When she was naked from the waist up, her breasts were big happy animals.

"Now the jeans," Melanie said.

She hooked her thumbs into the waist and shoved them down, along with the pale blue underpants. Her pubic thatch was black.

Melanie stood up. "Into the kitchen."

"Frank's going to be plenty pissed."

"Right," Melanie said. She retrieved the gun and gave Erica a shove.

Erica led the way into the kitchen. Tan blinds were drawn against the sunlight. The kitchen was hot. At a formica table were four chairs.

"Rope."

"Rope?" Erica said.

"Any kind."

"There's some clothesline in the closet there."

"Get it."

She didn't move.

Melanie had been staring at Erica's big sleek-as-dolphin tits. Now it was back to business. She took two short steps forward and swung the butt of the Luger against Erica's jaw.

"You fucking bitch!" Erica yelled through her blood and spittle.

Melanie kicked her in the shin, then backhanded her with the gun.

She slid a chair underneath Erica, who landed on the warm plastic seat. Her face was smeared with blood.

Melanie calmly walked over to the closet, found the clothesline, and lashed her arms and chest tight to the back of the chair.

"Now we're going to talk."

"I ain't gonna tell you anything."

"Oh, no?" Melanie said. "You're going to tell me everything I want to know. Everything, you understand?"

----

*One time you asked me how many abortions I've had and I was
ashamed to tell you so I said I didn't remember. But I did. I've
had twelve abortions, only three of them by real doctors. The most
frightening one I had was in the back of this old canvas-covered
truck where this very heavyset woman kept a cigarette stuck in
the corner of her mouth all the time she worked on me. She made
some kind of mistake and I knew I was bleeding a lot more than
I should have and I started to scream but she made a fist of her
hand and hit me right on the side of my head. By the time I woke
up, most of my body below my waist was covered with blood and
my purse was gone and I was real sick. Down near my feet, I
could see this rat kind of slurping up my blood. I tried to get up
but I couldn't. And then this old Negro man came along and
found me and said, "Oh, child. Oh, child." He got me into his
old car and to a hospital. I was real sick for three weeks.*

MAYHEW International Investigations was in a two-story building on Ventura Boulevard near several new antique shops. Mayhew's wife liked to shop here, though the slobs hanging around this end of Ventura made Del Mayhew vaguely sick. Beatniks: long unkempt hair, dirty scruffy clothes, and a patronizing glint in their marijuana-dulled eyes.

He parked in the lot behind the investigation firm, went in the back door and up to the second floor.

They had decent digs, he'd say that for them. Most investigative outfits he'd hired were squalid places, squalid as the way they made their money.

But International, with its Mediterranean furnishings, spoke of success.

The receptionist was a formidable matron with a cold eye and gray hair pulled into a bun.

"I'd like to see Mr. Samuelson, please," Mayhew said.

"Mr. Samuelson is out," the receptionist said. Mayhew smiled. "May I have your name, please?"

"I'm Del Mayhew."

She touched an intercom button and said, "Mr. Foyle? There's a Mr. Mayhew here."

Steve Foyle was maybe forty, boyish, enthusiastic.

"Are you familiar with my case?" Mayhew asked.

"I'm afraid I'm not, but we put a very good man on it."

"Mr. Tully?"

"Right. He used to be with Pinkerton."

"I was to hear from Mr. Tully at eleven-thirty this morning." Mayhew didn't mention the fact that he thought that the blackmailer with the muffled phone voice had been Tully—a double-crosser as well.

"And he didn't call?"

"No. And he's never missed calling at the exact time he promised."

"This is most unlike Mr. Tully. He also said he'd be in the office this morning."

"This is very important to me, Mr. Foyle."

"I'm going to see to this personally, Mr. Mayhew. I'll call you later in the day."

"Do that. It's very important."

LENIHAN There was a small stone Catholic church just off G Street where Lenihan liked to pray in the cool summer shadows of the early morning. He prayed here even though he was not, strictly speaking, a Catholic, not having made his Easter duty in perhaps fifteen years. But he liked the faint incense and flicker of the votive candles. The church made the real world seem distant.

But mostly he liked the empty church because he felt closer to Dulcie here. Little Dulcie, because she had died when she was only seven, and would always be that age in his mind.

Twelve summers ago, one steamy July day, she'd come home from playing in the park, and she'd climbed up on his lap and said, "Daddy, I don't feel good."

Heat, he and her mother Jean surmised.

Little Dulcie woke up the next morning with four degrees of fever, and numbness in her left leg.

At this time, years before Jonas Salk discovered his famous vaccine, there was a word that held primal terror for all parents: polio. And worse: *Bulbar paralysis*, the most virulent kind, an all-out attack on the nerve cells of the brain stem.

Within days, little Dulcie suffered stiffness in neck and back. Then she lost control of her eyes, tongue and face, even the ability to swallow.

She was put in a hospital iron lung. Jean and David Lenihan stayed with her around the clock. Sixteen days later, little Dulcie was dead.

A month after the funeral, he gave up his position in the CIA, where he had been a successful spook, and signed on with his old friend Jack Kennedy, who was then a congressman from Boston. The two men had met right at the end of World War II, where both had served in the South Pacific theater.

Jack said, "My father thinks I'm going to be president some day, David. That means I'm going to need somebody to be my trouble-shooter. You'd do a hell of job."

So David, with the help of a loan from Jack, bought a home in Georgetown, hopeful that the new job and new digs would start Jean and him on a new road. It was not to be.

David quickly discovered the real Jack Kennedy. The first three assignments David had were to "fix" woman problems. Jack had gotten one of them pregnant, so David had to convince her to have an abortion, for which she would receive a nice "bonus" from Jack.

The second was a husband who knew that Kennedy had slept with his wife and was threatening to go to the newspapers. The man turned down every offer of money, so David tailed the man for three days. The hot-headed mick bastard was a hypocrite. David got pictures of the man entering and leaving colored whore houses. The man dropped his newspaper threats.

The third involved a cop who had caught Jack putting it to a woman in the back seat of a car. The cop wanted money. David paid a visit to a D.C. councilman, a ruthless old black man who basically ran the District of Columbia behind the scenes. David paid him $3,500 to promote this cop to full-rank detective and let him know that Jack Kennedy was responsible. The old councilman grinned with gold teeth.

"That Kennedy better learn to keep his pecker in his pants," he said, "otherwise he'll get it gnawed off one day."

David Lenihan, the troubleshooter, was very successful.

As for David Lenihan, the husband, things did not go nearly so well. He had to cope not only with his own depression from little Dulcie's death, but also with Jean's alcoholism.

She'd never been good with booze, always getting angry or melancholy. Now she vanished from the house three or four nights a week. She left in the new Hudson he'd bought for her. Until she smashed it up. He'd hoped this would bring her around. And for a few weeks, she seemed chastened.

But then it was back to her nights out. There was a new addition now. Men. He smelled them on her, saw where they'd torn her clothes, tracked the scratches and bruises their fervid passion had left on her.

He pleaded and threatened, but it made no difference. He even got her into a sanitarium where she dried out for a month.

He had loved her since they were in grade school together. And he would always love her—or the memory of her. But ten years later, she was a demented middle-aged woman who sat in her upstairs room, cared for by the stern Irish maid who fed her alcohol, bathed her twice daily, and swaddled her in prison-plain housedresses. She had a nineteen-inch TV, and spent most of her days in front of it, sobbing over soap operas and melodramas of the thirties and forties.

So now, as he knelt in the back of the church, he prayed for them all, himself included.

An hour later, David Lenihan was standing in the Oval Office before Jack Kennedy's desk.

Jack Kennedy winced as he sat in his rocking chair. His back was out again. It had been ever since Lenihan had known him. You could see the pain lines around Jack's eyes and mouth, the gray streaking his otherwise auburn hair, the awkward way he carried himself. The White House staff now joked that the only thing Jack had strength for anymore was his women.

"Bobby is sure this Bellamy has got what he says he has," Jack said. "Are you?"

"Yes."

"How did he get them?" Jack asked.

"We need to find out."

"You need to go out there."

"When do you want me to leave?"

"Right away."

Lenihan nodded, thinking back to the phone conversation he'd had with the man named Bellamy four days ago. The White House operator had routed the call to Lenihan's office—Lenihan being a Special Assistant to the president—because Bellamy was a publisher and she didn't know where else to send it. "Vital information," Bellamy had called it. That kind of nut-ball call that came in all the time. But Lenihan talked to Bellamy, who was blunt and not at all intimidated by Lenihan's position.

"I've got something you and the president are going to want," Bellamy said. He told David what he possessed. "And you either pay me a half million dollars or *Time* magazine will."

The next forty-eight hours had been a frenzy of meetings for Jack, Bobby, and Lenihan, which finally concluded with Jack arranging for a half a million dollars in cash.

Lenihan began looking into Mr. Bellamy and learned that the whole matter was moving with dangerous speed.

A White House operative, who'd been checking out Bellamy at Lenihan's request, spotted a beautiful young woman named Melanie Baines lurking around Bellamy's office. Baines was known to be an unofficial agent of Edgar Hoover. If that frog-faced little bastard Hoover ever got his hands on what Bellamy had, J. Edgar could blackmail Kennedy and become the de facto president.

So, as in medieval times, the two powerful men dispatched knights to do their battles for them. Hoover had sent Melanie: Jack Kennedy, Lenihan.

Kennedy gave him his shark's grin. "You CIA guys know how to do stuff like this. If you can bring down a government, you can sure as hell nail Bellamy." Kennedy's allusion was to Guatemala, where the CIA had recently toppled a left-wing government and replaced it with a military man more disposed to the wishes of the United States.

The grin left Jack's face. "David, my ass is on the line here. You've got to make this work."

"I understand."

Jack sighed. "I fuck around too much." He looked at Lenihan. "But you get me out of this one, and I'll give up chasing women. I promise."

In the years he'd worked for Jack Kennedy, David Lenihan had dealt with union leaders, movie starlets, politicians who stood in Jack's path, and any number of other citizens who needed to be bought off or scared off or ruined. And after each one of them, Jack gave the same speech. How he was going to reform, quit chasing skirts. It was all bullshit.

Lenihan looked at his old friend across the years now and felt a melancholy for both of them. How fine and shiny and new they'd been at the end of the war. How the years had cost them: Jack's health and his almost pathetic need for new female conquests, Lenihan and his brooding sorrow for his daughter and wife.

Now, for Lenihan, there was just work—putting out all of Jack's fires.

Whatever the situation, Lenihan had always been able to handle it successfully; this one would be no different, he felt sure.

And he was grateful for the work because it was a splendid distraction. When he was playing the gumshoe, there was no time to think about his grief or his loneliness. There was solace in the knowledge that he was good at what he did. Solace, and even a modest pride.

"I'll be on the next flight out."

"You've got to nail this bastard," Jack Kennedy said, "right to the wall."

David Lenihan nodded and went home to pack.

SARA Was it that older woman she'd seen him with? Was that the one he was going to marry? Did he really love her? Was this marriage going to enhance his career?

There were so many things she had wanted to ask Michael when he'd called, but she couldn't—not and maintain self-respect, anyway.

Her intercom buzzed.

"Bellamy's on the phone," Jeff said.

She picked up the phone, trying to refocus quickly.

"Hi, kid." Bellamy sounded weak.

"Before we start on anything, Mr. Bellamy, I want to tell you that what you tried to do to Curtis Simmons is despicable."

"I've been hiding, kid. I got more important things on my mind than that Simmons bozo. This time I may have bought the farm."

She had no choice but to listen to him. "What happened?"

"Took too big a bite, and now I may choke to death on it."

She hated his gaudy melodramas. He was always embroiled in something.

"Where are you?"

"Better you don't know. People will be snooping around. I don't know just how I'm gonna handle this yet."

He should know that she'd given Curtis Simmons the photographs. "Maybe I'd better tell you—"

"You going to be home tonight?"

"Yes."

"I may need you to meet me, bring me what I need from the safe."

"Are the police involved?"
"Don't ask. I have to play my hand out my way."
"But Mr. Bellamy—"
"I'll call you at home tonight. Later, kid."

TOLSON "Clyde? Hal. Everything all right?"
"I could bullshit you, but it isn't."

"Well, my news isn't going to make you any happier. Our little friend Melanie has called Edgar at home four times in the past three weeks."

"Yeah? I figured."

"Anything else you want?"

"No. I'll have to handle things from here. But thanks for checking the phone records. And for setting up the shrink for me."

"Get what you wanted?"

"Enough to make me sick."

LOUELLA

"It's Mr. Gibbons," her maid, Maria, announced. Louella picked up. "I've waited two hours and forty-six minutes for you to return my call. Mr. Hearst always returned my calls promptly, even from ships and planes."

He sighed. "What can I do for you, Louella?"

"It's what I'm going to do for you, young man. For you and the entire Hearst organization."

"And that would be what, exactly?"

"The biggest scoop since Richard Nixon's slush fund in 1952."

"Can you get to the point?"

"I'm about to receive the secret tapes of a film star who recently died."

"Monroe? You're talking about Marilyn Monroe?" His voice perked up.

"Who else?"

"These tapes—what's supposed to be on them?"

"Oh, no, no. I don't say anything until you agree to my terms."

"What the hell are you talking about? We have a contract."

"First, I want the column that breaks the story to be run on the front page of every Hearst paper in the country. Second, I want my picture above the column. Third, I want both radio and TV advertising."

Momentary silence. "Louella, are you nuts?"

"I'm quite sane, thank you. You know the rumors about who Marilyn was seeing."

"Everybody's got rumors. I don't give a shit about rumors."

"But these tapes will prove that it's true. In their own voices—and sounds, I believe. Both of them."

"Holy shit! On the level?"

"Of course."

"I'll get to examine these tapes myself and give them to experts?"

"Of course."

For the first time since she'd met him eight years ago, Daniel Gibbons actually sounded excited about her work.

"Louella, you know how much I respect you."

Such respect. Forcing her into a two-year contract last time instead of her previous four-year deals, at a lower syndication percentage than Hearst used to give her. Pushing the younger columnists he'd brought aboard himself, instead of her, the queen.

"You'll meet my terms, then?"

"No sweat."

"I'll want it in writing."

"Since when do you and I need a piece of paper? I mean, if we can't trust each other, who can we trust?"

"I want a signature."

"Okay, okay, I want you to be happy, Louella."

Such a sickening boy now that he smelled a big story.

"I expect prompt responses to my calls."

"I promise." Pause. "When do I hear from you again?"

"I'll keep you posted."

"Louella, I want those tapes."

"I'm sure you do."

Excerpt from
American Goddess
by Louella Parsons

One thing you must remember about Marilyn is that the man who was her father, one Stanley Gifford, always denied that Marilyn was his. He gave her mother Norma no money; nor would he ever so much as hold the child who had been christened Norma Jean.

So, right from the very beginning you might say, Marilyn was in search of men who would approve of her and love her as she so desperately needed to be loved.

Her situation was not helped by a mother—well-meaning, said by many to be both intelligent and loving—who spent much of her life in mental institutions.

After the second of her breakdowns, Marilyn's mother was forced to turn the girl over to the state, which began putting her in various foster homes. Marilyn Monroe was three years old at the time.

Later, Marilyn would suggest to some very close friends that she remembered being sexually molested in one of these homes. She was also beaten—perhaps by one of the men who also sexually abused her—and told that she must have the "evil" driven out of her.

She didn't get along any better with the children in the foster homes, either.

One day, a little girl, jealous of how pretty five-year-old Marilyn looked in a party dress, got a group of children to tear Marilyn's dress off her.

Marilyn was humiliated and terrified and spent several days alone in her room dreaming of a handsome man, not unlike a prince, who would carry her off to safety and love.

SARA Jeff was getting set to leave the office. "Will you lock up?" he asked Sara.

"Sure. And thanks, Jeff. I really appreciate you looking after me."

"My pleasure."

Then he was gone, out into the hall and down seven floors in the elevator.

Before leaving, Sara decided to file away some old issues of *Insight* she'd been using as reference. Twenty minutes later, just as she was turning out the lights and getting ready to walk out the door, the call came.

"My name's David Lenihan, Mrs. Drury. I'm in Washington, D.C., but I'm about to catch a flight to L.A. I would like to see you tomorrow morning."

"In regard to what, Mr. Lenihan?"

"I need some information. Confidentially. Concerning Mr. Bellamy."

"What kind of information?"

"Mrs. Drury, I'm with one of the government security agencies. This is a serious matter and I hope you'll be cooperative."

"I don't mean to be uncooperative, Mr. Lenihan. But you're being pretty mysterious."

"Well, it's a mysterious world. I'll see you in the morning."

Sara scratched her head. Why would a government security agency be interested in Bellamy?

MICHAEL

He liked buying dolls for Laura. Nobody bought a kid more presents than a guilty parent, he thought.

He was in a toy store in Beverly Hills, the land of ermine and diamonds, gold plumbing fixtures and platinum cocktail shakers. He was looking at the new generation of Raggedy Annes when he felt eyes watching him.

A fur-wrapped matron was giving him a discreet look.

Today he played against type, wore a button-down shirt, no tie, and slacks. And they were paid for with his own money.

He had to do this every once in a while, go back to being Michael Drury from Omaha, the kid from behind the stockyards who had been a fair first baseman and who spent a lot of summer Saturdays fishing and a lot of autumn Saturdays hunting. And who loved the maiden fair Sara for her pure spirit and looks and midwestern values. And who had borne him that most lovely of earthly creatures, Laura.

He was in one of these moods this morning so the interested glance from the matron only disgusted him. He gave her a hard stare and went on looking at the Raggedy Annes.

Excerpt from Marilyn Monroe's personal tapes

I know you've heard the "salt" story about me. The terrible thing, Louella, is that it's true. My poor husband—my first husband— Jim Dougherty. He was this big Irish guy who really wanted me to be a regular wife for him. He spoiled me all he could, working overtime a lot, and then sending me his paycheck from overseas when he was in World War II. I really liked Jim; maybe not loved him in the way he wanted, but I liked him and respected him— and who knows, maybe I did love him. Anyway, one time I decided to make him this meal. So I asked this woman I knew for some cooking tips. I remember how shocked she was when I told her I didn't even know how to make coffee. She laughed. "Why, honey, just put a pinch of salt in it is all." I wasn't sure what she meant but I didn't want to ask her any more questions because I looked dumb enough already. At home, I made my very first meal, some scrambled eggs and bacon and coffee. I figured that I'd add a teaspoon of salt to the coffee pot because if a pinch was good then a teaspoon would be even better, right? Well, Jim took one drink of that coffee and ran straight to the sink and spit it out. And when he asked me what I'd put in the coffee and I told him, he started laughing, this big Irish laugh, and he took me in his arms and held me like I was the most precious thing he'd ever held. And almost everybody who called or came over the next few weeks, Jim told his "salt" story and roared with laughter and hugged me, as if he was really proud of me, as if I hadn't done anything stupid at all.

MELANIE Erica Dane's apartment was even hotter now than when Melanie arrived.

Melanie had been forced to get rough with her, a not unpleasant experience, and she was now working up a light sweat. The weird thing was, Erica still didn't give up Bellamy's whereabouts.

Even after Melanie had slugged her twice with her gun.

Melanie decided to use those big pleasurable breasts of Erica's as vehicles for pain.

She grabbed one and gave it a killer twist.

Erica blubbered.

"Where's Bellamy?"

"I haven't seen him for two days." Erica's head was down again.

"They do interesting things in South America to women they interrogate. I spent a little time down there and a couple of the generals taught me a few things."

Erica said nothing.

"One thing is to show the women these pictures of dead people with their eyes ripped out or their arms ripped off or their breasts sliced off. It's pretty scary."

Erica grimaced.

"Then they work people over with electric shocks. They shock them so bad that they pass out, but the generals keep this doctor on hand to revive you for more shocks."

Erica mumbled, "You're sick."

"You know what the weirdest one was, though? They strip these women naked and tie them down on their stomachs and stuff cock-roaches up the anuses. You should have heard those women scream."

Erica's head was still down.

"Erica?"

Erica still didn't move.

"I'm getting mad, Erica. I'm serious about finding your boyfriend. Are you listening to me? Last chance, Erica."

Erica did not respond.

So Melanie walked out to the living room and dug in her purse for a slender yellow can and came back into the kitchen.

"You want to watch, Erica?"

Her eyes stayed closed.

Sighing, Melanie sprayed the Ronson lighter fluid all over Erica's head. She quickly tied a gag over Erica's mouth, then lit a match and tossed it on the fluid-soaked pile of bottle-blonde hair.

Erica thrashed wildly, swinging the chair around under her bonds, her eyes now crazily open.

Her whole head was on fire.

The gag muffled her screams.

MAYHEW

He spent some time on the freeway in his shiny red Corvette, as he often did when he needed to escape, to think, to plan.

Not even radio music. Just himself and this fine piece of machinery. He was going 115 miles per hour without even thinking about the California Highway Patrol.

Then he got the idea, at which point he slowed to sixty, found an exit ramp and headed back to L.A.

"Afternoon, Mr. Mayhew."

"I saw Mr. Rossetti's car in the back. Thought I'd stop in and see him."

This was a private club near Laguna Beach. Very private. Not even a studio chief such as Mayhew rated much respect here. Mayhew had heard Rossetti mention it once. He'd decided to take a chance.

"I'm afraid he's pretty busy."

The man was an older, gray-haired gentleman with the nose, ears, and manner of a bouncer. "He really doesn't appreciate visitors."

"We're business partners. I'll take the responsibility."

The bouncer shrugged. "Up to you."

They stood in a shadowy nook off the lobby. Through a large window, Mayhew watched two men tee off on the nine-hole course, their talk enthusiastic but soundless; to Mayhew it was like watching a silent movie.

The bouncer walked down the rich blue carpet to a door and

knocked twice, softly, then stuck his head in. "I'm really sorry, Mr. Rossetti. A man's here. A Mr. Mayhew. He says he needs to see you."

There was a silence.

"Buy him a drink at the bar and I'll be along."

"Yes, sir."

Jonas bought Mayhew a drink. He was the only one at the bar. He could see in the mirror the door from which Rossetti would emerge. He was eager to tell Rossetti of his plan.

Fifteen minutes later, the door opened.

Rossetti came out. White curly hair, trim body, dark clothes, ominous intensity.

A girl came out the door after Rossetti. She was beautiful. She was also a Negro.

Just outside the door, Rossetti and the girl paused; their hands touched. The girl whispered something, then walked to the lady's restroom a few feet away. Rossetti watched her affectionately.

Mayhew was stunned. A mafioso at this level . . . with a black woman.

Rossetti came up the corridor, straightening his tie and unbuttoning his suit.

Mayhew turned on his padded bar stool to speak, but Rossetti's hand came from nowhere and smacked Mayhew's face.

His ears rang, and he tasted blood.

"I did not invite you here, Mr. Mayhew, and I resent your being here. Understand me?"

Stars danced before Mayhew's eyes. He started to apologize, but Rossetti hit him again. This time he fell face first on the floor.

MAYHEW The humiliation was worse than the pain. All Mayhew could think of was the long-ago day, back on the playground of a rural Pennsylvania school, when Bobby Jennings had pounded him to the ground and then sat on him so he couldn't get up.

The other kids, including the girl Mayhew had a crush on, stood around and laughed.

Now, feeling much the same way, he went to the men's room and washed the blood off his face and combed his hair and straightened his necktie.

It was all still unreal to him, what had happened in the bar. Such sudden violence.

He took several deep breaths and then returned to the expensive silence of the private club.

Rossetti sat at the bar. The other man, Jonas, was gone.

Mayhew was nervous walking in. Why were he and Rossetti alone?

"Del, I'm drinking bourbon and branch water. How about you? Still Scotch?"

"Scotch."

Rossetti went around the bar and fixed Mayhew his drink. He sat on the stool beside Mayhew.

"So, Del, what have you got?"

"I came here to tell you about an idea I had. What if I tell the police that Bellamy took something from my office and that I want him arrested. We'd have the entire LAPD looking for him. And when they find him, there's no way he can tell them about the tapes."

"So if the police have Bellamy, how do we get the tapes?"

"Tell him that I'll drop the charges if he hands them over."

Rossetti chuckled. "That's a great idea, Del—for the movies. The first thing wrong is that it gets the cops nosing around in our business. The second is that it assumes Bellamy is rational." He took a drag on his cigarette. "Do you think he's a rational man?"

Mayhew sighed. He felt like a child now. Rossetti was completely in charge—and scoffing at his ideas.

"Give that idea to one of your crime-picture writers," Rossetti said. "And never come here again unless you're invited."

Mayhew killed his drink in two large swallows. The liquor stung the inside of his mouth.

He looked out at the golf course. The players cast long afternoon shadows behind them as they moved along the green. There was no wind and the sky was very blue and the grass was impossibly green.

Mayhew wanted to project himself into that picture, into another dimension.

"Our agreement was twenty-four hours," Rossetti said.

Rossetti stood and clapped Mayhew on the shoulder. "Now I think I'll go for a swim. This place has a wonderful pool."

LAURA Today, Mrs. Grundy had asked her students to write down the name of their favorite cartoon show.

Laura Drury, always earnest, thought about the matter for nearly ten minutes before writing on her blue-lined white notebook paper: Bullwinkle. He was a dope who knew he was a dope.

Then, when school was out, she raced home to see Bullwinkle on TV.

Within two minutes of opening the apartment door, she had changed into jeans and was plopped down in front of the television, a bottle of strawberry pop in one hand, a small bowl of last night's popcorn in the other.

She hoped that her babysitter, Mrs. Gregory, didn't come down right away. She always talked right over TV shows.

The distinctive trumpet music sounded, and there was Bullwinkle prancing across the screen.

She smiled. Bullwinkle always made her feel good, especially when he opened the envelope and said, "Look here. Fan mail from some flounder."

No matter how many times she heard this particular piece of business, Laura always laughed.

The show started. Then stopped abruptly for commercials. They always teased you this way, the TV people did. They'd pretended that the show was really starting and then—wham! Right into the advertisements.

The commercials ran, all of them for cereals that her mom said were too sweet for her and would give her cavities.

The show started again. This time for real.

And then the phone rang.

Exasperated, she got up and hurried to snap up the receiver.

"Drury residence, this is Laura."

"Hi."

Susan! Her best friend! Unless Bullwinkle was on, that is. Then only Bullwinkle was her friend.

"I'll call you back, Susan. I'm watching Bullwinkle."

Laura hung up and ran back to the TV set.

When she watched Bullwinkle she could forget the problems of her mom and dad, all the screaming fights, all the tears she'd seen them both cry, all the grief the three of them had felt as their family began to disintegrate.

Laura always watched enviously on school-program nights when her friends came with their mothers and fathers. Real families. Mom tried hard but she was preoccupied and sometimes still bitter and lonely about the break up. And Dad tried hard, too, on the nights when he came over and rather solemnly took Laura out for dinner. Her father spent most of their time apologizing. He was sorry for all the fighting that Laura had had to listen to. Sorry for the break up. Sorry that Daddy and Laura couldn't live together until Daddy's life settled down some. And sorry that Daddy hadn't been a better father.

Laura would sit in the restaurant and watch her father.

Thinking about it made her sad.

The phone rang again. She couldn't believe it!

She got up from the TV and went over to the phone and picked it up.

"Is Mrs. Drury home?"

"Not yet. May I take a message?"

"Just say that Mr. Simmons called."

She reached for a pencil and wrote down S-i-m-m-o-n-s.

She went right back to the TV.

"Yoo-hoo!" a voice sang through the front door. It was Mrs. Gregory letting herself into the apartment. "Yoo-hoo!"

Oh, no, Laura thought. Bullwinkle was doomed.

BELLAMY He had never liked colored people. They were lazy, smelly, and stupid, just as his mother had taught him.

So now, as the black man brought him his fifth of whiskey and bottle of Coke, Bellamy said, "How come it's open? The Coca-Cola."

The black man, probably fifty, who seemed to be the odd-job person in this rotting motel, shrugged. "I just figured I'd open it for you."

"Well, you take that fucking Coke out of here, and come back with an unopened bottle."

"Yessir," the black man said.

When the man was gone, Bellamy grabbed the fifth of Old Crow and relaxed in the armchair facing the TV screen. It would be just like that colored bastard to take a drink of Bellamy's Coke.

He stared at the phone, wondering what Erica was doing. With those tits, with that dirty mouth. Usually, Bellamy didn't like women who talked dirty. But with Erica it excited him.

He tried not to think of his wife or what she'd be like when he finally got home after an absence of four, maybe five days.

He had neither loved nor desired her in many long years, but a divorce was too expensive. He'd worked too hard to let some former chippie from Kansas City, Missouri—who now weighed two hundred pounds and had clacking false teeth—take half his money. He'd stay married and fuck whoever he wanted. Much cheaper that way.

Of course, his life was about to change. After he got the half mil

153

for the tapes from the president's man Lenihan, maybe he'd take Erica someplace exotic.

The colored man brought him his unopened Coca-Cola.

Bellamy nodded to the bureau. "There's some change up there. Take a dime for yourself."

He picked up the telephone and dialed a Washington, D.C., number. David Lenihan's office.

Just to make the uppity bastard sweat a little, he was going to demand an additional $50,000.

But the secretary who answered said, "I'm sorry, Mr. Lenihan left for Los Angeles this afternoon."

Bellamy slammed the phone down. Los Angeles? What the hell was going on here?

But he knew just what was going on here.

Lenihan was going to try a sneak attack. Find Bellamy and take the tapes—at gunpoint.

Bellamy rubbed the sweaty gray hair matting his barrel chest. He'd show the bastard.

TOLSON Tolson—in his closed office, jacket off, tie loosened—had spent the past hour calling Los Angeles-area hospitals looking for a Jean Stephens, a woman Melanie had lived with back when Tolson had first attempted to discredit her to Edgar.

Now he called his sixteenth hospital.

"I'm trying to locate a nurse named Jean Stephens."

"She works in the hospice area. I'll connect you."

Finally! Lord, what ordinary agents went through every day of their lives, just to find people and ask them simple questions.

"Hello."

"Jean Stephens?"

"Yes."

"My name is Ben Wenwright and I'm an attorney. I believe you know a woman named Melanie Baines, is that correct?" For obvious reasons, he didn't want her to know who he was.

"We were roommates for a while."

"She's come into a small inheritance and we need to locate her."

There was a pause. "What did you say your name was?"

"Wenwright. Ben Wenwright."

"And you're with what firm?"

Clever. "Wenwright and Lauderber is the name of the firm, miss."

"In Los Angeles?"

"Chicago, miss."

"I'm afraid I haven't spoken with her in a while."

"When was the last time you saw her?"

"Oh, six months ago, I guess."

"You wouldn't have a current address for her? Or a current phone number?"

"No, sorry." Small, feminine, delicate laugh. "She often uses phony names."

"Phony names?"

"For her phone listings. She once called herself Elmira Johansen."

"I see."

"If I hear from her, I'll tell her I spoke with you. I'm sorry I couldn't be more helpful."

You're sorry. All this time wasted for a dead end.

"Well," he said, unable to stifle his sigh, "thank you."

LOUELLA Maria the maid and Juan the gardener stood beneath the den window, looking at each other in bewilderment.

From the window came the sounds of Louella's giggles as she talked to members of Old Hollywood, the ones she really loved—Walter Pidgeon had been called and then Greer Garson and then Van Johnson and then Judy Garland (who would be, of course, already loaded for the day).

Maria and Juan could not recall seeing Miss Parsons this happy since the time Khrushchev visited Los Angeles. Miss Parsons' invitation had gone astray in the U.S. mail. Not to get invited to such an event—the humiliation would have been devastating. For an entire week, the old bitch had sulked and fumed until one magical morning the postman said that he had found this envelope stuck in the back of his mail truck, where it had been lost since last week.

Miss Parsons had swept down on the envelope like a buzzard pouncing on its prey, tearing it open at once and letting out an exultant cry.

She had thrown a party for the entire staff, ordering Maria to the basement for champagne and Juan to the bakery for a fancy cake.

And now she was laughing again.

Ever since her phone call from Mr. Rossetti, she had been carrying on.

So Maria and Juan wondered what Mr. Rossetti could have said to Miss Parsons that could have made her this happy.

Excerpt from
American Goddess
by Louella Parsons

Between 1946 and 1949, Marilyn Monroe, as she was now calling herself, was dropped by several Hollywood studios. While she was both beautiful and sexy, the studios felt that Marilyn simply didn't have any talent that separated her from the hundreds of other beautiful and sexy girls who made the rounds of the studios.

Having worked in an aircraft factory during World War II, Marilyn again started looking for a steady job with a steady paycheck. At times she even considered the possibility that she'd made a mistake in leaving her first husband, James Dougherty, a big Irish-Catholic guy who had wanted her to forget about a movie career and just be a housewife.

At this same time, a photographer she'd known for a few years asked, for at least the fifth time, if Marilyn would do a nude spread for him.

She surprised him by saying yes.

At this point in her career, she was desperate for any work that would support her fantasy of being an actress. She had already done a lot of bikini modeling for a reputable Los Angeles modeling agency, so modeling nude was not that big a deal.

Over the years, many people have noted how insecure Marilyn was. That was true all her life. The morning of the modeling, an hour before she was to take the bus to the photographer's studio, she began douching, wanting to be very, very clean for the man. In high school, a boy had once remarked about Marilyn's "smell." She'd been menstruating at the time. Ever since, she was very conscious of her body odors, which was why she was so fastidiously clean.

On this day, she even daubed a few drops of perfume on her vagina. Today, she wanted to feel totally self-confident.

MELANIE Melanie realized that she'd gotten a little carried away. She'd planned to scare Erica Dane by setting her hair on fire, and then put it out right away. But Melanie had become so fascinated with the burning hair, and how Erica squirmed and jerked in her ropes, making the chair clump across the linoleum floor, that she just kept watching and watching. Like a TV show.

Now that the damage had been done, ol' Erica definitely had third-degree burns. The thin flesh across her skull had been reduced to naked nerve and fiber and bone. Definitely not pretty. Erica probably wasn't going to live very long. Her heart would start pumping too hard to compensate for the shock, and she'd croak.

The kitchen stank of hair and burnt flesh. Melanie opened a window, found some Air-Wick, pulled the tongue up and set it on the kitchen counter.

Erica rolled in and out of consciousness every few minutes.

Melanie untied the gag around her mouth.

"Fucking bitch," she slurred.

"Real nice, Erica. I take your gag off and you call me a name."

"Frank's gonna . . ." Erica's eyes rolled back. She had drifted away again.

She looked awful: this charred, bloody skull cap on her head, her arms and legs all trussed up.

Melanie went to the sink and filled a Skippy peanut butter glass with cold water. She poured it into Erica's mouth. It was like trying to feed a baby who didn't want to be fed.

Water ran out of the mouth that Melanie had bloodied earlier. Erica moaned, and then her eyes appeared again. "You fucking bitch."

"You know, you might attract a better grade of man if you didn't swear so much. And dressed a little more modestly."

The wall phone rang.

Melanie dragged Erica's chair across the floor, snatched the receiver from its cradle, and put the phone to Erica's ear and mouth. Then put the Luger to Erica's head.

"Hello," Erica mumbled.

"I'm fine. I need . . . to talk to you. . . ."

A faint male voice in the receiver.

Melanie hung up the phone. Talking had completely drained Erica. Her chin slumped to her shoulders and a faint mewling bubbled up her chest and throat.

She wasn't going to make it, ol' Erica wasn't.

But she'd been useful. Frank Bellamy was surely on his way over here right now. Melanie couldn't ask for more than that.

"Fuck . . . fuck . . ." Erica moaned.

Darn, but Melanie hated coarse language like that. She went into the living room to wait for Frank Bellamy.

K I D The factory shift let out at three o'clock. The old man usually didn't make it home till seven-thirty, eight o'clock. Till then the kid was free to play his ten-year-old games without a fight erupting between his parents.

Sometimes the fights got so bad that half the block would congregate on their front porch and force the two apart. The old man, when he was drunk, used his fists.

When he was an even littler boy, the kid used to cry about the fights, go to his room and lie on the bed and sob so hard that the mattress would shake.

Now the kid just left when the fights started.

Today, he walked the open L.A. sewer system.

You found all sorts of neat stuff in the sewers. One time the kid found a gold wristwatch that ticked if you shook it hard enough; another time he found three steelie marbles that some other kid must have lost.

The kid stayed in the sewer an hour and a half.

Then he went to his second-favorite place, the block of abandoned warehouses, where he liked to climb up in the loft and smoke the Lucky Strikes he'd swiped from the old man.

Today, he took the warehouse in the center of the block, walked up the stairs in back, climbed through one of the shattered windows, and crawled out to one of the wide beams that spanned the place. Then he had himself a cigarette.

And then he looked down and noticed on the floor a wide stain,

161

shaped somewhat like the continent of Europe as he saw it in history class.

He wasn't sure what it was. The stain widened as it neared the large barrels lined against the wall.

Blood?

The kid hoped that was it.

That would be a neat story. And it would be even neater if he found something to go with the blood. A body, say.

The kid crawled back along the beam and went down the ladder and over to where the swath darkened the floor.

He stooped down. Touched the stuff. Still fresh. Sticky.

Blood! It was blood for sure.

He straightened up and stared at the three barrels aligned by the wall.

He made his way along the edge of the blood continent to the barrel with the blood smears down its side. He slid the lid off, and it clanged to the floor, making him jump.

He had to stand up on tiptoe to look inside.

He saw the body. He gulped, frozen to the spot.

The guy shoved down inside had his head twisted, and one blue eye stared upward. His left eye. His right one was just a bloody, ugly hole.

The kid started to sweat. The smell was pretty awful. The guy had shit his pants or something.

The kid stood still for another minute, not wanting to stare but not able to stop.

And then he ran. Out of the warehouse and down the long cracked sidewalk to the next block to a greasy-spoon hamburger joint where there was an LAPD car parked. In through the door, up to the counter where two cops with creaking holsters and giant guns sat drinking coffee and smoking cigarettes.

"Dead," the kid said, so out of breath he couldn't get out the second word.

"Huh?" one cop said.

"Dead," the kid tried again. "Man."

"Dead man?"

"Where?" the second cop said.

"Dead man in the warehouse!"

A moment later, he was sitting in the back seat of an LAPD cruiser, guiding the cops to the scene.

TOLSON J. Edgar Hoover said, "You've been spying on me, Clyde."

His face was red, even in the low light of this Georgetown restaurant.

"No, Edgar, I have not been spying on you."

One way to piss Edgar off—something Tolson liked to do once in a while, to keep their friendship on an even keel—was to strike a reasonable tone in the face of one of Edgar's dramas.

"You went into my office—"

"Looking for you."

"—and looked through my desk—"

"Looking for something I needed."

"—and then made this terrible accusation that I've been in contact with Melanie again!"

"Meaning that you haven't been in contact with Melanie again?"

"Absolutely not."

"Then why were her name and number written on your pad? And why has she called you at home four times in the past three weeks? No, Edgar, I haven't been spying on you. I've been checking up on her."

"You had no right—"

"So you are dealing with Melanie again, aren't you?"

Edgar spluttered.

Tolson sipped the very good white wine following their delicious pork chops and wild rice.

"Do you remember Chicago, Edgar? Or Miami?"

"I don't want to talk about it."

"Melanie killed three people in those cities alone."

"She gets the job done."

"She's insane."

"In *your* opinion."

"What job is it this time, Edgar?"

Edgar gritted his teeth. "I'm not going to tell you about it."

"Very well."

Tolson was being clever. Edgar loved to have secrets pried out of him. But Clyde wasn't playing his usual role.

"I'd rather not know, actually. One day she's going to do something that'll drag you and the entire Bureau down with her. Maybe this time." He stood up. "I'm going to the men's room."

Tolson smiled to himself. He returned five minutes later.

Edgar's face was still red. "I'm going to tell you why I'm using Melanie and you're going to listen."

Tolson knew enough to listen.

And when Edgar finished, Tolson said, "My God, if Melanie can get them, you'll have Kennedy right by the balls."

"Then let's see him try to get me out," Edgar said, his voice raspy with anger. "Let's just see him try."

S A R A   "Mom? Do you know where Daddy's going to take me?"
"I don't, honey. But I'm sure it'll be someplace fun, with food you like."

"Last time he took me to Disneyland."

"I remember. You had a great time."

"And the time before that he took me to a movie."

"Yes, and you enjoyed it."

"And the time before that—"

Sara laughed and held her arms out for Laura, who climbed up on her mother's lap.

She weighed barely seventy pounds, and even in a faded Mickey Mouse T-shirt and red pedal pushers, she was heartbreakingly beautiful. Nothing was as sacred to Sara as her daughter and her greatest fear was that something might someday happen to Laura.

"I wish you could go with us tonight."

"This is for you and Daddy."

"Will you and Daddy and I ever go anyplace again together?"

"Maybe someday."

"Like we used to?"

"Maybe, honey."

She glanced up at the wall clock. "You'd better get washed up and change those clothes. Your dad will be along in half an hour."

Laura gave her a hug. "I love you, Mommy."

For a moment, Sara clung to her daughter. Things had changed so much in this past year and she had not yet been able to deal with all the pain and confusion and fear she felt.

Then Laura ran off to get ready.

In one of the foster homes I was in, the mother got very angry whenever I dressed up because her husband doted on me so much. This was when I was eleven or so. The husband was a very nice, honorable man, a businessman who always came through the door whistling and carrying his briefcase. He'd always wanted a daughter—they had three sons—and he saw me as sort of a substitute, I suppose. Anyway, the mother hated me so much after a couple of weeks that she took twenty-five dollars from her husband's wallet and then put it in one of my drawers. When the husband realized the money was missing, the first thing the wife said was, "I'll bet she took it." And then she marched straight into my room and started going through my drawers and there was the money. The orphanage picked me up that night. The husband didn't even look hurt and disappointed. When the orphanage people asked me if I had taken the money, I said yes. I knew they wouldn't believe my story anyway. Sometimes it's just easier to take the blame and get it over with, even when you're innocent.

VANESSA

"I'm Detective Brinkman."

"Detective?"

"I'm calling about your husband, Mrs. Tully."

"My husband?"

"I'm afraid there's been some trouble."

So here it was. You're so happy you can scarcely believe it, but something will surely spoil your happiness.

"Mrs. Tully? I wondered if I could stop by and give you a ride."

"To where?"

"I'm afraid you'll have to identify him."

"Then he's dead?"

"I'm afraid so, Mrs. Tully."

She began to tremble. "I don't know if I could do that, Detective Brinkman."

"Is there somebody else you could recommend? A relative or—"

"I know I don't sound very grown up."

"It's all right, Mrs. Tully. I know how difficult this is."

"How did he die?"

"We don't have the medical examiner's report yet, but it appears he was shot."

"Where?"

"A warehouse out near Long Beach."

"Long Beach? He always liked it out there."

"I'll be there in twenty minutes, Mrs. Tully."

"He was dead when you found him?"

169

"Yes, ma'am."

"On the floor?"

"No, actually, he was—well, inside a barrel."

"My God." She felt so confused. "Do you know who did it?"

"Not yet, ma'am."

"In a barrel," she said. "In a barrel."

She sank to the couch and let the phone drop to her lap. *In a barrel. In a barrel.*

S A R A Michael arrived five minutes early and a little too dressed up for taking his daughter out.

When she saw him in the doorway, all got up in a blue suit red tie, she thought back to their wedding day, and how young and appealing he'd looked.

"Hi, Michael. C'mon in."

Michael stood like a nervous suitor near the door, hands folded in front of him, rocking back and forth on his heels.

"This place looks nicer every time I'm here," he said. "I like those drapes."

"Laura picked them out," Sara said.

"You've even got a little office."

He walked over to the card table in the corner, where sat Sara's portable Underwood typewriter and the stacked pages of the script she was working on. And a collection of screenplays by Billy Wilder.

"Still reading Wilder, I see."

"My patron saint. I'll get Laura for you."

Laura, in a fresh white blouse and red skirt, stood with a mirror in one hand and a brush in the other, stroking through her long hair.

"Your dad's here," Sara said.

Laura smiled. She put down mirror and brush and took Sara's hand and led her down the hall. "Oh, I forgot. A man named Simmons called, Mom."

"Simmons? I wonder what he wanted?"

171

BELLAMY You didn't reach Bellamy's status without being insightful and clever, Bellamy frequently told himself.

Take tonight. When he called his girlfriend Erica, she said she was fine. But he knew immediately that something was wrong. So he needed to get over there right away. But he wasn't about to bumble into a situation where some guy might be standing there holding a gun.

So Bellamy, being clever, parked a block from Erica's house. He walked around to the alley. And then started his sneak-attack in the gathering dusk.

In Erica's backyard, he took the .45 from the waist of his trousers, and started across the grass. He eased the back door open and went inside.

The small back porch smelled of apples. He edged up to the kitchen door and peeked through the gauze-like curtain.

The kitchen was empty. He stepped in and closed the kitchen door behind him. He stood in the shadows, listening intently.

Something was wrong here. Really wrong. Erica always had the TV on when she was home. Even when they were in the bedroom balling, the TV was on.

But the TV was not on.

Just the *thrum* of the refrigerator, the hum and drip of the air conditioner.

Maybe he should run.

But then something odd happened to him. He realized that he was actually worried about Erica.

If it had been his wife, he would have run and not given her a thought.

But with Erica it was different.

He edged closer to the alcove, on the other side of which was the living room.

He knew better than to call out to her. He took a deep breath. Maybe she wasn't here at all.

He stepped across the threshold, and gasped.

Erica sat naked, bound, and gagged in a straight-backed chair, her head horribly charred.

Melanie stepped out of the shadows and brought the butt of her weapon down on Bellamy's head.

VANESSA She was in hell. This version was not hot but meat-locker cold. And instead of flames there were odors. Stomach-turning odors of chemicals disguising the smell of dead human meat. And the devil was not a horned madman, but a thin young doctor in a spotless white medical smock.

Their footsteps rang on the tiled floor as he led her to the rear of the morgue. Here, she was not self-conscious about her crippled leg; she did not care.

Corpses on the steel tables. Three of them uncovered, two of them men, and the sight of dead men's genitals was disorienting. Next to the woman was a small pile of dark material, her innards. Vanessa was nauseated.

Now she kept her eyes only on the back of the doctor's smock. She ached to escape.

He took her to a wall where wide drawers were built, four across and three deep. He went to the middle drawer in the second row and pulled it open.

She froze, could not take another step. Could not walk over there and see what lay inside.

"Are you all right, Mrs. Tully?"

Detective Brinkman took her arm. He had white hair and kind blue eyes.

"We'll make this very fast," Brinkman said.

"I don't know if I can."

"You'll be okay, Mrs. Tully."

She stared at his blue eyes. "I don't want to remember him this way."

"I lost my wife a couple of years ago in a traffic accident."

"You're kind."

"C'mon now," Brinkman said, "and we'll get it over with."

He led her to the drawer and she looked down and broke into sobs. She put her head against Brinkman's chest and he held her.

They had their answer.

The man in the drawer was obviously Tully.

In the parking lot, as Brinkman was leading her back to his car, a man stepped from a jaunty Ford convertible.

She looked up. "Steve?"

"I stopped by your place. Your neighbor told me . . ." He nodded to the morgue. "Was it . . ."

"Who are you?" Brinkman said.

"Oh. Sorry." He put forth his hand. "Steve Foyle, International Investigations. I worked with Tully."

"I just want to go home now," Vanessa said.

Steve kissed her on the cheek. "I'm sorry, Vanessa. You know how much I liked him."

Brinkman led her away.

Foyle got in his convertible and drove three blocks to a corner phone booth. A Beach Boys song blasted from a nearby record store.

"Mr. Mayhew, Steve Foyle. I saw you at the agency this afternoon."

"Oh. Right. Have you found Tully?"

"I'm afraid we have. He's dead."

"What?"

"Murdered."

"What was found on him?"

"Pardon?"

"Did they find anything on him?"

"Nothing unusual that I know of. Why?"

"I'd better go."

Foyle wondered what Mayhew was so anxious about. Maybe Tully and Mayhew had made a private deal between themselves.

The phone booth smelled like a toilet.

Foyle was happy to get back to his red convertible and the fresh night air. Fresh as it ever got in L.A., anyway.

Excerpt from Marilyn Monroe's personal tapes

One time when I was nine I went to visit my mother in the mental hospital. As usual, I brought her a poem I'd written for her and some flowers I'd picked. In this particular hospital, we usually went out on this veranda where you could see down into this valley. It was very pretty, especially on days like today. There was usually a man out there, one my mother was always very respectful of. She'd told me that he was a concert violinist who suffered from schizophrenia. Of course, at that time I had no idea what schizophrenia was. I just knew that it was something terrible because the man, who was quite handsome, actually, always looked so sad. One day when we came out on the veranda, he was sitting in his chair and he asked my mother if she would bring me over to him. She did. I still remember standing in front of him and him very gently touching my cheek and saying, "Your beauty will bring comfort to other people, Norma Jean. Always remember that." And as soon as we got back to my mother's room, I wrote down what the man had said to me so I wouldn't ever forget it. But what he didn't tell me that day was that sharing my beauty would also bring comfort to me—I make men feel better about themselves, and that makes me happy, Louella.

177

MAYHEW The Negro maid had just served dinner. Mayhew's wife Sheila was sipping her wine when the phone rang in the den.

Mayhew had a dire premonition of who was calling.

And moments later, the maid said, "Sir, it's Mr. Rossetti."

"Tell him my husband will call him back," Sheila said. She was a manor-born woman who grew fat with resentments as she aged.

"No," Mayhew said, more gruffly than he'd intended. "No, darling, we're having problems at the studio and I need to talk to him." He spoke in as courteous a tone as he could muster. He wanted to slap her, a reckless impulse he had every so often.

"My father would never let anybody interrupt his family dinner."

He went into the den and picked up the phone.

"I wanted to tell you about Tully," Rossetti said.

"I just heard about him," Mayhew said.

"I wonder where the tapes are."

"I'm going to make some calls."

"You know Bellamy, that sleazeball sonofabitch at *Insight?*"

"Of course."

"There's a little club I own on Santa Monica Boulevard. People don't know I own it. Bellamy hangs out there a lot. Five days ago, he met Tully there. Tully may have been trying to double-cross his detective agency and sell the tapes to somebody." He paused. "You know what's on them, Del. I want those tapes made public."

Mayhew wondered what Kennedy had done to make the mafioso hate him so much. Early in the presidential campaign, Rossetti had contributed hundreds of thousands of dollars and introduced Kennedy to dozens of powerful men across the United States. Kennedy and Rossetti had been photographed on yachts, at movie premieres, playing tennis.

And then, for no reason Mayhew knew, Rossetti turned enemy.

One day last month, Rossetti had asked Mayhew to dinner at the fashionable Coconut Grove. After making the rounds of the Jimmy Stewart table, the Alan Ladd table, the Cary Grant table, Rossetti came over and sat down and said, "My friend the president of the United States is laying the rail to Marilyn Monroe."

Mayhew had been stunned. "Christ, you really think so? Taking a risk like that?"

"You don't know Kennedy. The bigger the risk, the more the excitement."

Rossetti had smiled. Picked up a manilla envelope. Took out three large black-and-white photographs. Handed them over.

The photos showed Kennedy in swim trunks on a yacht. He was standing next to Marilyn Monroe who wore the briefest of bikinis. In the second photo, Kennedy had his arm around Monroe's shoulder. The third shot showed the two embracing. Obviously more than a friendly kiss.

"These were taken last month. He was flying out here as often as possible. Or meeting her in New York on the pretext that he had business at the United Nations."

"He's crazy."

"He loves danger. I want to nail him."

"How?"

"I want you to hire a private detective to bug Marilyn Monroe's bedroom."

"We're talking about the president of the United States."

Rossetti smiled. "I don't want my name involved. As far as anybody knows, this is your idea. She's under contract to us. Tell the investigators that we need a bug in her house because we think she's negotiating a deal with somebody else. The night Kennedy's supposed to be there,

I'll tell you. Then you tell the guy who planted the bug that you want those particular tapes delivered to you immediately, that same night—before he gets a chance to hear them himself. You understand?"

And so it was done. Mayhew had hired International Investigators and was assigned a man named Tully. Tully taped nine nights running and got very little. The tenth night Kennedy was to show up. Mayhew was alerted. He told Tully to retrieve the tapes as he usually did—after Marilyn Monroe had gone to the studio where she was shooting a picture—but instead of taking the tapes back to International and listening to them, he was to bring them straight to Mayhew's office.

But Tully hadn't done that.

Mayhew's best guess was that Tully had listened to the tapes and realized what he had. But Tully knew his limitations, knew he couldn't parlay them into a lot of money without help . . . so he brought Bellamy in.

Bellamy—a professional blackmailer.

Now Tully was dead and in all likelihood Bellamy had the tapes. And Mayhew had no doubts what Bellamy would do with them. He had the brains and the balls for it. Bellamy would shake down John Fitzgerald Kennedy.

He had to find Bellamy, and thus the tapes of Kennedy's visit to Marilyn Monroe.

So now, Rossetti said: "I want you to get those tapes because I'm going to give them to Louella Parsons."

Mayhew almost laughed. Louella Parsons! Rossetti didn't want money. He wanted revenge. Rossetti was insane when it came to Kennedy. What the hell could the guy have done to Rossetti that was that bad?

"I'm going to handle it. Believe me."

"I don't care what you have to do, Del. Are you listening to me?"

"I'm listening."

"I don't care what you need to do. Or what kind of dough you have to spend. I want those tapes."

"I understand."

"I don't need to threaten you."

"I appreciate that."

"But everything is on your shoulders, Del. The whole ball of wax."

"I'll get the tapes. I promise you."

"Okay. Now I'll be able to sleep. Knowing that everything is in your capable hands. And you'll do the right thing."

Rossetti hung up.

He was being threatened, Mayhew realized. There was no need for that. He'd get the job done. He was determined. He would make it work.

"Your food's cold," Sheila said, as he seated himself at the table.

He didn't look at her.

"I really do think it's rude of you to leave the table for a phone call."

He ate. Said nothing.

"Did you hear me?"

He still didn't look at her. "I heard you."

"Well?"

"I want you," he said, looking up at last, "to shut your mouth or leave the fucking table."

She sat there, stunned.

He had never talked to her like that before. It felt wonderful.

MELANIE

Melanie watched Bellamy come unglued. It was fun.

"What happened to her head?"

"Her hair caught on fire."

"You bitch," he sobbed.

Melanie had to admit that ol' Erica, though still breathing, wasn't doing too well at the moment.

Bellamy stood next to Erica's chair, head down to hear the ragged breath escaping from her lips. He seemed at a loss about what to do or say—overwhelmed.

Melanie stood by the front door, her gun pointed at Bellamy's heart. She had already decided that these two deserved each other.

"What about infection?" Bellamy said in a quaking voice. "Erica could get all kinds of poison from setting her hair on fire." He was like a lost child.

Melanie shrugged. "I'm not here to talk about Erica, I'm here to talk about you."

"I love her. I do want to talk about her."

Melanie smiled. For a sleazy guy like Bellamy, a man without scruples, a faithless husband, a shakedown artist—to see Bellamy crumble like this made her want to barf, especially when he tried to be noble.

Melanie smirked. "You love her, huh?"

"Yes, I do."

"She's got nice breasts."

He gave Melanie a puzzled look. "You keep your hands off her," Bellamy said.

Melanie moved away from the door. Over to where poor Erica sat slumped and unconscious in her chair.

"Mr. Bellamy, I want the tapes you cheated Tully out of. I figure Tully brought them to you and tried to make a deal. But then you double-crossed him and took the tapes for yourself. He started following me around because he figured that I was going to get the tapes from you."

"Why do you care about the tapes? I don't know where they are."

Melanie said, "I'm getting tired of all this, Mr. Bellamy. I want to get it over with."

Melanie put her pistol, with its four-inch silencer, to Erica's head. "I'll kill her. Somebody who'd set a woman's head on fire might actually kill her, don't you think?"

"My office," Bellamy said.

Evidently, he'd decided that Erica was more important than the tapes and his half mil.

"Your office?"

"I'll take you there and give you the tapes."

Melanie nodded at Erica. "You really love her a lot, Mr. Bellamy."

"I do."

Melanie squeezed off three quick shots with her silenced gun.

Erica's body jerked and then was still. The exit wound on the far side of her head looked like an ugly flower. Blood and brains were spattered on the wall.

"She wasn't a very nice person, Mr. Bellamy. She used filthy language all the time. Now, let's take a cruise over to your office."

HOOVER

End of a long, grinding day.

J. Edgar Hoover sat at home with his drink and let the memories roar and tumble like a churning rapids through his mind.

The candy stores and silent-movie houses and hiding places of youth. He could hear the boys and girls he played with calling him for a game of pom-pom pullaway, a game he'd excelled at.

Tommy. Best, truest friend he ever had. Darla. Oh Lord what a crush he'd had on her. Going to bed so many nights and tenderly holding his pillow as if it were Darla. And Jamie—

Abruptly, he pulled himself back to the present.

He would be with the ghosts soon enough.

But before he joined them he would show this town, and the smartass national press, that you couldn't just toss J. Edgar Hoover aside once he'd given this nation every drop of selflessness, wisdom, and patriotism he possessed.

Hadn't *Reader's Digest* recently stated that without J. Edgar Hoover, this nation might well be in the clutches of the Communists?

Now, there was just the remaining task—getting the tapes. Screw Clyde if he didn't like it. Clyde was just jealous of Melanie.

He sat back. Sipped his drink. Smiled.

Then he'd pay an Oval Office visit to the president and mention it casually: "Say, Mr. President, somebody sent me these tapes and said you might want to hear them."

And then he'd watch the handsome young president's face grow tight and dismayed as the tapes began to play.

J. Edgar Hoover finished his drink and fixed himself another one. Lovely.

MELANIE

Poor Bellamy. He obviously kept reliving Erica's death. Seeing her jerk and jump when the bullets entered her brain. He kept shaking his head, trying to banish the image from his mind forever.

"Now, Mr. Bellamy, I expect complete cooperation. Do you understand?" Melanie said. She wanted to get this over with.

"You didn't need to kill her," Bellamy said, his voice dazed and distant.

They were in Bellamy's cherry-red Caddy near the NBC TV studios in Burbank. This time of night, there were still tourists passing by and pointing.

"Yes, I did."

"You're crazy," he said matter-of-factly. "Aren't you?"

And then Bellamy couldn't take it any more. Right there at the stoplight, he went crazy.

First pounding his fist against the dashboard. Then grabbing for Melanie's slender neck.

Melanie rammed her gun into the curve of Bellamy's big belly. And he was done.

Vomit poured from his nostrils and his mouth and covered his chest and lap.

"I'm sure glad we took your car instead of mine," Melanie said. She rolled down her window.

All he could do was sit there, hot reeking vomit all over himself.

"You didn't have to kill her," he said calmly. "You didn't have to."

Melanie stopped at a gas station and took him into the men's room, like a mother with a naughty son, and cleaned him up as best she could.

Then, they reached the building housing the *Insight* offices. As they rode up in the elevator now, the stench was still bad. Not to mention the looks of his shirt and trousers. They walked down the hall to the door marked INSIGHT in gold lettering on dark wood.

Bellamy wasn't doing too well. It was all gone from him now, the money, the pleasure of shaking down the president of the United States, the plans for his final years.

He didn't care about anything any more. He wanted to give Melanie the tapes and get rid of her. And then get a fifth of bourbon and go to some motel room alone and stay drunk for several days.

And stop thinking about Erica, naked and tied up, jerking around as the bullets exploded in her head.

He was coming to his senses.

They went into his office. It smelled of stale air and cigarette smoke. Bellamy went over and swung the painting to the right, exposing the safe. He dialed the combination.

He opened the safe and put his hand in and felt around and said, "Fuck!"

"What?"

"They're gone!" Bellamy was fully alert again. Where the hell were the tapes?

"This was stupid, Mr. Bellamy. Lying to me like this."

"They were here, I swear they were here! I put them here myself!"

The silencer was good for three more rounds. She spent only two.

She put two bullets right into Bellamy's head, pretty much the same as she'd done to Erica.

Bellamy slumped to the floor.

She sighed. Now she had to start her search for the tapes all over again.

PART THREE

"The way to power
is to take it."

——*William Marcy 'Boss' Tweed*

JEFF He thought about her all the time, in the moony, sad way of a young man in love for the first time. He was a New Hampshire boy from a solid family and was, if not a great catch, at least a decent catch for the right woman. If he could just find the right woman. And now he thought he had.

But he seemed unable to sway Sara. Even though her marriage was over, she still seemed to hold on to hope. But soon Sara would have to accept him in a serious way, or he'd give up and find somebody else.

He was five minutes late, but for once didn't worry about it, didn't start forming an excuse for Mr. Bellamy, who sometimes got there right after dawn.

He greeted all the usual people on the elevator, and proceeded to the solemn, locked door marked INSIGHT.

Jeff took out his keys, opened the door, and went inside. The smell hit him. He gagged.

With reluctance, he went on through the front office and into Mr. Bellamy's private domain.

He found Bellamy sprawled behind his desk, bloody and covered with flies attracted to the feces that had filled his pants.

He glimpsed Bellamy's bullet-blasted head, then looked quickly away.

He had never seen anything like this before. He felt panic, and great fear.

Dazed and slow, he went to the outer office and called the police.

SARA At the same time that Jeff was calling the police, Sara was dropping Laura off at school.

The playground was bustling. Girls jumped rope and played hopscotch; boys ran around and threw a yellow rubber football. Kids were on the swings.

But not all girls and boys were thus occupied, of course.

In the corner of the playground was the tall, awkward girl who didn't feel good enough about herself to join the others; the boy with his head buried in the comic book, indifferent to the clamor of his peers; three black girls already artificially segregated, jumping rope by themselves. There would be others already driven from the main group for any number of reasons: because they lisped or limped, because they were so stupid that the other children laughed at them, or because they came from home environments so strange they felt like aliens visiting another planet—and were perceived by their peers to be just that.

Here and there were teachers speaking to their favorites. And one couldn't blame them. Teachers had every right to have favorites.

And as Laura opened the car door, Sara remembered what it was like to be her age, what a wonderful time it had been for her, and would be for these kids, too—even some of the outcasts would recall their school days fondly, forgetting (at least for the most part) all the cruel things their peers had done to them.

"Mommy?" Laura said, as she grasped the door handle.

"What, honey?"

"Last night with Daddy? I think he wishes you would've been there with us."

She pretended that Laura's words hadn't stirred her. "You do, huh? Why do you think that?"

"Just because of how he was acting." Her blue eyes were wistful. Every day she said something about them getting back together.

"Did he say anything special?" Ridiculous, pumping her own daughter for a hopeful word or two.

"I could just tell. The way he looked at me."

So he hadn't really said anything.

Now Sara felt ridiculously disappointed.

"Maybe next time."

"You always say that, Mommy."

"It's true. The next time you two go somewhere, I'll ask if I can tag along. How's that?"

She stared at Sara. "Really?"

"Really."

"That'd be great."

Sara smiled. "Have a good day in school, hon."

Laura got out of the car, one more kid in brown and white saddle shoes and white anklets and the school uniform, hefting her Bullwinkle lunch pail in her right hand and her books in the other.

She vanished into the throng of kids.

MELANIE
Melanie waited until she saw Sara leave, then she swung her rental car to the back of the school.

Yesterday afternoon, she'd checked out the school and found that, on returning to class after recess, Laura passed right by a large lost-and-found board that was five feet from the door to the basement.

In an envelope marked "Laura Drury" she had put a note: "Laura: Wait for me here after the bell. Miss M."

Now she found the rear door to the basement, and went inside, the envelope in her pocket.

She found the stairs leading to the first floor on Laura's side of the building. She peeked out in the hall, found it empty, went out and pinned the envelope to the lost-and-found board, and snuck back down the steps, leaving the door ajar so she could see out.

LENIHAN

Lenihan got in late to L.A. and went to his suite in the posh Fenwick Hotel. He took from his suitcase his framed photograph of little Dulcie and set it reverently on the nightstand.

He sat in his underwear, smoking an L&M filter cigarette, staring at little Dulcie and remembering her silver laughter when they'd played hide-and-seek. He could always find her because of her laughter. No matter where she hid in their big back yard, even if she hid in the garage, she could not stop herself from giggling, and so finding her was easy. He would always lift her up then and hold her with a devout love that had frequently brought tears to his eyes. He knew what was important in this life. Little Dulcie.

Staring at the photo now in a threadbare Los Angeles motel room, a hairy middle-aged man in boxer shorts, he recalled little Dulcie's laughter exactly. As if she were in the room with him at this very moment.

Then he spoke to her as he did each night, in the perfect thoughts he carried like jewels in his mind.

He turned off the light, lay down wearily in bed and fell into a ragged sleep.

He wasn't sure what time the argument started. It wasn't even that loud an argument, but it woke him. He lay for a time listening to the hurtful words being spoken on the other side of the wall between husband and wife. She started crying. The man finally slammed out of their room after she repeated for the tenth time that she would not give him the divorce he wanted.

Then, in the ensuing silence, Lenihan lay wide awake in the lonely air of the hotel room. In the lonely dark.

For once, he thought neither of his daughter nor his wife, but of his last operation for the Office of Strategic Services in the waning months of World War II, when he received two Purple Hearts.

With thirty other men, Lenihan had parachuted behind enemy lines on Manchuria, where the Japanese Army was holding four thousand American prisoners in concentration camps.

They spent four days killing Japanese soldiers. They killed them with bullets and knives and bayonets. They killed them singly and in bunches. On the second day it rained so hard that some of the corpses they'd put in shallow graves floated free. They knew the war was nearly at an end. They just prayed it would come soon.

By the time they reached the main camp, their own number had shrunk to twelve.

On the evening they were to raid the camp, loudspeakers announced that the war had ended. Cheers went up from the American prisoners. Lenihan was dispatched to persuade the Japanese in charge of the camp to surrender. By dawn, four of the top Japanese had committed suicide rather than surrender.

Lenihan and his men went through the cells where the Americans were held. It was gruesome. There were men who weighed no more than seventy pounds. Men with arms and legs being eaten by gangrene. Even the heads of two men who had been executed by decapitation.

After the war, Lenihan stayed with Colonel "Wild Bill" Donovan as the OSS became the Central Intelligence Agency. The wartime pact between the United States and Russia was fast disintegrating and the U.S. government meant to check communism around the world. But Lenihan was not by nature a political animal and was not disposed to killing some poor Thai peasant who called himself a "Communist."

So, in 1946—a year after John Fitzgerald Kennedy had been elected the congressman from Boston's Eleventh District—Lenihan met Kennedy at a Georgetown cocktail party, and a month later went to work for him as a troubleshooter.

And now, he was on yet another mission, the most important of Jack Kennedy's political career.

Excerpt from Marilyn Monroe's personal tapes

I always have the same nightmare. I'm walking down a street and a very handsome man stops me and asks me for my name and I tell him—but I'm speaking in a language he's never heard before. Then he looks more closely at me and hurries away. He looks upset and frightened. When I told my psychiatrist about this, he says the dream is about my fear of going insane. A lot of people know that my mother spent a good part of her life in and out of institutions, but what most people don't know is that my maternal grandmother and her husband were also put away several times. It's in my family, all the way back, and sometimes when I get depressed, I'm afraid I'm going to lose control, the way my grandparents and mother did sometimes—just lose control totally and they'll put me away forever.

S A R A The boxy white ambulance was parked at an angle to the curb and was flanked by four police cars.

A crowd formed outside the police cordon in the bright sunny morning, watching.

Sara knew instantly that there was something wrong in the tall, shining office building that held *Insight*.

She went up to a cop and said, "I'm Sara Drury. I work inside. At *Insight*."

"You'll want to see Detective Rabinowitz. He's in charge of the investigation."

"Did something happen at *Insight*?" Sara felt an adrenalin-rush of panic.

"You'd better ask Detective Rabinowitz."

Uniformed officers were stationed throughout the lobby, asking people questions, pointing them to the elevators.

When Sara stepped from the elevator on her floor, she saw a handsome, older man with a good haircut and a good suit talking to Jeff.

All the other men and women wore the dark uniforms of the LAPD, the white smocks of the medical examiner's office, or the rack suits of the crime lab.

Jeff nodded at her. The man stopped talking and motioned Sara over.

"Somebody killed Mr. Bellamy in his office last night," Jeff said.

"Mrs. Drury, I'm Detective Rabinowitz. I'd like to talk to you, after Jeff and I finish."

She forced herself to remain calm. God—Mr. Bellamy dead. "Of course. I'll wait in my office."

The offices were crowded with people and equipment. Flash bulbs blazed every few moments and men with tape measures and small whisk brooms and small clear evidence bags worked everywhere. She almost peeked into Mr. Bellamy's office, but stopped herself. She did not want to see something so horrible she might never be able to forget it.

She couldn't relax, of course. She went to the window and looked out at Los Angeles. She could see buildings that had been built in the early 1920s and were now slowly coming down in urban renewal projects. She could see faded advertisements painted on their backs— for cough syrup and pipe tobacco and a Pilsner beer. The ads dated back to her favorite period in L.A. history, just when the talkies had reached their zenith.

"Mrs. Drury?"

She turned to Detective Rabinowitz.

"Is now okay?"

"Of course," Sara said.

Rabinowitz sat in the chair on the other side of Sara's desk. He told her what had happened.

Sara got scared, deeply scared, learning, as if in a vision, the true nature of the universe—dark and completely unpredictable.

MELANIE Melanie waited at the top of the basement stairs, peering out behind the door into the hall of the school. The corridor was alive with children laughing and shouting and shoving.

"Help you with something?"

Melanie turned, startled, and looked down the concrete basement stairs to where, near the furnace, a uniformed janitor stood amidst cobwebs and dusty sunlight.

"Just going to see the principal about my little girl. Thought I'd take a shortcut."

The janitor, bald and hawkish, looked skeptical. "This ain't a shortcut." He sidled left, toward a black wall phone.

"Wait right there, please."

He reached for the phone.

"Would you like to see some identification?"

She was already moving down the steps, hand on the iron banister.

"No, no, you just wait right there."

She leaped.

Her feet touched the basement floor as the edge of her right hand slashed into the janitor's neck with a blinding karate-chop.

Dentures flew from the man's mouth as his head struck the wall by the phone.

The receiver dangled free, the dial tone loud in the dusty basement.

She hung up the receiver and dragged the janitor over to a dark corner where he wouldn't be found for a while.

The class bell rang.

Melanie then went back up the stairs to the door. The hall quickly cleared. At first she couldn't see Laura anywhere.

And then she saw her, just where she wanted to see her.

At the lost-and-found board, holding the note.

Melanie opened her purse and took out a clean, white handkerchief. Then she took out a small bottle of chloroform and doused the handkerchief with it.

VANESSA So many things helped define Tully.

Tully had been Wildroot Hair Oil, Cavalier cigarettes, *True* magazine, Montgomery Ward underwear, Thom McCann black wingtips, blue Arrow button-down shirts, a Merchant Marine photo of himself and three mates, his First Communion rosary, a deck of cards with photos of topless women on the backs, a photograph of his uncle who had been killed fighting the Japanese near the China mainland, and his Tom Mix Club membership card, issued July 14, 1932, from radio station WPIK.

Vanessa didn't know what she was looking for.

But she sensed that eventually, whatever it was, it would show itself as a symbol or a sign from God.

She did pretty well, really, breaking down only twice so far as she quietly went about searching the drawers and cabinets and closets and pockets and hat bands that had belonged to her beloved Tully.

Every phase of his life was in these drawers: boy, teenager, and man.

She was still unable to quite believe that it had actually happened; that Tully was actually gone.

But then the cold suffocating odor of the morgue would fill her nostrils and she would know that, yes, he was dead.

She kept on searching.

SARA As soon as Detective Rabinowitz had finished with her, a tall, quietly handsome man knocked on her office door and said, "I'm David Lenihan. From Washington." He reminded her that he was from a federal agency that had been investigating Mr. Bellamy, and was here to talk to her for a few minutes.

"Oh, right. C'mon in."

He sat and stared at her for a long moment.

"Mr. Bellamy was murdered, I understand."

"Yes, so we've been told."

"Do you have any idea who might have done it?"

"Why, no, I don't. I would have told the police."

"I didn't mean to insult you, Mrs. Drury. I just thought you might take a guess."

"I can't, Mr. Lenihan. I just don't have any idea at all."

His brown eyes smiled, but behind them was a hard, cold intelligence.

"I understand the safe was open, Mrs. Drury."

"Yes."

"Do you know if something was taken?"

"I'm not sure."

"But $2,500 was left behind in his desk?"

"Yes."

"So the police don't think it was a normal robbery."

"I guess not."

"You know the combination to the safe?"

"Yes."

The sad smile again as his eyes lingered on the framed photograph of Laura. "She's a beauty."

"Thank you."

"Reminds me a little of my own daughter."

"Oh. How old is she?"

His eyes shifted to her. "She died several years ago. Polio."

"Oh, I'm sorry."

"Have you ever opened the safe?"

"Once."

"When was that?"

"Uh, yesterday."

"Would you mind telling me why you opened it?"

"I had to get something for somebody."

"Oh?"

She had to lie. She didn't want Curtis Simmons implicated in any of this. Not with his wife dying of cancer.

"Mr. Bellamy asked me to open it."

He watched her carefully.

She knew that he knew she was lying.

"To take something out?"

"Yes, to take something out and put it on his desk. An envelope."

"I see. And was that the last time you spoke to Mr. Bellamy?"

She nodded. "Yes." She paused. "May I ask you a question?"

"Of course."

"Why are you investigating Bellamy?"

He stood up. "That's one question I can't answer, Mrs. Drury. I'm sorry."

He nodded and left her office. She had the impression that she'd inadvertently told him more than she meant to.

Then she thought of his face when he'd mentioned his dead daughter, and the shaky quality of his voice. Several years, and he still wasn't over her.

But then you'd never get over the loss of your child. Never.

MELANIE Had to be quick. Right in the middle of a school like this.

She took four long steps from the basement door and said, "Hi, Laura."

And Laura turned from the lost-and-found board. "Are you Miss M?"

"Yes."

Melanie glanced down the long hallway. Clear.

She was four steps from Laura. "I've got a surprise for you, honey." Three steps. Two. Now—

She slapped the chloroformed handkerchief to the girl's face and held her tight. Laura wriggled against her, and gasped so hard Melanie feared Laura was going to throw up.

Then she was still. Inert.

Melanie picked her up and carried her under her arm like a puppy back down the basement steps, past the sprawled janitor, up the far steps to her car right outside.

She dropped her onto the back seat, closed the door and slid behind the wheel.

She was soaked with sweat and panting so hard she was disgusted with herself. Really had to lay off the fats and the sweets.

LENIHAN Del Mayhew looked the part of a studio executive, suave, $25 razored haircut, $1000 custom-made suit, steely grip, and a smile to rival Burt Lancaster's.

"I've got to admit, Mr. Lenihan, you've got my attention. All the way from Washington just to see me?"

"I'll come to the point, Mr. Mayhew. You hired a private investigative agency recently."

"You've been doing some homework."

"A man named Tully did the work."

"Yes. Tully."

"He was murdered yesterday."

"I heard that."

Lenihan studied him a moment and then said, "I know what he was looking for, Mr. Mayhew." He paused. "And so do you."

Mayhew pursed his lips in thought. "I don't have them."

"But maybe they will come into your possession eventually."

"I'm not optimistic, I guess."

"Let's be honest, Mr. Mayhew. You're turning Los Angeles upside down to find them. And so am I. I even know who's putting the heat on you." He paused. "Rossetti plays rough, but I play rougher. I have all the resources of the government."

"Are you threatening me?"

Lenihan did not smile. "I guess that would be a matter of interpretation, Mr. Mayhew."

Lenihan picked up a note pad from Mayhew's desk and wrote down the number of his hotel.

"You can reach me there, Mr. Mayhew."

Lenihan rose to go. He didn't offer his hand.

VANESSA In the golden morning sunlight, she finally stopped in her search and broke down. Sat in the recliner Tully had liked so much and started sobbing.

She opened one of Tully's drawers for one of the white handkerchiefs she had always kept ironed for him.

And that's when she found it, the little black address book.

The pocket-size book protruded slightly from inside the three-ring notebook in which Tully kept his job and expense ledger. She must have missed it before and jarred it loose now.

She carried it carefully, as if it were a fragile heirloom, back to Tully's recliner.

Even before she opened it, she knew that she'd found something important.

Tully had probably slipped the small notebook inside the larger one by accident. He had always been tucking one thing into another and this tendency, coupled with his absent-mindedness . . . well, he'd spent a lot of time calling, "Hon, could you come in here and help me find something?"

Perhaps that was the role she'd valued most with Tully. Being his mother. She liked lover and wife and friend very, very much but there was something endearing about seeing a big, blunt otherwise self-sufficient Irish guy like Tully reduced to a helpless little boy.

"Hon, could you come in here and . . ."

She heard the ghostly words now. Out of the bedroom they came, past the small dining room with the good mahogany table Tully had proudly paid cash for, into the living room with its twenty-one-inch blonde Admiral console and its shelf of *Reader's Digest Condensed* novels.

And then she had to smile.

Tully had finally rejoined her. She could feel his presence right next to her. Tully was with her now.

She opened the small black notebook and saw neat rows of blue ink names and blue ink phone numbers.

Some of the entries had dates next to them, indicating, she supposed, which investigation they belonged to.

There were so many pages of names and numbers that it would take her a while to find any that could help her.

But she didn't mind, now that Tully was keeping her company.

She made herself some Butternut drip coffee. She no longer resented the sunlight. Or the noisy birds. Or the fact that the world had gone right on spinning after Tully's death.

Indeed, she was filled with a great peace and purpose as she stood at the window watching a pair of cardinals perched on the clothesline.

The little black notebook was right there in Tully's chair, waiting for her. She had a clear, true purpose for her life now, and thanked God for it.

ROSSETTI Rossetti knew all about the Hollywood-Mob connection. Frank Costello was a good friend of Harry Cohn at Columbia Pictures. Jimmy Durante and George Raft could often be seen in the company of Lucky Luciano. Producer Bryan Foy, at Warner Brothers, often held parties that included the likes of Mickey Cohen and Big Al Polizzi.

Rossetti even remembered how, in the late forties, a reporter for one of the Hollywood dailies attempted to prove this conclusively. Before he could finish the first installment of his promised "racket-busting" series, he was found in the trunk of his car minus his nose, fingers and penis. And his heart. They'd ripped it right out of him.

A few years after Senator Estes Kefauver tried to dig up some of the same connections the reporter had been investigating. All of this came to naught until Attorney General Robert F. Kennedy began investigating the connection between organized labor and organized crime, and the hold James Hoffa had on the Teamsters union.

Mob bosses feared that Kennedy, if he got Hoffa, would be encouraged to look for Mob connections with other labor unions—including Hollywood labor unions, which had been tightly controlled by the Mafia since at least the early 1940s.

It was well known in Mob circles that Carlos Marcello, the head of the Mob's New Orleans family, wanted the Kennedy brothers dead. Robert Kennedy had come after Marcello directly and personally, using the attorney general's office to not only harass and inhibit the Mob, but to put its leaders in federal prison.

Rossetti had heard it whispered in late 1961 that Marcello was planning the assassination of president John Kennedy. "Cut off the head of the snake and the tail will die, too." Meaning that if John were killed, Robert would be rendered powerless. Lyndon Johnson— JFK's successor—hated Robert Kennedy as much as Marcello did.

But, it was explained to Rossetti, other Mob bosses leaned on Marcello to try some other means of bringing down the Kennedys. If Americans ever discovered that the Mob was behind the assassination of the beloved president, the Mob would be destroyed for sure.

And so Marcello devised the idea of publicly exposing John and Robert Kennedy as the reckless playboys they were.

Rossetti was asked to have Marilyn Monroe's bedroom bugged by someone who couldn't be traced to the Mob. He was to get her on tape with either John or Robert. Rossetti's employers didn't care. Once his bosses had those tapes, the Brothers Kennedy would be politically dead, their reputation and careers destroyed, abandoned to the dust-heap of history.

His orders weren't Rossetti's only reason for wanting the president to tumble. Rossetti had been careful to present his Negro lady friend not as a whore or even as a mistress but as a serious and intelligent woman he both respected and loved. But even knowing this, John Kennedy, who was happy to trade the most noxious race jokes, once quipped to a yacht-load of people, well within the lady's earshot, "Rossetti goes for the dark meat when he carves up a turkey."

There was no recourse. One didn't upbraid the president of the United States, particularly when you were a guest on his yacht.

No, one waited for a chance at vengeance.

Rossetti, who was always reading the classics in an attempt to improve himself, lived by the words of Francis Bacon: "Revenge is a kind of wild justice . . ."

Rossetti was at last ready to defend his true love's honor. And at first the plot had gone well. He had entrusted the job to Del Mayhew, who had hired a private investigator, and they had actually gotten some tapes proving that John Kennedy had been seeing Miss Monroe and—well, no administration could stand that kind of scandal.

But things went wrong. The private investigator tried to cut himself in on the action. And now the P.I. was dead and God only knew where the Mob's Marilyn tapes were.

Rossetti was halfway through his breakfast of bran flakes and grapefruit when the maid appeared, cradling the white phone like a priest his chalice and trailing a phone cord behind her.

"There's a call for you, Mr. Rossetti. He said it's urgent."

"Thanks."

She set the phone down in the sunny breakfast nook where Rossetti liked to sit and watch the golfers on the back nine of his country club.

"Hello."

"Morning, my friend. Beautiful day, isn't it?"

Rossetti's breath caught in his throat.

He had talked to this man, the West Coast boss of bosses, perhaps three times in the decade Rossetti had been out here.

"It's a great morning," Rossetti said.

"Great, great." His voice had the oily vigor of a TV minister's. Suddenly the voice was hard. "We put a lot of trust in you. Word I'm getting is that things aren't going so good."

"Just a temporary problem."

"Losing the fucking tapes is a temporary problem? Bellamy had them, but now where the fuck are they?" He paused. "I promised my doctor and my wife I won't get upset. Fucking ulcers. You're a young man. You don't have to worry yet—not about things like that."

No, thought Rossetti, not about things like that.

"I'm getting a lot of heat."

"I'm sure," Rossetti said.

"A lot of people think, a man in my position, nobody gives him heat. But I get heat. I'm getting heat from friends of ours in the midwest who are unhappy about certain things going on in Washington."

"I realize that."

"You know what I got in addition to ulcers?"

"No," Rossetti answered dutifully.

"I got hemorrhoids, I got constipation and I got gout. And you know how old I am? Seventy-one. I shouldn't have any of this bullshit till I'm at least eighty."

Rossetti wasn't sure what to say.

"You know why I'm telling you all this?"

"Why?"

"So you'll know that I'm not in the best of moods. So if somebody was to fuck up an important assignment, I would not have much patience."

"I understand."

"I hope you do, my friend. Because I like you. You got ambition and you learn, and you got class. That impresses me."

"Thank you."

"But the heat I'm getting, that's what's making my body act up this way. Your fuck-up is my fuck-up. You understand?"

"Yes."

"A couple of our people wouldn't mind taking a run at me. They could use this. 'He gives the job to Rossetti and Rossetti fucks it up. He don't even give the job to the right guys any more. He's too old.' That's what they'll say."

"I'll handle it."

"You got twenty-four hours."

"Don't worry."

"Tell that to my gout. You ever know anybody with gout?"

"An uncle once, I guess."

"He dead?"

"Yes."

"Well, if he had gout and he's dead then he's a lucky man to be dead. We got an understanding, my friend?"

"Yes. Guaranteed."

MELANIE As she pulled the rental car into the garage, Melanie checked again to make sure that nobody followed her. The road along the ocean was empty. She was safe.

She got out and opened the back door and pulled Laura out. The girl was sweaty.

She carried her out of the garage and quickly up the back stairs. The ocean rolled in behind her.

Somebody could be walking on the beach.

Or out on a boat with binoculars.

She couldn't afford to take any chances.

She hurried unlocking the door, getting the girl inside.

She carried her straight through the small house to the bedroom she'd arranged for her.

She'd done the bed up nicely, going to Penney's for pink sheets and blanket, and a plump brown teddy bear so maybe she wouldn't be so scared when she came out of the chloroform.

She laid her on the bed, listening to Laura murmur and faintly moan in her sleep.

Melanie got her all tucked in and stood up and looked at her for a time and then left the room.

"Mr. Drury?" said the female voice.

"Yes."

"I need to talk to you about your daughter. Your wife's phone is busy at the moment so I decided to call you instead."

"Who is this?"

"A friend of your daughter's."

"What about her?"

"I have her. She's safe, but I have her."

She could hear his small gasp.

"Is this a joke?"

"No joke, Mr. Drury."

"But why?" His voice rose. "Who are you? What do you want?"

"I want the tapes that were in Bellamy's office safe and you'll have to help me."

"Help you do what?"

"Convince your wife to find those tapes for me."

"I don't know what you're talking about. I don't know about any tapes."

"You tell her that if I don't have those tapes by nine o'clock tonight, I'm going to kill Laura."

"No, no, please, wait!" Drury was frantic now. "I need to know who you are."

"Who I am doesn't matter."

"But you have Laura now?"

"Yes."

"And she's all right?"

"Just sleeping."

"Please, don't do anything. . . ."

"This is strictly business, Mr. Drury. Once I have the tapes, your lives will return to normal. Here's my number." She rattled it off. "And no cops, of course. You know what'll happen if you call the cops."

She hung up.

LOUELLA

Louella was in the screening room of her house. Universal had sent over a copy of the new Sandra Dee–Robert Goulet–Andy Williams movie in hopes that she would boost it in her column. But even by Louella's tolerant standards the picture was terrible.

She stopped the film to take the call from Gibbons, the man from Hearst.

"Good morning, Louella. How are things going?"

"Things, Mr. Gibbons, are going fine."

"Then you got the tapes?"

"Not yet."

"But you know when they're coming?"

"Not exactly."

A hesitation. "Oh. I thought you'd have them by now. I thought you said—"

"Very soon, Mr. Gibbons."

"So everything's on track, then?"

"Everything's very much on track, Mr. Gibbons."

"Okay, okay. And the things you expect from us? Your photo. The guarantee of front page. No problem, Louella. I'm keeping all this under wraps, of course."

"Fine."

"You're a sweetheart, Louella."

"I'm hanging up now," Louella said.

Excerpt from
Marilyn Monroe's
personal tapes

A couple of weeks ago, I had this terrible argument with Bobby Kennedy. I saw that he wasn't ever going to leave his wife for me. Not ever. I think he wanted to, but there were so many things he had to overcome—his friends and family and the Catholic church. I just stayed drunk for three days after that argument, and then I had this friend over and I showed him something I'd never shown anybody, this diary I kept with some of the things John Kennedy and Bobby Kennedy had both told me about government—about who was crooked and taking bribes, about who was homosexual, about who was working for the Mob and who was spying for Russia—all kinds of terrible things like that. After I showed it to him, my friend took my hand and said, "Marilyn, if anybody ever finds out about this diary, they'll kill you. They'll kill you right away." That was the first time I ever got scared about knowing John and Robert Kennedy.

TOLSON Had Edgar gone around the bend?

Last night, Clyde had pretended to be intrigued with Edgar's efforts to get his hands on the Monroe tapes, to get at the Kennedys. But that was a stall for time. Actually, it was a terrible idea. Worse, it was an incredibly dangerous idea. Melanie was a psychopath. And it would be up to Clyde to stop her.

So he'd gotten up seven times during the night. Seven times.

He'd sat on his bed and smoked a lot of cigarettes.

And wondered how he could stop Melanie.

At work in the morning, Clyde was groggy until he'd had his third cup of coffee.

The roses came just after eleven, brought in by a neatly dressed Negro man. All the secretaries in the front office turned to look at the resplendent red flowers, so regal in their green wrapping.

Who were they for, and why?

The buxom receptionist carried them to a small, frail woman in the back who immediately broke into a smile.

Then the entire office knew who'd sent the roses. Not a lover or a regretful husband, but Clyde Tolson. The only executive who had the tact and taste to treat the office workers as real people.

The small woman's name was Mindy. Her four-year-old daughter was in the hospital for some tests. Clyde was a nice guy.

Today he was already in his office when the women arrived. His phone lights showed that he was busy making many brief calls.

Curious that Clyde had gotten to the office so early. And even more curious that he didn't come out and say hello to them, as usual.

"Sonofabitch."

He wasn't much of a swearer, Clyde. Back on the farm where he'd been born and raised—Laredo, Missouri, in the year 1900—Clyde had been taught the Good Book, which meant keeping a pure mind and a clean tongue. He had abided by these rules all the way up: from his brief years in a Cedar Rapids, Iowa, business college; to his years as confidential secretary to Secretary of War Newton D. Baker; to his years as associate director, the number-two man in the FBI.

But this morning, so much was at stake. Edgar was getting wilder and crazier in his attempts to hold on to power. And God only knew that Melanie was up to out there in Los Angeles.

So this morning he'd come to work an hour before even the most zealous employee showed up, and started dialing the number for Melanie he'd found in Edgar's office.

By now, he must have dialed her twenty times. He decided to try once more.

"Hello."

"Hello!" Tolson exclaimed. "Who is this?"

"Conchita, the maid."

"The hotel maid?"

"Si."

"Is Miss Melanie Baines there?"

"I give you the front desk."

A male voice said, "Desk."

"I'm trying to find Melanie Baines, who was staying in Room 408."

"Yes, sir. She checked out yesterday afternoon."

"Any idea where she might have gone? Any forwarding address or phone number?"

"No, sir."

Tolson hung up and then dialed a two-digit interoffice number. Edgar's private number.

"We need to talk, Edgar."

"Believe it or not, Mr. Tolson, I'm busy," Edgar snapped.

"We need to talk now," Tolson said.

He slammed down the phone.

He had never treated Edgar this way before. Never had the nerve. Now there was no choice.

MAYHEW

"Mr. Murchison, please."
Moment.

"Del, how's it going today?" Murchison said.

"I need a quarter million dollars in cash and I need it right away," Del Mayhew said.

"My God, Del, what the hell is going on?"

"I wish I could tell you but I can't."

"But a quarter of a million, Del. That's a fortune."

"The studio has at least that much cash on hand."

"I suppose. Yes."

"Then you know I'm good for it."

"But that money's not yours, Del. You'd need the approval of your board."

"You could fix it for me, Hugh. I think I've done a lot for you the past couple years. Brought you big accounts."

"Yes but—"

"And now I need a favor, Hugh. There's a lot riding on it."

"It would take me a while."

Mayhew smiled, knowing he'd get his way. "Two hours."

"Two hours?"

"That's all the time I have, Hugh. I'll see you then."

This was Mayhew's last best try to get the tapes. If anybody beat him to possession of them, it would be the government man, David Lenihan.

And with a quarter of a mil, Mayhew knew he could buy Lenihan off.

On a government salary, a man would be a fool to reject a quarter of a million dollars.

MICHAEL His first reaction was to deny the truth that Laura had been kidnapped, to consider the phone call a hoax.

He stared out the huge window of Kathryn's Malibu house, dimly aware of the beach below and a sailboat on the horizon.

Somebody had kidnapped Laura.

He had to call Sara.

The phone rang six times before she picked it up.

"Hi, Michael. I'm afraid this isn't a very good time to talk. Somebody killed Bellamy. Murdered him. Jeff found the body here this morning."

"Wow. Listen . . ." Stay calm, he thought, to help Laura. "I need to see you. Right away."

"Tonight?"

"No, sooner. Something's happened, Sara, and I have to talk to you face-to-face."

"Are you all right, Michael?"

"I'm okay. I can meet you at the Hideaway restaurant near your office in forty-five minutes."

"I'll see you then."

He left a brief note for Kathryn and finished it with several Xs for kisses. She was a sentimental lady and liked things like that. The note said only: *I need to help Laura with an emergency. I'll call you tonight. Love, Michael.*

He got into the T-Bird Kathryn had bought him and drove quickly to the freeway.

SIMMONS Only when he was drunk could you take full measure of the actor, Curtis Simmons.

He would (in his cups) tell you about the time he appeared in a 1946 picture with Sonny Tufts and Tufts got top billing and three times as much money. Or the picture with Gloria Swanson when she said, during a kissing scene, in front of the entire crew, "You have breath like a pig, Curtis!" Or the time (by now his career was sinking fast) he made a juvenile delinquent picture at American-International (playing the fey high school teacher) and was told by a sweaty, illiterate graduate of the Method that "you, Daddy-O, are no longer relevant."

Or how about when he had paid down on a new home, counting on a large salary from a picture with Elizabeth Taylor, only to have Taylor suffer one of her mysterious illnesses and force cancellation?

Dear God, he'd lost seventeen-five in earnest money!

Nowhere, it seemed, was there a thespian more ill-starred than Curtis Franklin Simmons.

Last night he was supposed to be at his dying wife's bedside in his demi-mansion Colonial home, in his silk smoking jacket with his expensive brandy. The English lord in his manor.

But he'd looked at her in so much pain, wasted to little more than bone, blue eyes glassy with the disease burning through her, and all he could feel was . . . guilt.

He had ceased loving her long ago, and had never been faithful. He found her company dull, sick or not.

And so he'd fled to his den.

And out of monotony (Maren, his true love, was in Las Vegas, doing a vocal turn in the lounge) he decided to play the tapes he'd taken from Bellamy's office. He wanted to hear them once before destroying them.

He put one of the tapes on the reel-to-reel machine, made himself comfortable in his chair, and raised his brandy glass.

The tape began to play. The quality was bad. At first he didn't recognize the voice. But surely it wasn't him and it wasn't Maren. Sara had given him the wrong tapes.

Then he realized who he was listening to.

Marilyn Monroe. Oh good God.

And one of the Kennedys. Yes. Absolutely.

It sounded like Robert.

Simmons sat straight up, wide-eyed.

He spent the next several hours in his den, playing all the tapes, nervously smoking cigarettes.

And then, transformed into a festive mood, he went into his wife's room and sat by her side and held her hand until she went to sleep.

He spent the rest of the night in the den, trying to reach Maren in Las Vegas. He wanted to tell her that their money worries were over—that after his wife's death there would be plenty of money. Plenty.

But he couldn't reach her.

Finally, so drunk he could barely walk, he flopped down on the couch, an old Rudy Vallee picture flickering on the TV, and slept the sleep of a happy man.

By noon, the worst of the hangover had waned.

The nurse was here to see to the Mrs., and Simmons had finished his half-hour exercise program of light weightlifting and running in place. While he was no longer a star, he hoped to continue working. Staying in shape was important.

Now, dressed in a yellow shirt, white duck trousers, and brown leather sandals, he took the white telephone out by the pool.

He lit a cigarette and dialed the number.

"Good morning, Mrs. Drury. I want to thank you for yesterday. We need to talk about the tapes—"

"I can't talk right now, Mr. Simmons. I'm heading out the door.
You'll have to call me later."

She hung up.

And Simmons was left staring at the phone.

MAYHEW The agent sitting in front of Mayhew's desk was tough, but Mayhew liked him. For his top star in a picture like the one Mayhew proposed, the agent didn't want a simple salary. He wanted "participation," a piece of the profits right off the top. Gary Cooper did this with *High Noon*; likewise Bing Crosby, Danny Kaye, and Irving Berlin in *White Christmas*.

"Del," agent Harry Solomon said, "we're sitting here talking a payoff of millions of dollars and you're not paying attention." Something was woefully distracting Del Mayhew.

"Home life?" Harry Solomon said.

"Home is fine, Harry."

"Mistress making you crazy?"

"I don't have a mistress, Harry."

"What kind of studio head doesn't have a mistress?"

"It's just sinuses." Mayhew felt himself blush. He really needed to pull things together. He was losing it.

His intercom buzzed.

"Excuse me a minute, Harry."

"A Mr. Murchison from your bank," his secretary said.

He took the call eagerly.

"Del, Hugh Murchison here. I've got it for you. All new currency in hundred-dollar bills. I've even put it in a leather valise for you."

"I appreciate this, Hugh."

"I could really get my tit in a wringer for doing this. Maybe I should be reporting it to the FBI. There's no kidnapping or anything involved, is there?"

"Not at all."

"You coming to get it?"

"Yes. In an hour."

They hung up.

The call gave him new encouragement that he was going to get the tapes soon.

"So why don't you have a mistress?" Harry Solomon asked.

"No time."

Harry shook his head. "All these beautiful girls all over your lot. And all going to waste."

Mayhew leaned forward. Now he was hungry to negotiate hard. "Your contract is bullshit."

"Del, do you have any idea how hot Steve McQueen is just now?"

"Not a million and a half hot, not when he also gets ten per cent of the gross."

"You want to know how bad Zanuck wants him, the kind of dollars Zanuck is talking about?"

"I'll think about it."

"I promised Zanuck a call back by noon tomorrow."

"Well, we certainly wouldn't want to keep Zanuck waiting, would we?"

"He's a nice guy." Harry grinned. "Some of the time, anyway."

Mayhew stood up. "I have to leave. But I'll call you before noon tomorrow with my answer."

Ten minutes later, Del Mayhew was on the freeway, roaring toward his bank and the valise containing $250,000 in cash.

Excerpt from
Marilyn Monroe's
personal tapes

I had a small affair with a Los Angeles cop named Tom just after I split with Joe DiMaggio. It was strange how I met him. I was sprawled in the middle of a dark side-street at midnight in the middle of a cold April downpour. I was also half-naked and drunk.

I had started drinking that afternoon, alone in my bedroom. At one point I looked out and saw this teeny-tiny kitten, this calico, and I went out and got her. I fixed her warm milk and then I took a comb and got her all cleaned up and then I got under the covers and put her down next to me. She was like my baby sister. We just slept and slept and slept.

When I got up the house was dark.

I started drinking again, too. And because I hadn't had much to eat that day, I got drunk pretty fast.

I went in to pick up the kitty but she scampered ahead of me into the kitchen. I'd left the door open when the kid had brought groceries earlier in the day. The kitty went right out the door, into the night and the pouring rain.

I went after her. All I had on were my mules and this very thin silk robe. Outside, the robe caught on the vines and the latticework and got torn pretty bad.

But I didn't care. All I could think of was the kitten and how it would get run over by a car. I ran down the center of the street crying for the kitten but I couldn't find her anywhere.

At that moment the only thing that mattered to me in the whole world was that kitten. I knew she loved me the way I'd *always wanted to be loved—because I was good and kind and helpful, not just because I had a wicked smile and a big pair of tits—and I had to find her so we could spend our lives together, had to.*

Anyway, a while later, Tom found me. He was on duty, in his police car. He took me back home and got me dried off and put in bed. I was so depressed, all I could think of was killing myself.

Then he came in with the tiny little kitty in the palm of his hand.

He'd found her on the floor, meowing.

Apparently, she hadn't liked the world out there after all.

She wanted to be with me.

SARA Sara reached the restaurant before Michael and waited for him in one of the booths, the walls of which were covered by framed black-and-white celebrity photos. She thought maybe he'd called her today because he wanted to get back together.

He walked quickly in and sat down and said tensely, "It's about Laura."

"Laura?"

He nodded. His eyes burned.

He wanted to tell her everything but the waitress intruded to give them menus. "Two fries, two Cokes," he snapped, so they would be left alone.

"What's wrong?" Sara said.

"Laura. Somebody's—taken her."

"Taken her?"

In a hushed voice, he told her.

As he spoke, she felt her insides clutch, and she fought to restrain her anxiety in this public place. She felt dizzy, and the walls pressed in. She forced herself to stay logical and clear.

The waitress delivered their Coca-Colas and french fries, and went briskly away.

Sara looked at her french fries and felt nauseated. No food now. No way. "You never heard the woman's voice before?"

"No."

"Did it sound long-distance?"

"No. I don't think so."

232

"Could you hear Laura in the background?"

"No."

"She didn't describe the tapes?"

"Just that Bellamy put them in his office safe."

"The only tapes in there were ones he was using to blackmail Curtis Simmons, the actor."

"Bellamy blackmailed people?" He blinked.

"Simmons came in with a gun and demanded some audio tapes and some photos."

"Then Bellamy is really into something dangerous," Michael said. "And now *we're* into something dangerous." He inhaled his cigarette smoke deeply. His hands trembled. "And maybe it's the same thing."

She reached across the booth and touched his wrist and said, "We'll get her back, Michael. I know we will."

"I don't know what to do."

She had never seen her husband look older or sadder. Not even his handsome Rodeo Drive clothes could make him look happy now.

She wanted to cry but stopped herself.

"We need to think, Michael," she said. "And think hard. Now tell me about this woman's voice again."

Michael didn't have the strength for this situation, but thank God she did.

LENIHAN Sara and Michael left the restaurant, walking as calmly and coolly as they could. Neither of them noticed the man parked several cars down, watching them.

Lenihan watched them walk to their car. He thought of Laura, the girl in the framed photograph on Sara Drury's desk. A nice family.

As Lenihan and his wife and little Dulcie had once been a nice family.

Lenihan started the engine to follow them.

KENNEDY His wife Jacqueline and the children were out of town, so President John F. Kennedy ate lunch alone and hastily returned to the Oval Office where he continued dialing David Lenihan's hotel room in Los Angeles.

This morning had been taken up with four meetings: Secretary of State Dean Rusk, Secretary of Defense Robert McNamara, Ambassador Henry Cabot Lodge, and General Maxwell Taylor, chairman of the Joint Chiefs of Staff. Discussions had ranged from the worsening situation in Vietnam—the Chiefs were asking for more troops—to how unhappy Vice President Lyndon Johnson was with his routine duties. He wanted "something major" according to McGeorge Bundy, one of the few Kennedyites able to get along with the harsh, vulgar Texan.

But now there were more pressing problems to worry about than Lyndon Johnson and Vietnam.

Kennedy peered through the horn-rimmed glasses perched on the end of his nose at the afternoon edition of one of the Washington papers that had just been brought to him.

Near the bottom of the front page was the headline: PUBLISHER SLAIN IN OWN OFFICE.

The story then described how the man, named Frank Bellamy, had been murdered.

He was the same man who had called David Lenihan and asked for half a million dollars for the Marilyn tapes.

All the president could think was that J. Edgar Hoover's unofficial agent Melanie had gotten to Bellamy first. A full-fledged psychopath, she had murdered before.

And if Melanie had the tapes, Hoover would have them soon.

And if Hoover had them . . .

He took his glasses off and leaned back and vigorously rubbed his eyes.

VANESSA The address she'd found in Tully's notebook was of a beach house out near Malibu beyond the section where movie stars and studio executives lived.

Next to the address was the name "Baines." The day before he died, Tully had mentioned Melanie Baines to her, said that this Melanie had been following him around. Tully had wanted to find out who the woman was and what she wanted from him. So Tully in turn had started following Melanie and, after checking out the local Hertz offices and getting the name of the redhead renting the car, ended up at the beach house.

Vanessa sensed she had found the name she was looking for.

Along the beach below, in the hot sun, a woman in a red bikini rode a chestnut mare through the edge of the waves and a few surfers rode their boards.

The drive in the battered old Chevy had taken Vanessa twenty-two minutes.

She looked down the wide stretch of beach and saw the house, a relatively new home with a garage beneath. Even from here, she could see that the curtains were closed. Somebody didn't want to be seen.

Because of the open area of sand, she couldn't sneak up to the house. She'd have to drive up and invent some lie to get herself inside, so that once she was facing Melanie she could take out the gun and make her tell her the truth.

She angled the car off the highway and drove down the narrow road to the beach house.

The garage entrance was around back, and she saw that the door was open and the garage was empty.

But she sensed that somebody was inside the house.

Watching her.

LAURA Once upon a time a man lured a little girl into his black car. He told her that something bad had happened to her mother and that he would take the little girl to her. But the man was lying. He just wanted the little girl. He took her to a dark woods and did naughty things to her. Then he took out an axe and hacked up the little girl into pieces.

Years ago, her friend Betsy Coughlin had told Laura this story and it was the first thing she thought of as she emerged from the depths of the chloroform.

Then she remembered the lady who'd grabbed her and clamped a handkerchief with something bad-smelling on it over her face.

She didn't remember anything else.

She awakened in this room, bound at wrists and ankles, a gag stretched tight across her mouth.

She smelled the new pink sheets on which she lay.

She saw beside her, in the dusty beam of sunlight from the high window, a teddy bear.

She heard ocean waves and the rough sound of her own breathing behind the gag, which was soaked with her warm saliva.

And she heard a car coming close to the house, stopping.

Maybe it was her mom.

And then she thought that maybe it was the woman coming back. Maybe she had gone to get an axe.

She heard somebody climb up the back stairs.

And knock.

Somebody was knocking!

If it was the woman with her axe, she wouldn't knock. She would just come in.

Laura tried to scream, but nothing much came out, just a hum.

Please, please hear me, Laura thought. And tried to scream some more. But all that happened was that her throat started to hurt.

Then the knocking stopped.

Was the person going to give up and go away?

Please don't go. Please stay. Please come and help me.

VANESSA She felt self-conscious, standing on the back porch, knocking on the door every thirty seconds or so, and looking out at a lonely gull black against the hazy afternoon disc of sun.

She knocked again. She didn't really expect an answer. Curtains were drawn over the door window and the room window.

If anybody was inside, he or she was being quiet.

She'd thought of breaking a window and getting inside. But if Melanie caught her inside, she'd most likely kill her just as she'd killed Tully.

Dying didn't scare Vanessa. But the prospect of dying without avenging Tully did.

For a moment, she thought she heard a faint, plaintive sound, like a muffled animal bleat. She stood still, listening.

Then the gull she'd been watching emitted some distant squawk.

The gull, she thought. That's what I heard.

She walked down the porch and put her ear to the room window. She heard nothing.

She went down the steps and got in her battered Chevrolet and drove off to a hill where she could look down on the beach house.

She stayed there a long hour, waiting to see if anybody came out or went in. But nobody did.

TOLSON Tolson knocked once, then came right into Edgar's office.

Edgar hurriedly hung up the phone as Tolson shut the door behind him and threw a newspaper on Edgar's desk.

Edgar ignored the paper.

"Look at it, Edgar."

Edgar's bull-dog face seemed ready to growl. Nobody talked to J. Edgar Hoover this way. Not even his only friend and confidant, Clyde.

He picked up the paper.

"Bottom of the front page," Tolson said.

Edgar turned the paper over and scanned the stories. His eyes fell on the article about the murdered publisher. He read it quickly. He kept his face clear of expression.

"And just what does that prove?"

"Bellamy," Tolson said, "the man in the middle of this tape business—what that proves is that Melanie is at work again. Killing people."

"Maybe she had to. If she did."

Tolson shook his head. "Maybe she had to? But that's not all, Edgar. Did you see the L.A. *Times?* Page seventeen." He dropped another paper on the desk.

Glumly, Edgar laid the newspaper flat on his desk and turned the pages. "PRIVATE INVESTIGATOR FOUND SLAIN?"

"Right. A Mr. Tully."

"So?"

"Melanie moved from her hotel. The clerk there told me that a Mr. Tully had been looking for her." Tolson ran a hand across his face. "I think she's killed two people on this case so far, Edgar. How many more will it be?"

"You're shouting!"

"So are you!"

Tolson sighed and turned away to the window and looked out at Washington, D.C. After World War II, the city had started to lose some of its elegant charm. There were too many people, too many crass souls. The kindness was gone from the city now, the cordiality. Only the greed remained.

He turned back. His voice was sad. "I want us to retire together, Edgar, and do exactly what we want and be in public favor. We've worked hard for all these years, and we deserve a good retirement."

Edgar stared at his desk, sullen.

"Edgar?"

"I'm listening." He didn't look up.

"Call her off. I don't know how to get ahold of her. I've tried."

"I can reach her."

"Will you do it?"

"I want you to leave now, Mr. Tolson."

Edgar kept his head down. Only when he was very, very angry did Edgar call Clyde Mr. Tolson.

"Take care of this, Edgar," Clyde said. "Right away."

Tolson closed the door quietly.

SARA

"You sure you want to do this?" Sara said, her voice trembling.

"Very sure," Michael answered. "I grew up with guns."

"It scares me."

"We're both scared, but it'll be fine. You'll see."

Sara stared out the window of Michael's car, a plush new baby-blue Thunderbird.

He took her hand and looked at her somberly. "If we could go to the police, I wouldn't need a gun, but we can't go to the police. Otherwise, Laura will be—" he paused and said, more softly, "I'd feel better with a gun."

She nodded, silently. She knew, after all, that Curtis Simmons had one. And she knew almost as surely that he had the tapes—those she had given him by mistake—which was why he had been trying to reach her. Now they would have to go to Curtis Simmons' house and get the tapes back, at gunpoint if necessary.

Michael got out of the car and stood by the door as traffic streamed past.

He'd passed CLARK'S GUN-A-RAMA many times. He hadn't paid it much attention other than to think that the place was probably packed with John Birchers and other right-wing lunatics. Michael was an Adlai Stevenson Democrat. GUN-A-RAMA wasn't the kind of place he frequented.

He saw a hole in the traffic, dashed across, and went into the gun shop.

Waist-high oak-and-glass display cases lined either wall and racks of shotguns and rifles were arrayed at the rear. The store smelled of gun oil.

Oddly, an FM classical station filled the air with gentle Debussy.

If he'd had to predict the kind of guy who worked here, Michael would have leaned to the beer-bellied, tattoo-armed, greasy-haired redneck you always saw at truck stops. But the man behind the counter was tall, and wore a striped button-down shirt and an elegant Rolex watch.

"Afternoon. Help you?"

"I'm looking for a handgun."

"I see. Well, why don't we step over here?" They walked to a display case filled with handguns.

"May I ask what you want this for?"

"Uh, protection."

"In your home?"

"Yes."

The man looked at him carefully. "Are you trained with firearms?" Michael nodded.

The man smiled. "I wasn't. I wouldn't be here if my father hadn't died and left me this store." He laughed. "Not all the gun people like me. I guess they resent me force-feeding them Debussy. Tried to sell this store when my father died, but I couldn't get a fair price so I decided to run it myself."

Michael nodded again. He just kept thinking of Laura.

"How about that one?" Michael said.

"That .45? It's a Colt model from World War II." He smiled again. "See? I'm learning this business after all."

He reached down and brought up a silver-plated Colt .45.

The last time Michael had handled a gun was back in Omaha, when he'd shot at targets with his old man.

He sighted along the barrel, curled his finger around the trigger.

"This is fine. And some ammunition."

The store owner studied him a moment. "You look kind of upset. Maybe you should come back tomorrow and buy this gun."

Michael smiled at him and leaned casually against the case. "I'm fine."

The owner's gaze lingered a moment. "That'll be fifty dollars."

Michael walked out of the store with a .45 in one suit coat pocket and a box of bullets in the other.

LENIHAN

The man had been in the gun shop ten minutes now. Sara sat in the car waiting for him.

Lenihan watched her from his car down the block.

Then the man was back. Trotting across the street to the car. Inside, he leaned to Sara and showed her something. A gun, probably. Sara shook her head, seemed to argue.

Maybe Sara didn't want him to have a gun.

By now, Lenihan was assuming that the man was Sara's husband, Michael.

Michael steered the car out from the curb, heading south, and Lenihan was not far behind.

MELANIE She was afraid the ice cream would melt. She'd picked up a quart of peppermint at the supermarket. What little girl could resist peppermint? She figured it would calm her down a bit. The object was to scare the parents, not Laura.

She pulled off the ocean highway, moving down the narrow road to the house.

She saw the fresh tire tracks.

She drove the car around back to the garage, pulled inside, and walked back to the tire tracks in the sand.

Somebody had been here during her short trip to the supermarket.

She squatted and examined the tracks closely. New tires, from the look of them, but that didn't mean anything. Somebody had been here.

She stood up and stared at the house. She was a professional. Who could possibly have found out where she was?

Maybe the whole caper was coming undone by some subtle mistake. Happened sometimes. Even to the most careful of professionals. She might have botched the job.

She hurried back to the car, grabbed the ice cream, and scampered up the stairs, drawing her Luger from her jacket pocket.

Everything was locked up tight. No sign of anybody trying to force a way in.

She put the key in the lock, turned the knob.

Not a sound in the place.

Quietly setting the ice cream inside the door, she checked room by room as she headed for Laura's bedroom, her Luger leading the way. Nothing.

Finally, she came to the locked door. She silently unlocked it, paused, then kicked the door open.

Laura lay tied up and gagged on her little pink bed next to her fuzzy brown teddy bear. Laura stared in horror at the Luger.

Melanie was so happy to see her, she immediately shoved the gun back into her pocket and said, "You wait right here, honey. I've got something for you."

She laughed at herself. What a dumb thing to say. Where could Laura go?

By the time she brought the peppermint ice cream and two spoons back to the bedroom, it was half-melted.

She and Laura would have themselves a nice little party anyway.

Excerpt from Marilyn Monroe's personal tapes

It's funny how people look at movie stars. When I lived in Los Angeles County Orphanage, I'd see some of them on the street because RKO was nearby. And they looked different to me—they had a kind of poise and glow that us mortals just couldn't have. I especially liked it when they would lean out of their limousines and wave to us kids on the sidewalk in front of the orphanage. It was like watching gods pass by in chariots. One day I saw Rita Hayworth, who I always thought was the most beautiful of all the movie stars. And she looked right at me and smiled. But that night I had a really strange dream—this limousine was passing by in the street and it stopped and the window started to roll down but instead of a movie star there was just this horribly grinning skeleton wrapped in an evening gown. I never had that dream again until I was a movie star—and then I realized that the skeleton was me . . . that movie stars weren't special people at all, just people with a lot of problems. One time when I went to Tahoe for the weekend, I had to get special medication on top of my sleeping pills so I could sleep. Every time I'd close my eyes, I'd see that skeleton leaning out of that limousine.

WINONA In the beginning, she had been terrified. First there was the word "cancer," the most imposing and chilling word in the entire vocabulary, and then came two failed operations and then the gradual retreat of her closest friends—as if they might catch it from her breasts.

Tears had not nourished her, nor prayer, nor rage, nor self-pity.

Nor had her husband, that celebrated, sophisticated rake, Curtis Simmons, a.k.a George Smythe from Dalton, Illinois, where his family had been so poor they'd had to use a two-holer out back.

What a prize Winona had been then, the lovely, refined daughter of a genuine Californian who could trace his roots back five generations, and who had been smart enough to invest his modest inheritance in real estate on what would become Wilshire Boulevard.

She was twenty-six by the time she met Curtis Simmons at one of her mother's charity functions, and already burdened with the knowledge that she could never have children.

Two months later, Winona totally bedazzled, they were married. He changed quickly. He woke up to find himself in the best of all possible circumstances. He had a booming career as an actor and was now married to the daughter and fortune of the Reynolds family, one of the hallowed names in Los Angeles society.

It was three years before she caught him cheating, though of course he had been doing it virtually since their honeymoon.

An indiscreet starlet had sent a perfumed letter to the house. She was a chorus dancer who was pregnant with Curtis' child, and desperately hoped he'd been serious when he said he'd leave his wife for her. Winona felt great pity for both the dancer and herself. She took $500 cash from a drawer, wrapped it in paper, and put it in an envelope addressed to the dancer, with a note: *Use this however you see fit.*

She said nothing of this to Curtis.

He ran to patterns down the years, two "serious" romances per year with chippies to fill in the gaps. She should have left him long ago, but she was not self-confident enough. Sex was not pleasurable to her, and she loathed social evenings with preening movie stars. So she said nothing. And pretended to know nothing.

She always lived as if this would change some day. As if one fine shining morning she would rise to find that her husband had come to love her as tenderly as she'd always hoped, as tenderly as she'd loved him in those first years.

But that was not what happened at all.

One fine shining morning, at age fifty-one, she woke up to find that she was dying of breast cancer.

"How are you today?"

As usual, he came in and kissed her on the forehead. Still handsome, quick, charming.

"May I ask you a favor, Curtis?"

"Of course, darling."

"Will you burn our bed after I die?"

"What?"

"Because you won't have enough respect for my memory to keep your whores out of our bed."

He looked stunned. "Oh God, Winona, you're not in another of those moods, are you?"

He gave her another peck on the cheek. "You're always crabby in the morning, darling. You'll be feeling much better in a few hours."

He strode from the room.

He had not listened to anything she'd said.

He would bring his whores here and they would sleep in this very bed and he would not think of her at all.

I went to see my mother one time after she got out of the mental hospital. I was doing some modeling then and an assignment took me to Portland, where my mother was living.

I knew right away that something was wrong because the rooming house where she stayed was the sort where derelicts bought rooms by the night.

She was up on the top floor, where the roof slanted, so there wasn't much standing room.

She was sort of cool to me, at first. My mother was a very intelligent woman but she never believed that I had inherited her intelligence. She had on this faded gray housecoat and worn slippers. She looked frail and old. She hadn't tinted her hair lately, so it was almost completely gray.

She asked me how my life was going and I suppose I exaggerated how good things were. I didn't want to worry her.

And then I said, "Mom. You haven't touched me. I tried to give you a hug when I came in but you pulled away. Aren't you glad to see me?"

"Of course I'm glad to see you. You're my daughter."

And for some reason when she said that, sitting there in the afternoon light through her grimy window, I saw my mother clearly for the first time in my life.

I saw that my mother was insane.

It was in the eyes. And in the way her lips always seemed to be mouthing silent words.

I felt guilty. I'd blamed my mother for so many things in my life. . . . Every time I got seriously unhappy, I'd hate my mother for not taking good care of me when I was growing up.

I fell at her feet and wrapped my arms around her hips and put my face in her lap and began sobbing.

She started rocking a little, and singing some old lullaby, strange and a little off-key, and when I looked up, I saw that she was crying, too, soft tears on her wrinkled cheeks.

And I hugged her all the tighter.

I had never loved my mother as much as I did at that moment.

MELANIE

Melanie had to feed Laura like an infant. She was, after all, tied up.

"Taste good?"

Laura nodded silently.

"Peppermint's my favorite kind." Melanie thought a moment. "It was Jessica's, too. Sometime I'll tell you all about Jessica." She sat on the edge of the bed, feeding Laura.

"I don't want anymore ice cream," Laura said. "I want to go home."

"You can't go home. Not now. Now have some more ice cream."

She put the spoon to Laura's mouth again but Laura abruptly turned her head away.

Without thinking, she hit Laura in the face and temple with a closed fist, slamming the girl's head against the wall.

For a moment, Melanie felt good about what she'd just done. Laura had deserved it.

But Melanie began to wonder if Laura's head hit the wall too hard. Laura lay there still as death, her eyes closed.

She hurried into the bathroom, soaked a washcloth in cold water, and came back. Placing the cloth on Laura's forehead, she untied her bonds, plumping up a pillow for her head.

She felt for her pulse. It wasn't strong.

Laura didn't stir.

Melanie shook her gently.

"Laura, Laura. You need to wake up now. I'm really sorry I hit you so hard."

Melanie leaned closer, searching for any sign of life.

"Laura, you can have all the ice cream to yourself."

The phone rang.

She ran out and picked up. "Yes?"

"Melanie?"

"Who is this?"

"It's Edgar. Who do you think it is?"

She swallowed. "Yes, Mr. Hoover?"

"Melanie, I think we should just forget this whole assignment. Things are getting sticky."

"What things?"

"I don't have time to explain. I just want you to stop what you're doing. All right?"

Usually, she did exactly what Mr. Hoover asked her to. But not this time.

"I've been working hard for you, Mr. Hoover, and I can't give up on something this far along. I'm sorry, but that's the way it has to be."

And then Melanie Baines did what almost no one on the planet had ever done: She hung up on Mr. J. Edgar Hoover.

SARA In the 1930s, when the studio star system was at its peak, a few movie icons were not merely appreciated, they were cherished. The studios were so apprehensive that exuberant fans would break into the stars' homes that they asked Beverly Hills police to have special patrols in these neighborhoods around the clock. And the police did just that, circling certain neighborhoods in open Chevrolet touring cars, with binoculars and extra weapons.

Sara remembered this from research for her articles.

While Curtis Simmons had never been one of those gods, he hadn't done badly as the perennial second-lead at MGM. And while he didn't have the largest house in Bel Air, his white Georgian home was beautiful in the soft afternoon sunlight, the green grounds of rolling, flawless beauty. A winding brick drive ran past the columned front, leading to full shade trees in the back.

Michael parked in back, next to a blue DeSoto convertible.

He picked up the gun from the seat.

"You sure you want to take that with us?" Sara said.

"Positive," he said.

They got out of the car and walked around the west end of the house on a narrow walk to an ornate wooden side door, where he knocked.

A small woman in the gray dress of a maid opened the door. "Yes?"

"We'd like to see Mr. Simmons please. Tell him it's Mrs. Drury."

"Very well."

The interior was a traditional but elegant European motif, with period furnishings and an Aubusson rug in the living room, Chinese porcelains and flowered, upholstered sofas.

They sat on one of the sofas, where they could look out at the pool.

They fell silent. The big house was very quiet. Sara felt intimidated and scared.

And then Simmons was there, looking very much like the sophisticated second-lead he'd played throughout his long career, all gussied up in a paisley dinner jacket and peach-colored ascot.

"Well, I have to say this is a surprise," he said. He looked and sounded scared.

KENNEDY Lyndon Baines Johnson had been in the Oval Office now for more than fifteen minutes, trying to get Kennedy to help out a former constituent of the vice president.

"He's about to go to prison, Jack. And he's a good family man." Which, translated, meant that he probably didn't ball more than six, seven workers a week.

Johnson usually called the president "Jack" when they were in the White House. Johnson was dressed in his standard blue serge suit, garish patterned tie, white shirt that he had custom-made by the dozens, and snakeskin cowboy boots. Few of the easterners who worked for Kennedy actually liked Johnson, viewing him as vulgar, mean and relentlessly corrupt.

Kennedy sighed. "I'll see what I can do, Lyndon." Then he smiled. "You sure know a lot of people who're in trouble. Don't you know any honest people?"

Lyndon smiled right back. "Now where would I get the chance to meet any honest people? I'm a Democrat."

Johnson sat forward in his chair. "You should learn to call on me more often, Jack. There are a lot of things I could take care of for you, if you wanted me to."

But Kennedy's mind had begun to wander again. He wondered what was going on in Los Angeles. Why the hell hadn't David Lenihan called?

He stood up. "I'll keep that in mind, Lyndon."

"And you'll talk to Bobby about my friend?"

259

"I'll do what I can."

Robert Kennedy, the attorney general, was Lyndon Johnson's sworn enemy. If Lyndon Johnson wanted any favors from the Justice Department, he'd have to go through Jack Kennedy. He'd never get any help from Bobby.

As was his custom, Kennedy walked Lyndon to the door, shook his hand good-bye.

Then Kennedy went back to his desk, lifted the receiver and dialed the number of David Lenihan's hotel room.

SARA "Would you care for a drink?" Curtis Simmons said. Sara shook her head. "No, thanks. Is there a private place to talk?"

"The den, I suppose. You seem upset."

"We'll talk in the den," Sara said.

Simmons led the way to a room filled with bookcases.

"I think I'll have a sherry," Simmons said. "Sure you won't join me?"

"We're sure."

Simmons poured sherry from a cut-glass decanter, then toasted them in the arch manner of an actor in a sherry commercial.

In the theatricality of this performance, Sara was able to see that Simmons' tears of concern for his dying wife yesterday had also been a performance. He simply hadn't wanted to pay blackmail.

Simmons parked himself on the edge of his desk.

"Now you'll tell me why you're here."

"I want the tapes," Sara said.

"The tapes?"

Michael finally spoke. "Our daughter's life is on the line here, Simmons. That's all we can tell you. We just want the tapes."

Simmons looked as if he might deny any knowledge of what they were talking about, but then decided against it. "Surely, Mr. Drury, you realize how much such tapes are worth."

"You don't understand. Our daughter's life is being threatened."

261

Simmons smiled. "This all sounds like a thriller, doesn't it?" He glanced at Sara.

Sara was breathing raggedly. "For our daughter, Simmons, we'll do whatever we have to do." She meant it to sound like the threat it was.

She didn't notice Simmons slide his hand into the wide pocket of his smoking jacket until it was too late. Now he pointed a small revolver at Michael's chest.

"I've had a lot of practice with this particular scene," Simmons said. "When you've played the cad as many times as I have, you're quite comfortable pulling a gun on somebody. And ordering him out of your house."

He gestured toward the door with his gun.

"Come on now, the fun's over."

"We meant what we said," Sara said.

"Whatever you'll get for them, it isn't worth a little girl's life," Michael said.

Simmons frowned. "I do what I have to to survive. Don't try to make me feel guilty."

He edged around them so that he stood with his back to the door. Sara saw Michael try to ease his own gun from his pocket but Simmons was watching him too closely.

Suddenly Michael drove his shoulder into Simmons' chest. The revolver spun from his hand.

Simmons slammed back against the door, and the two tumbled to the floor. They rolled around, scrambling for the gun.

Simmons managed to get off a right-hand punch that dazed Michael.

Michael brought his knee up hard between Simmons' legs.

Simmons grunted in pain but kept inching his hand toward the weapon.

Sara was just about to dive for the pistol when a woman's voice barked, "Stop it! All of you!"

Winona Simmons stood gaunt and pale in the doorway. She wore a formal royal blue robe and house slippers. In her right hand, quite steady, was a large handgun.

"Get up, Curtis."

"Darling, you should be in bed," Simmons said, trying to catch his breath.

Winona looked at Sara and said, "I can imagine what you're going through, Mrs. Drury, and I'm sorry. Curtis has always been a selfish and duplicitous ass, but I never thought he'd be capable of anything like this—where a child's life is at stake. Curtis, you get those tapes right now."

"I don't owe these people anything," Simmons said, sullenly picking himself up from the floor.

"Get the tapes, Curtis," Winona Simmons said, "and please shut up."

Simmons silently cursed his wife—why couldn't the bitch just die?—but he got the tapes.

LOUELLA

She called his business office, his social club (where he often spent time with his beautiful, colored girl friend), his country club, and even his home.

Rossetti wasn't anywhere.

Her call from Gibbons at the Hearst office bothered her more than she'd thought. She now shared his anxiety. When were the tapes actually going to be in her eager hands?

With the tapes, Louella would once again be the top gossip columnist in the nation. Even more, she would play a major role in the history of her country.

Louella dialed a number from her small, leather-bound, gently perfumed book marked PRIVATE.

"Good afternoon."

"Has Mr. Rossetti come back yet?"

"Is this Miss Parsons?"

"Yes."

"I'm afraid not, Miss Parsons."

"Is Monica there, then?"

"Monica?"

"Please. I know all about Monica and Mr. Rossetti. We're friends. Would you ask her to come to the phone?"

"I can't do that."

"You mean you're refusing me, young man?"

"I'm sorry, Miss Parsons, but those are my orders, directly from Mr. Rossetti."

"Put her on the phone, please, or I'll see that you lose your job."

"Don't say you talked to me."

"Don't you worry about it. I'll take responsibility."

"Hold on, then."

A minute later, a soft, cultured voice said, "Good afternoon, Miss Parsons."

"Nice to speak to you again, Monica."

Monica had started out as a cocktail waitress, and that was still her cover in case Rossetti's wife (or the attorney Mr. Rossetti's wife might someday hire) got nosy.

"I understand you're looking for Mr. Rossetti."

"Yes."

"He's supposed to be back here in an hour or so."

"You've spoken with him lately?"

"About twenty minutes ago."

Louella sighed. At least he hadn't mysteriously vanished or been killed, which was always possible with his type. "I've been leaving messages everywhere."

"He did say he was working with you on something pretty big."

"Did he say how it was going?"

"I gather it was going all right."

"You're very sweet, Monica. You'll have Mr. Rossetti call me?"

"Of course. As soon as he comes in."

After hanging up, she stared at the phone, thought of calling Gibbons to give him a status report.

No. Let the bastard sweat a little more.

Excerpt from
American Goddess
by Louella Parsons

The irony did not escape Marilyn. She was now in a mental hospital (Payne Whitney Psychiatric Hospital in New York) at about the same age her mother had been when committed for the first time.

She had had an affair with Yves Montand during the filming of *Let's Make Love*, in 1959.

Marilyn felt sure that the affair was blossoming into a real relationship and would lead to marriage, that Montand would divorce his wife and marry her.

But then, one day, she heard an astonishing thing on the radio. Yves Montand was saying to a gossip columnist, "I want to stop these rumors about Marilyn Monroe and me. I have a wife and family. Marilyn is spreading these rumors, not me. She's mentally ill, and I want nothing to do with her."

Marilyn lost the next six days in a fog of prescription drugs and alcohol. Her situation was not helped by the fact that every time she turned on the TV or radio, there was Yves saying he was happily married, and that Marilyn was just some kind of "pain freak" so strung out she "frightened" him. Not enough for him simply to dump her and dash her dreams of marriage; like DiMaggio, he now wanted to destroy her.

When her maid found her, Marilyn was crawling around naked on her bedroom floor. She had fouled herself and her pale body was streaked with feces.

She acted completely insane, calling out for Stanley Gifford, the man who had never admitted that he was her father; and her first husband, James Dougherty, the big Irishman who had always treated her so lovingly.

Her maid got Marilyn cleaned up and phoned her doctor.

MELANIE
Laura was alive.

By the time Melanie returned to the bedroom after talking to Mr. Hoover, Laura was sitting up in bed. The ropes Melanie had stripped from her lay like dead snakes on the floor.

"You really had me scared for a minute," Melanie said, coming through the door.

"Was that my mom on the phone?"

"No, honey, it wasn't."

"Will you call her?"

"Your dad's going to call me."

"When?"

"I'm not sure just when." Melanie paused. "How's your head, Laura?"

"Hurts. How come you took me here, anyway?"

"I'll see if I can find some aspirin for you."

"How come you took me from school?"

"I thought we could be friends."

"Couldn't I just talk to my mom or my dad?"

"Laura, just relax and everything will be all right. I promise."

Melanie knelt down next to Laura and daubed at the girl's forehead with a damp cloth but, without any warning, Laura sprang from the bed and was racing for the living room, slamming the bedroom door behind her.

Melanie walked out and looked in the living room.

Where had Laura gone? Outside?

She opened the front door and looked out.

Laura was nowhere to be seen.

Then she heard a faint, brief, shuffling sound behind her.

As she turned, she smiled.

Laura was still in the house. She was in the closet.

Melanie went to the sofa and took a fresh silencer from her purse and affixed it to the Luger.

"Laura?"

No response.

"We're going to have some fun, Laura. I'm going to start shooting bullets into the closet. I've only got six of them but I'll bet I can hit you at least once. Even though I can't see you."

No response.

"Are you ready, Laura? On the count of three I'm going to start firing. One."

She raised the Luger and sighted it downward slightly, right where a little girl would be if she were sitting on the floor, then raised it slightly to aim above. She wanted to scare her, not kill her.

"Two."

She steadied her hand.

"Three."

She fired.

Laura's scream filled the house.

MAYHEW Ordinarily, the first thing bank vice president Hugh Murchison did was put out a hand and offer a hearty cliche. But not today.

He waved Mayhew into his office.

"Shut the door, Del."

A small leather valise sat in the middle of the desk.

"Two hundred and fifty thousand dollars," Murchison said, grimly.

"Good job," Mayhew said, reaching for the valise.

A strong hand clamped his wrist. "It's not that easy, Del."

"I really don't want your hand on me."

Without loosening his grip, Murchison said, "Then tell me what's going on."

"I can't."

Murchison sighed and removed his hand. Leaning back in his chair, he lit himself a Winston. He inhaled a deep drag and exhaled it slowly toward the ceiling.

"Del, you deal in fantasy, I deal in reality."

"I don't have time for speeches."

"I've got a board of directors. I can't just make a quarter million dollar cash withdrawal without telling them something." He leaned forward. "Has one of your stars been kidnapped?"

"No."

"Is one of them being blackmailed?"

"No."

"Goddammit, Del, we have to cut the bullshit here."

269

"Hugh, I'm a loyal customer who keeps a big balance on hand for the studio. Now I need a personal favor and I deserve it. If you want my house for collateral, I'll be happy to put it up."

Murchison took another drag on his cigarette. The collar of his blue button-down shirt showed dark signs of sweat.

Del Mayhew was indeed a valued customer. He had also set Murchison up with several beautiful young women he said were contract players at the studio. Actually, they'd been expensive call girls but they'd loved the fantasy that they were "starlets" and Murchison had loved it even more.

"Why the hell do you need this much cash?"

"Call it an opportunity."

"A business opportunity?"

"Yes, if you like."

"When a customer withdraws this much cash, I'm supposed to inform the police and the FBI."

"I'd appreciate it if you didn't."

Murchison stubbed out his cigarette in the ashtray.

"You owe me one," Murchison said.

Mayhew got to his feet, hefting the case full of cash, and started toward the door.

"Right, Hugh," Mayhew said. "A big one."

S A R A She could scarcely believe it.

Lying on Michael's lap was a manilla envelope, inside which were the tapes that were going to free Laura.

As they were backing out of Curtis Simmons' winding driveway, Michael said, "It's over now, Sara. Everything will be fine."

He looked pale and anxious, and she supposed she looked as bad. "I guess I'm not as sure as you. I need Laura in my arms before I'll feel right again."

He steered toward the gates.

"It's nice being with you again, Michael—even under these circumstances."

He smiled at her. "I feel the same way."

When he reached the gates, he waited for a break in the traffic.

"You're a good man, Michael," she said.

"Not good enough. Not after the way I've treated you and Laura."

Suddenly the car sank—first one side and then the other. The tires—

David Lenihan's face appeared at Michael's window. He was closing the blade of a pocket knife.

He had punctured the tires.

He leveled a pistol at Michael. "Roll down the window, Mr. Drury." The gun had a fat silencer on its barrel.

"Sonofabitch," Michael muttered. His gun was still in the glove compartment.

Michael rolled the window down.

271

Lenihan leaned in. "I've been following you most of the day, Mrs. Drury. I knew you'd eventually lead me to what I'm looking for. Give me the tapes."

"No," Michael said. "Our little girl is being held hostage for them."

Lenihan stared icily. "I have some appreciation for what you're going through. But I have to take the tapes. I'm sorry."

As before, Sara heard the curious sorrow in the man's voice. But his manner was absolutely firm, cold, scary.

He put the tip of the gun to Michael's head. Sara felt grief, rage, despair.

She handed the manilla envelope across the car to Lenihan.

HOOVER One night long ago, when he had been reading an inspiring history of the United States, Hoover asked the chief of Capitol Police, Captain Leonard H. Ballard, if he could tour the Senate building late at night by himself. If any senators were present, they would curse him or brownnose him, depending on their politics. They would spoil his visit.

"Well, you won't actually be alone, Mr. Hoover. I've got ninety men assigned to night patrol. But nobody will bother you except for the ghosts—and all they do is give speeches." Ballard had laughed heartily.

And so on a rainy Tuesday evening, Hoover had toured the building and let himself be suffused with its history, from the quiet dignity of the Rotunda to the stillness of the Capitol Prayer Room to the eerie echoes of the Senate Chamber with its wooden desks and ceremonial snuff boxes and the spittoons that a visiting author named Charles Dickens found so repellent.

He had walked through some of the underground chambers built in the last century, and heard the ghosts that Captain Ballard had warned him of.

The ghosts had spoken to him.

They had told him that for most people, death meant the indignity of extinction. Yet for a few there was a life afterward—for those who had been strong or cunning enough to make their mark on this great nation's history.

Walk the halls and look at the faces in the portraits and sculpture.

273

Make note of the eyes. They tell you of a special need to be remembered, and that went for somebody as dynamic as Daniel Webster and as self-effacing as that little bastard Harry Truman.

Make your mark. Avoid utter extinction. Be remembered.

But Clyde was right, Hoover thought now. He'd screwed it up. Putting Melanie on the job. My God, he must have been crazy. . . .

The phone interrupted his memories.

"Yes?"

"It's Clyde. Edgar, I realize that you're still angry, but—"

"There's something I need to tell you, Clyde."

"You got ahold of her?"

"Yes."

"How'd it go?"

"Not well. She wants to go through with it. She hung up on me, Clyde."

"Oh God," Clyde Tolson said. "Oh God."

MELANIE
"Laura? Laura!"
Still nothing.

"Laura! Laura, you answer me right this minute!"

Silence again. And the drifting acrid smell of gunsmoke. She'd pumped four bullets into the door.

"Laura, if you don't say something I'm going to start shooting again."

Silence.

She could go right in there and pull her out, of course, but that would be missing the point. She wanted Laura to come out on her own. To submit, show that she was a good little girl.

Silence.

Melanie groaned in frustration. She took aim.

"Last chance, Laura. All right?"

She squeezed off more shots. The air was raw with gun smoke. She was careful to keep her shot high. Didn't want to hit Laura. Her gun was finally empty.

She listened carefully, wanting to hear a whimper of submission, wanting Laura to yield to her.

But nothing.

Then she saw the puddle of red blood spreading from beneath the door.

"Oh no," she said. "Oh good Lord, no."

HOOVER

Every once in a while, even though he knew it was a sin, J. Edgar Hoover went into his private bathroom and emptied out his prostate gland.

Just doing what his doctor told him to. Keep that prostate of yours cleaned out, Edgar.

Edgar hoped The Man Upstairs understood that he was just following doctor's orders.

Usually, he thought of Darla, the girl he'd loved when they were in sixth grade.

Down the years, the FBI had confiscated lots of hardcore porn, thus Hoover had access to raunchy stuff. He'd come in here and spread a few of the photos out on the edge of the sink, bare breasts and exposed vaginas, but it wouldn't work. To Edgar, they were just sinful women who should be ashamed of themselves.

Images of Darla always helped him get his prostate cleaned out. But now it wasn't working.

He knew the problem. He couldn't stop worrying about the tapes Melanie was after and all the risks involved. How could he empty out his prostate when he had that weighing on his mind?

Try to look on the bright side of it, he finally said to himself. Suppose she calls and says, "I've got them, Edgar." Boy, would he have cause for celebrating then. He wouldn't have any trouble cleaning out his prostate if that happened.

With a reluctant sigh, he gave up. Zipping his pants, he turned out the light and left the bathroom.

PART FOUR

"Power is the measure
of manhood."
—*Josiah G. Holland*

Excerpt from Marilyn Monroe's personal tapes

You always wanted me to tell you about the time I locked myself into my trailer while I was making the movie with Yves Montand.

It wasn't a "temper tantrum" as Hedda Hopper said. I was scared.

I had been told by a lawyer who worked for one of the Senate investigating committees that I was probably going to be called to testify during Senate hearings on the Mafia in the United States.

If I refused to testify, I could go to prison. I would also lose the faith of my fans. They wouldn't like it if I didn't testify.

On the other hand, if I did testify . . . well, I have to be honest and say that I had several friends in the Mob. Real friends, including Mickey Cohen. Friends who took care of me.

The other thing was . . . people who testify against the Mob . . . well, sometimes there's retaliation. I was worried about that, too. There were actresses who used to go with certain Mob members, and if the actresses ever fell out with them . . . well, the mobsters saw to it that the actresses' careers were over.

. I have to admit, there was something pretty special about Mob guys.

Even studio heads were always upset because somebody wasn't getting in line. Well, when Mob bosses gave orders, that was it. Their orders were carried out to the letter. Nobody argued back. Or disobeyed them, because they knew what would happen if they did.

Anyway, I stayed in my trailer because I was afraid that some-body would try to serve me with a subpoena.

I knew I was getting myself in trouble with the studio and the director—there goes crazy Marilyn, having another one of her fits, that's what they were saying—but I was just scared was all.

Don't think I didn't say a lot of prayers that day. I know I haven't been a very good person most of my life, but I felt that if I asked God a favor this one time, he'd understand.

And he did.

Because that night, I was sitting in my trailer—I'd decided to sleep there over night—when I got a phone call from this Senate lawyer who said that his boss had decided to drop the hearings and that nobody was going to be subpoenaed.

I was real, real lucky, Louella.

LENIHAN He should be happy. Next to him on the seat were the tapes so desperately wanted by his boss, Jack Kennedy. Tapes that few other men would have been able to track and seize the way he had.

There was a 6:35 flight this evening. He would go back to his hotel room now and pack.

He looked down at the manilla envelope. You wouldn't think that a package so small could be so important.

He tried not to think of Drury's little daughter.

SARA No way they could drive after the tires had been slashed. Michael shut off the engine and sagged in his seat.

"We didn't have any choice, Michael."

He shook his head miserably. "I don't know what we're going to do."

"The first thing we do is get out of here," Sara said. "Then we can find out where he's staying." She opened the door. "C'mon. We have to find some kind of transportation."

"I wanted to kill him," he said, as they started walking.

"So did I."

MELANIE She stood there frozen, a fragile girl-woman in the throes of despair. She had killed a little girl. Mr. Hoover was going to be furious. She had to keep him from finding out.

She stood there and watched the blood seep forth from beneath the door.

She hadn't really wanted Laura to die. Just show a little respect, a little . . . fear.

"Laura."

She put her hand on the doorknob. She would see a sweet little girl with bullet holes in her chest. Or, maybe even worse, in her face.

She shouldn't have gotten so angry. But Laura had been misbehaving.

Now just the roll of ocean, the cry of the birds.

"Laura, I'm going to open the door now, all right? I promise I won't hurt you."

Slowly, she opened the door.

She peered into the shadows of the closet.

Oh, my God, my God, Laura. My God in heaven.

SARA The cab ride took almost an hour. Sara and Michael sat silent, holding hands, the whole way.

The Fenwick was several blocks from Wilshire, near its chief rival, the Ambassador. It was surrounded by rolling lawns that ran on for three square blocks. The Fenwick boasted its own self-contained world with a swimming pool, movie theater, six restaurants, bank, brokerage office, post office, doctor, nurse, art gallery and more than twenty-five shops right on the grounds.

As the cab swept into the winding drive, Sara looked up at the towering structure. On the top four floors, each room had a veranda.

Michael led Sara inside to the front desk.

"Has Mr. Lenihan returned? Room 1756?" Michael asked.

The desk clerk dialed Lenihan's room.

Sara turned around for a quick look at the lobby. The ornate pillars and vast expanse of carpet gave the lobby the feel of a set from *Ben Hur*.

And then she saw him. Coming in the east door, fast. David Lenihan.

Lenihan didn't see them. He bore toward the wide bank of elevators.

A man was pursuing him, coming closer now as Lenihan reached an open elevator. The man carried a dark valise.

Sara recognized the man, of course. Everybody who worked in Hollywood knew him as one of the key players, Del Mayhew.

Why would Del Mayhew be trotting after David Lenihan?

Mayhew hurried aboard the elevator and the doors closed just as the two men started to argue.

"He doesn't seem to have returned yet, sir," the desk clerk said.

MAYHEW

Del Mayhew got inside the elevator, panting and sweating, just as the doors rolled shut.

He had been trying to catch up to David Lenihan from the parking lot.

"What the hell do you want, Mr. Mayhew?"

"I want to talk to you."

"Why didn't you say anything this morning when I visited you?"

"I needed to think things over."

Lenihan smiled. "Well, you're a little late, Mr. Mayhew. I've taken care of everything now."

The elevator stopped at the sixth floor. An older couple in tennis whites got on. Mayhew and Lenihan stood silently facing the front of the elevator. The couple rode to the twelfth floor and then got off.

When the elevator started moving again, Mayhew said, "This afternoon you waited for the Drurys outside of Curtis Simmons' house. I know what you took from the Drurys."

"You do, eh?"

Mayhew thumped his valise. "I have a quarter of a million dollars in here. In unmarked bills."

Lenihan tried not to react to the dollar number, but he couldn't help but glance at the valise.

"The money is for you, Mr. Lenihan."

"For me? Why?"

"I knew you'd eventually lead me to the tapes. And now I want to buy them from you."

"They're not for sale."

"Come on, Mr. Lenihan. A quarter million, unmarked. Think about it."

They reached the seventeenth floor. The doors opened and Lenihan said, "Our business meeting is over, Mr. Mayhew. So long."

He stepped off the elevator and started down the empty, plushly carpeted hall to his room.

Mayhew held the elevator doors open, considering what to do next. Only one thing to do.

He stepped off the elevator and walked after Lenihan, who was fumbling with the door key.

Mayhew took the gun from his pocket and stuck it into Lenihan's back.

He was about to ask Lenihan for the tapes right there, but a woman came out of a room down the hall and walked toward them.

"Why don't we go inside and have a few drinks and talk about it some more?" Mayhew said in a normal voice. "We can probably wrap this up in a few minutes."

Lenihan opened the door and stepped through.

As Mayhew entered behind him, Lenihan suddenly swung the door back, cracking Mayhew on the forehead and driving him to his knees.

"You sonofabitch," Lenihan said, as he flung Mayhew into the room and slammed the door shut.

He turned and aimed a kick at Mayhew's jaw.

MELANIE

Laura was propped up against the back of the closet, vivid red blood staining her blouse.

"Oh, no," Melanie said. "Oh, no."

All she could think of was what Mr. Hoover would say when he found out.

It wasn't easy lifting Laura out and carrying her over to the couch. Melanie didn't want to get blood all over herself. She didn't like the inert, lifeless feeling of Laura in her arms. Melanie had handled a few corpses in her time and she knew what *dead weight* was.

What if Laura's parents demanded to speak to her before they handed over the tapes?

She laid her on the couch as if she were the most precious thing in all the universe. She knelt next to her and put her ear to Laura's mouth.

She couldn't hear or feel any breathing.

She put her hand on Laura's chest, detecting no movement.

Then Laura moaned.

"Laura? Laura, can you hear me? This is your friend Melanie and everything is going to be fine."

Maybe she could escape Mr. Hoover's wrath yet. . . .

"Mommy," Laura mumbled.

She didn't open her eyes. She lay on the couch, one side of her white blouse soaked with blood, and muttered "Mommy" over and over again, as if it were a magical incantation.

She was very pale and had a fever; her forehead was hot.

Melanie soaked a towel with cold water and laid it over the girl's body. She decided to put her in a place where nobody could find her for a long, long time. If ever.

Melanie needed to get out of the country before the police found out what she'd done to Laura. Not even Mr. Hoover would be able to help her then.

"Laura, everything's going to be fine now."

Her blue eyes opened.

"Mommy?"

"No, Laura. But I'm your friend and I'm going to help you."

"Mommy?"

She saw that Laura was delirious.

"Just rest now."

"Mommy?"

She was tired of Laura now. Didn't want to see her any more. Or hear her whining. She went into the kitchen where she found a thick roll of tape. Perfect for what she had in mind.

HOOVER

As the day wore on with Hoover never leaving his office and taking no calls (except for Clyde's), the director felt some brief solace contemplating the life he would have once Melanie delivered.

And after John F. Kennedy heard the tapes.

I've been thinking of a new office building for the Bureau, Hoover would say.

I've been thinking that perhaps you should create a new cabinet post for me.

You know, Mr. President, I've got some friends I'd like to see get good jobs in your administration.

Then let's see that bastard smirk at Hoover again. Or whisper behind his back.

Or ever refuse the director anything again.

Say, Edgar, I was wondering if you'd like to spend a weekend at Hyannisport. . . .

Say, Edgar, how would you like to spend Easter weekend at the Florida compound?

Say, Edgar, we've got a foreign affairs problem that I could really use your input on.

That would be one of the first things Hoover demanded. He had pleaded with FDR during World War II to be put in charge of foreign as well as domestic intelligence. But FDR had never liked

Hoover and so he created the OSS, which eventually became the CIA, and foreign affairs had forever been put out of Hoover's reach.

Until now.

MAYHEW He wasn't going to be stopped. He was going to get the tapes and take them straight to Rossetti. He grabbed the foot that David Lenihan had just landed on his jaw and jerked Lenihan off his feet.

Both men got to their knees and grappled in the lavish front room of the suite. Mayhew caught Lenihan in the mouth, hard enough to cut his lip with his big Masonic ring and bang Lenihan's head back against the wall.

He then connected with Lenihan's solar plexus. Lenihan exhaled like a deflating balloon.

Mayhew looked down at him. "You don't give me those tapes, Lenihan, I'm going to kick your face in."

He hauled back with his leg and swung it.

Lenihan, however, ducked, caught the ankle, and bit his calf so hard that Mayhew screamed.

He drove his fist into Mayhew's crotch, and Mayhew collapsed, sobbing.

Mayhew looked like he was finally finished. Lenihan sighed with relief. It was all he could do to stumble backward toward the open veranda doors. He wanted fresh air.

Then, much to his horror, Mayhew was on his feet, charging Lenihan, shoving him across the veranda.

Kneeing Mayhew's face, Lenihan broke loose and dove to his left, rolling up against the veranda wall.

Mayhew's momentum carried him into the low wall . . . and over it.

Seventeen floors, straight down.

"Jesus," Lenihan muttered.

Mayhew shrieked all the way down.

His screams stopped when he caved in the top of a black vintage '51 Packard.

Lenihan stared over the veranda rail and felt sick.

S A R A Seconds before Del Mayhew pitched over the veranda and fell to his death, Sara and Michael reached the doorway of David Lenihan's suite.

The door was ajar. Hearing the battle inside, they waited a few moments before entering the room. One of the two men would be the victor, and that one would emerge with the tapes. They'd just wait for the winner and take them from him.

Suddenly they heard the fading scream.

Easy enough, even from the corridor, to tell what had happened.

One of the men had fallen from the veranda.

As the man screamed all the way down, Sara pressed her face into Michael's shoulder.

Then there was silence.

The survivor was in the suite. With the tapes. Not expecting any visitors. Now was the time.

Easing the door open, pistol ready, Michael looked around.

Through the open doors of the veranda he could hear people yelling below. In the distance, a siren already wailed.

Had both men fallen to their deaths?

Then he heard water running in the bathroom.

"Wait here," he whispered to Sara.

Michael edged toward the bathroom. He tried to see through the small opening of the door, but all he got was a sharp angle of mirror with nobody's reflection.

He steadied the gun in his hand. Would he really be able to use it?

Yes. For Laura's sake.

He eased the door open a few inches. Lenihan was washing his face at the sink.

Two quick strides across the bathroom tiles, and Michael raised the pistol by the barrel. He hammered Lenihan's head with the butt.

Lenihan fell back against the sink, blood streaming from his scalp.

Michael pinched Lenihan's nose and shoved the business end of the gun into his mouth.

"You awake?"

Lenihan nodded, gasping.

"So where are the fucking tapes?"

When Michael eased back the hammer, Lenihan shuddered.

LOUELLA

Maria the maid and Juan the gardener were amazed at how the day had turned out.

In the sunny morning, kittens and puppies and rabbits had played in the back yard, and Miss Louella had been so happy you would have thought her husband had come back from the grave and promised to take her out to a nightclub.

Even in the afternoon, Miss Louella had walked through the house smiling at anybody she saw.

But now, at dusk, they did not see Miss Louella at all.

She had been in the den for nearly two hours, ordering a cocktail every half hour or so, brooding, angry.

Couldn't the staff do anything right? she fumed. Didn't they know she liked ice in her drinks? Didn't they remember that she wanted the short-stem cocktail glasses, not the long-stemmed ones? Didn't they have any respect for her, a woman who slaved to support not just a daughter, a staff, a mansion—but a legend? Didn't they know how difficult it was to be Louella Parsons when so many people wanted to cut you down, wanted to see you fail and humiliate yourself?

Did they have any idea at all of how heavy a burden this all was?

She dialed her phone.

"Hello." It was a young man's voice.

"To whom am I speaking?" she asked.

A sigh. "Miss Parsons, right?"

"Right."

296

"He hasn't come in yet, Miss Parsons. As soon as he does, I'll have him call you. Just like I promised."

"I'd like your name please. When I finally do talk with Mr. Rossetti, I'll be able to tell him the name of the insensitive young man who was so uncooperative."

"You've called four times in an hour and a half, Miss Parsons. It's just that I'm busy. Mr. Rossetti left me all this ledger work to do."

"I don't like whiners."

"I'm sorry, Miss Parsons. You want my name?"

"No, you seem to have learned your lesson. The next time I call, I trust I'll be treated much better."

"Yes, Miss Parsons."

She sat in the awful, lingering silence of her den.

Where the hell was Rossetti?

Excerpt from Marilyn Monroe's personal tapes

I don't handle Christmas Eves very well. I always drink more than I should and I cause a scene sometimes.

I'm thinking of four years ago, at this producer's house in Brentwood.

The man and his much-younger wife had a seven-month-old baby. Everybody was taken up to the nursery to see it.

When I looked down in the baby's bed, I started crying. I'm not even sure why. I was just suddenly overwhelmed by the sight of the child. By how innocent and sweet and pure she looked.

The mother gave me a very funny stare. I was drunk but I didn't think I was that drunk. She seemed relieved when her husband led me out of the room.

Downstairs, I kept drinking. Just couldn't stop.

And then I found myself back up in the baby's room. Didn't even remember going up there.

But there I was, sitting in the rocking chair the mother used when she breast-fed her little daughter. . . . There I was in the same chair with the baby in my arms.

I didn't mean any harm. I was just rocking her and singing a lullaby and the mother came in and got hysterical. Started screaming.

Her husband came in and snatched the baby from me and then the wife started slapping me.

I kind of blacked out. She was slapping me real hard. Then one of her friends was pulling her back.

"I don't want that lush to ever touch my daughter again! I want her out of my house right now!"

I remember I had a hard time standing up, because I really was pretty drunk and because she'd hit me so hard that I'd teared up and couldn't see very well.

Somebody—I don't know who—helped me get downstairs where a chauffeur was waiting.

God, I can remember how everybody looked at me. Like I was some kind of pervert.

I just wanted to hold that baby.

HOOVER Clyde Tolson sat at his desk at home and picked up the ringing phone. It was his private line.

"Yes, Edgar?"

"Clyde, I'm scared."

"Maybe things will work out."

"You know better than that."

"There's at least a good chance they will."

"Why don't you come over to my office? We'll have a drink."

"I don't want a drink. I've got a stack of paperwork here."

"Maybe we should fly out there. Maybe we can help."

"To L.A.? It's too late. Whatever's going to happen is going to happen."

"I don't like that attitude, Clyde."

"I don't either, but right now that's the only attitude we can have. We'll just have to wait and see."

"I hate waiting."

"There isn't a choice."

"Clyde. I'd really appreciate it if, as my best friend, you'd come and have a drink with me."

"For Christ's sake—"

"You know I don't like blasphemy. Just one drink."

"All right. One drink."

"If you had to bet, which way do you think it'll come out?"

"Fifty-fifty. Melanie is a psychopath, Edgar. You knew that when you sent her out."

"I think she'll be fine."

"I'll be over right away, Edgar."

"Good boy."

S A R A Three blocks from the hotel was a Hertz office. Michael emerged jangling a set of keys to a green Pontiac sedan.

Shutting her door, Sara said, "We need to call her. I saw a phone booth a block down."

He pulled out of the parking lot in three violent jerks.

The evening traffic had started. Moving a single block took eight minutes.

"We'll take Laura out for dinner tonight," Sara said vacantly, as if talking in her sleep. "It'll be just the three of us."

He found the phone booth and pulled in.

When he got out, Michael saw that a young man with a beard had slipped into the booth first.

For the next four minutes, Michael paced while the young man went through a symphony of facial expressions. Then, abruptly, he kicked the door open and stomped out, cursing.

Michael dove into the booth, closed the door, took the piece of paper with the phone number on it from his shirt pocket, and splashed his coins on the small metal ledge.

He dropped a dime in the slot with trembling fingers. He carefully dialed the number.

The line was busy.

"Sonofabitch," Michael said.

He immediately hung up, scooped his dime from the coin return and inserted it again.

He must have dialed the wrong number.

Kidnappers were supposed to keep their lines clear at all times.
Busy again.
Shit.
Again.
And again. . . .

MELANIE She knelt next to Laura.

Laura smelled pretty bad. Not only from the blood, but she'd peed on herself.

Melanie had once kept a wounded guy she was torturing six days in a garage. Gangrene set in. The guy smelled so bad Melanie gagged when she got near him. But she got her information, and when she was finished with the guy she cut him up into fourteen chunks, put the chunks in a dark plastic bag, and rowed the bag out to the middle of the river and dropped it over the side. Mr. Hoover had been very happy about the information that Melanie had obtained, but suspicious when she told him that she hadn't used excessive force on the guy. The man's body was never found.

Suddenly, Melanie noticed something. Laura wasn't moving. She shook her gently, as she had before, trying to wake her.

But the little girl did not move at all.

Melanie leaned forward, trying to hear if Laura was breathing. Nothing.

She put her thumb to Laura's wrist, felt for a pulse. Nothing.

She slowly set Laura's skinny arm down.

Ten-year-old Laura Drury was dead.

Excerpt from
Marilyn Monroe's
personal tapes

One night I miscarried and I wouldn't let the guy I was with clean it up. I was pretty drunk and taking a lot of pills and when I felt myself getting sick and losing the baby, I started crying real hard and I put my hands in the mess I'd made on the bed and I felt that there was this ghost of a baby, my baby, in the room. The guy, who was a contract actor at Warners, finally hit me and knocked me out. When I woke up, my doctor was there. I guess I owed the actor a favor but for some reason I never wanted to see or talk to him again. I guess I always associated him with losing my baby.

HOOVER

J. Edgar Hoover sat in his office doing deep-breathing exercises.

He had recently seen a TV show in which a psychologist said that the best way to forestall panic was to close your eyes, begin inhaling deeply, and exhaling slowly.

Impulsively, J. Edgar Hoover, Director of the Federal Bureau of Investigation and one of the world's most respected men, jabbed his finger down on his intercom.

"Any calls for me from California?"

A frustrated sigh. "No, Mr. Hoover. Not since you asked me three minutes ago."

"You didn't leave your desk?"

"No, Mr. Hoover."

"Very well," Hoover said gruffly. "Carry on."

Breathe in.

Slowly exhale.

Why the fuck hadn't he heard from Melanie?

Think about being with Clyde on the Colorado river, fishing on a warm summer morning.

She could be so goddamned irresponsible, Melanie could.

Gently breathe in.

Gently breathe out.

He stabbed the intercom button. "I'm expecting a call from California. I want it put through the moment it comes in."

"Yessir. I've written that down, sir."

How could Melanie do this to him?

MELANIE Getting the dead girl rolled up in a small rug and loaded into the trunk took five sweaty minutes.

She had to move fast so nobody from the highway would see, and carefully so she wouldn't get blood all over her. She'd saturated a bath towel with blood.

Some time ago, the phone had started ringing.

It would either be the dead girl's parents or Hoover.

Either way, she wasn't going to answer. She had taken it off the hook.

The drive to the woods took fifteen minutes. She followed asphalt roads till she found an area that plunged down to a deep ravine.

She wheeled the car off the road and drove deep into the woods, stopping when the trees got too thick. She got out and went over to the edge of the ravine and looked down. A narrow blue creek ran through the bottom. There was maybe a mile of timber here, cedars and spruce and hemlock.

She spent ten minutes checking out the nearby land, making sure that nobody was around.

She took the shovel from the back seat and went half way down the ravine and started digging.

Her hands blistered immediately. For all her expertise with the martial arts, she had the palms of a princess.

And then there were the Bluebirds.

She didn't even hear them till they were right at the edge of the ravine, cute little girls in their cute little Bluebird uniforms led by some birdy middle-aged woman with a whistle that tweeted every few minutes.

Melanie dropped to the ground and lay flat.

They wouldn't be able to see anything unless they came right down here.

"Girls," the leader said, "let's go on up the road there to the water fountain and fill our canteens."

And they took off.

She waited a few minutes to make sure and then pushed himself to her feet.

Had to hurry now. Finish. Get out of here.

She picked up the shovel and fitted it into her bloody hands and started shoveling again.

Twenty minutes later, she went back to her car, and took the dead girl out of the trunk and carried her quickly over to the ravine and down to the shallow grave.

She began shoveling dirt onto Laura's sweet, dead, rug-covered body.

S A R A They found a restaurant nearby. They ordered only Cokes. There was no way Sara could eat. The place was mock-Italian, with Chianti bottles holding candles on red-and-white-checkered tablecloths.

The phone was ten feet from their booth.

Every couple of minutes, Michael put down his cigarette and went to the phone.

It continued to be busy.

Something had gone wrong.

Returning to the booth, he said, "Maybe she wants us to keep calling."

"Laura's dead."

"Sara. Listen to me. The woman doesn't have any reason to kill her. She has every reason to keep her alive."

"I'm just so scared." Her eyes filled with tears. "Maybe you should try again."

"Right."

They had been in the restaurant for nearly an hour now.

"Hello," a woman's voice said.

"This is Michael Drury!" he spouted with relief.

"I've been waiting for your call."

"I've been trying to get through for the past hour."

"What about the tapes?"

"We want our daughter."

"You know the deal, Mr. Drury."

"We have the tapes."

There was a pause. "You'd know better than to lead any policemen here, wouldn't you?"

"Of course. All we want is our daughter. We don't care about anything else."

"Write this down." She sounded young, bright, confident.

"Just a second," he said. He wrestled out his small notepad and pen.

"All right," Michael said.

"Here's the address."

Michael wrote it down.

"I'll give you an hour and a half to get here."

"I want to speak to my daughter."

"You'll see her soon enough. She's fine."

The woman hung up.

He walked back to Sara, took her hand and together, in an eager panic, they scurried back out into the clamor of the fading day.

ROSSETTI

He was on the way to his private club, in the massive black Cadillac that his employees kept so shiny and fine, when the phone signalled. He reached to the dashboard and picked it up. He always drove himself. Chauffeurs made him uncomfortable. Having chauffeurs suggested that you worked for the Mob. Except for movie stars and an occasional tycoon, the only people who had chauffeurs were mobsters.

Nobody ever called him on the car phone, except with an emergency. So this would not be good news.

It was Karla, the efficient secretary.

"Have you been listening to the radio?"

"No, I haven't, Karla. Why?"

"Your friend, Mr. Mayhew."

His chest tightened.

"What about him?"

"He had some kind of accident. At least they're calling it an accident. Apparently he fell from a veranda at the Fenwick. Seventeen stories."

"Oh, Christ."

"He's dead, of course. I figured you'd want to know since you two called each other so much lately. Should I send flowers to his home?"

"Please. That would be nice."

Of course it was no accident. Somebody had gotten to Mayhew.

And now somebody would try to get to Rossetti.

He drove for a while in stunned confusion, missing his exit ramp and not even noticing it for eighteen miles.

His superiors had counted on him, and now that he had failed, they would punish him. A quick death did not frighten him. Death was darkness and nothing more. But he hoped they would not torture him because then he might die without dignity. He feared he would beg and sob and foul himself the way he had seen other men do when their deaths were long and painful.

Kill me quickly. Let me have my pride.

He decided not to wait for his superiors to come to him. He would go to them.

At the next off-ramp he came around and back in the direction of downtown Los Angeles.

He lifted the phone receiver. There was someone he needed to call before he spoke with the godfather. She was one more person he had let down.

SARA She saw the house from the highway. Against the backdrop of ocean and darkening sky, the place looked lonely. Somewhere inside was Laura.

"You want to hand me the gun?"

This time she didn't protest. If killing somebody was the price for getting Laura back, so be it. She took it from the glove compartment and set it on the seat beside Michael.

He veered left on the road leading to the house. He went all the way to the end of the road and pulled up beside the garage.

"I don't see any lights," Sara said.

"She said to go to the back door," Michael said.

They got out.

There was a car in the garage.

They started up the creaking stairs to the back door.

He knocked. He knocked again.

"I just want to go in there and get her," Sara whispered. "Why isn't she answering?"

He knocked a third time.

He tried the doorknob. Locked.

The stairs creaked.

"Michael," Sara hissed.

Up the stairs came a sleek red-haired woman, not much over twenty. The gun looked silly in her hand, a young girl playing at an adult's game.

"Hi," the woman said brightly. "You must be Laura's parents."

"Where is she?" Sara said.

"Gosh, why don't you relax a little? We'll talk about Laura in a minute. But right now I want you two to stand about three feet apart."

"What?" Sara said.

"I speak plain English, Mrs. Drury. I want you to stand three feet apart."

Sara and Michael parted.

"That's fine."

She came over to them cautiously, keeping the gun aimed at Michael.

She patted him down efficiently. She had no trouble finding his weapon.

She stuffed his gun in the waist of her skirt.

She moved to Sara. "You're very pretty."

Sara swallowed hard, controlling her desperation.

"Laura got your looks. She's lucky."

The young woman's hands felt obscene on Sara's body. Pat, pat, pat. Looking for weapons. But lingering, too.

"I take it the tapes are in your car."

"Where's our daughter?" Sara said. "We want our daughter first, at least to see her."

"I'm the one holding the gun, Mrs. Drury."

Melanie took a quick step toward Michael, grabbed him by the back of his neck and pulled his head down while she brought her knee up into his face.

Michael's nose dripped blood.

She drove her knee up between Michael's legs.

He sagged to his knees and doubled over.

Sara lunged toward her but Melanie stopped her with the gun in her face. "I'll kill you and your husband right here, unless you give me the tapes."

"Don't do it, Sara," Michael said from the floor.

"You're smarter than that, Mrs. Drury. Go get the tapes."

Sara nodded and set off down the stairs.

On the way down, Sara tried to figure out a way to take the woman's gun away when she returned.

Only when they had disarmed her were they going to find their daughter.

Something was in the garage, scuffling around.

She hesitated, listening, then continued to their car.

She reached into the glove compartment, took out the manilla envelope, and closed the car door.

A woman stepped out from the shadows at the rear of the garage, holding a gun and putting a *shush*ing finger to her lips. When she came forward, she limped on her right leg, as if crippled.

The woman leaned in close. She wore a blue windbreaker and jeans. Sara assumed that the woman had parked her car somewhere up the highway and had snuck back here.

"I'm going to help you," the woman said. "My name's Vanessa Tully. That woman killed my husband. Just wait here and be quiet."

Vanessa Tully went over to the stairs and started climbing them in her awkward way.

MELANIE Everything was going to work out fine. In a few moments, she would have the tapes and be gone. Mr. Hoover would be happy. They wouldn't find Laura for years, if ever. Europe would be fun.

She looked down at Drury.

She should give him an extra kick in the groin just for existing. She hated handsome men.

One extra kick.

No harm in that.

She kicked him.

MICHAEL

For Michael, there was just the slow roll of tide and the breeze from the ocean.

And the pain.

Then, without any warning, the woman stomped on his balls a second time.

He heard himself yowl. He was just a trembling animal now—afraid of the pain and afraid he would die.

And then he saw the other woman, sneaking up the stairs.

A slender, limping woman, with a gun.

The redhead had her back to the top of the stairs, enjoying the misery she had inflicted on him.

The second woman, now on the porch, said, "Turn around slowly and put the guns on the railing. Yours and Mr. Drury's."

Melanie hesitated, her shoulders hunched in surprise. The other woman took a couple of steps closer and put the pistol against the back of Melanie's head.

"The guns, Melanie."

She reluctantly obliged.

"Now turn around and face me."

Michael crawled over to the porch railing and hauled himself to his feet.

"Where's the little girl?" Vanessa asked Melanie.

"In the house."

Sara appeared at the top of the stairs. She walked past Vanessa, Melanie, and Michael, straight to the back door. Michael joined her.

"Give them the key," Vanessa said.

Melanie took out a key and handed it over to Sara.

The Drurys went inside. They searched the house.

"Laura! Laura!"

Their voices came back to them in awful echoes.

In one of the bedrooms, Michael found the rope that had been used to tie Laura up. In the living room, Sara found blotches of blood that had soaked into the couch. In the bathroom, Michael found a towel that had been used to soak up blood.

In the front closet, Sara found bullet holes and blood spots on the walls.

"In here!" she called.

Michael knew he was going to see something he did not want to see.

VANESSA

Vanessa couldn't help herself. She smacked Melanie on the mouth with the butt of her gun.

"What did you do with their little girl?"

"She's in there," Melanie said through bloody lips.

"You're lying." Vanessa smiled icily. "Tell me the truth, Melanie, or I'll kill you. Where is their little girl?"

She hit Melanie even harder this time and at long, long last Melanie told her the truth.

MICHAEL Michael peered into the closet. Six bullet holes. And a hint of gunsmoke odor in the air.

"She killed her, didn't she?" Sara said.

He took her in his arms and let her sob into his shoulder.

MELANIE Melanie looked at Vanessa and grinned. "It's too late, you may know where Laura is but it's too late."

Vanessa shouted for Sara and Michael to come out of the house.

A decade of martial arts training had not been in vain. With the speed and precision of a ninja, Melanie ripped the gun from Vanessa's hand.

Then Melanie jumped on her.

VANESSA Vanessa fought back. She heaved herself forward, slamming Melanie back against the porch railing. The old wood cracked and they both plummeted to the sand below.

The gun flew out of Melanie's hand.

Vanessa scrambled to get it.

Melanie tackled Vanessa and threw her down.

By the time Michael and Sara were on the porch to see, Melanie stood with her back to the house, holding the gun on Vanessa.

"You'll be sorry you ever found me," she said.

"You killed my husband."

"Was that such a loss?" Melanie smiled.

Vanessa was raving. "He was my husband and he loved me!"

Melanie put two bullets in Vanessa's belly and one in her chest.

Vanessa slumped to the sand.

At the same instant, Michael leaped from the porch onto Melanie's back, throwing punches as he wrapped himself around her.

Melanie was incredibly strong. She took Michael for a bronco ride down the beach, trying to throw him off her back. Finally she fell and Michael was pitched over her head.

Michael got to his feet while Melanie was still on her knees. She was raising her gun when he kicked it from her hand. It tumbled into the scrub growth.

Michael dove after it, found it, and whirled around.

Melanie came sailing at him.

Reflexively he pulled the trigger.

The bullet exploded Melanie's heart.

"No," he said, realizing what he'd done. "No, no!"

He leaped at the dying woman as she fell over on her back.

Michael started slapping her face back and forth.

"Where is my daughter, you bitch?"

Blood spread across Melanie's chest.

Sara dropped to her knees next to Michael. She gently touched his arm and said, "There's no use."

"Dead?" Michael shook his head. "She can't be dead."

He grabbed Melanie by her blouse, pulled her up and shook her violently.

"What did you do with our daughter!"

Gradually he calmed down, letting Melanie slide to the sand.

"Let's go, honey," Sara said.

"I didn't mean to kill her. I wanted to tell you about Laura." He sounded insane.

"I know," she said, helping him to his feet.

MELANIE

At first there was just blackness. It was very cold. Melanie was afraid. She felt vulnerable, the way she'd felt when she was five.

There was no more pain. But there was terror. Oh, yes.

It was freezing. She felt herself shivering. She wished there were some light, even faint starlight. It was like being submerged in dark, deep water.

And then she saw her.

Just ahead.

Walking down a long white tunnel.

Calling her name. Beckoning.

Jessica.

"I love you, Jessica! I love you!" Melanie cried out.

And Jessica kept walking toward her.

Smiling now.

MICHAEL The pain from Melanie's first assault was worse when his senses returned, and it took them a long time to reach the beach house.

"We'll find her," Sara kept saying. "We'll find her."

The sound of the waves obscured Vanessa Tully's moaning as they passed her, and they almost didn't hear her.

But Sara heard, and steered them over to her.

"She's dead," Michael said.

"Maybe not."

Sara dropped to her knees and put her head close to Vanessa's face. Moonlight gave Vanessa's face a ghostly pallor.

"Vanessa."

No movement. But then a slight moan.

"We're going to get an ambulance for you, Vanessa," Sara said. "Can you hear me?"

Vanessa's eyes flickered.

"Did she tell you where our daughter is?"

Vanessa was able to tell them in a halting, whispered fashion. Then her trembling hand reached out in the sand. And beyond her stretched fingertips lay the envelope containing the tapes.

Right where Sara had dropped it.

Sara kissed Vanessa on the forehead, then took her hand as the woman crossed over into death.

Michael went to the beach house, called for an ambulance, and gave a quick rundown to the police. Then he went downstairs to the garage.

Inside Melanie's car, on the floor of the back seat, he found a small spade. He touched the dirt-caked edge of the metal. The dirt was moist.

Taylor Park, Vanessa had told them. Michael stared at the fresh dirt. A terrible conclusion suggested itself. Laura had been killed and buried.

L O U E L L A "Telephone, ma'am. It's Mr. Rossetti."
"Oh, thank you." She'd had more to drink than
she'd intended and had fallen asleep in the armchair in her den. She
had given up trying to find Rossetti.

At last. She'd be able to call that little prick Gibbons and rub his
face in it.

She got up from the armchair with difficulty and tottered to her
desk phone. "I hope you know how hard I've been looking for you,
love."

"Louella, it's bad news."

"What're you talking about?"

"I didn't make my connection."

"You don't have the tapes?"

"No."

"And you won't be getting them?"

"I'm sorry, Louella."

"But I've already told the newspaper—"

"You shouldn't have done that."

"But what could possibly have gone wrong? You sounded so sure
about it."

"The source fell through. That's all. I'm sorry."

He hung up.

She sat for a long time next to the phone, the famous Louella
Parsons, who would now have to endure Gibbons' humiliation.

No tapes. No boxed column, photo inside, carried on the front pages of the biggest dailies in America. Nothing.

A very old woman now, lost in her loneliness, she began to cry.

When she was finished crying, she called Gibbons and told him. He was every bit the sneering prick she thought he'd be.

LAURA

Darkness. Nightmare.

She was in her room and it was so dark that not even moonlight peeked through the curtain. And something in her sleep had scared her. Maybe it was the cute little dog that turned into the hissing, lashing snake. The nightmare she had so often.

Darkness. And she hurt.

But this was not her room. This was . . . somewhere else.

Dirt. Taste of—dirt!

And then she remembered.

The terrible woman. Her melting ice cream. Banging her head against the wall. Hiding in the closet. Then gunshots. Rocking, trying to escape them.

And then—

The woman wrapping her in a blanket or something and packing her in the car.

And then—

The piney air of a forest. She loved forests.

And then—

She was being pushed down into a hole in the ground. Unable to talk. Something clanking. Feeling pressure, weight on her. And dirt hitting her face. . . .

All the while trying to scream. But nothing came out.

Then all the light went out, and she was breathing dirt.

Just darkness now—heavy, black.
And she couldn't breathe.
Mommy. Please come and get me, Mommy.
Darkness.

SARA The cops beat them to Taylor Park, three squad cars with cherries blazing into the blackness, splashing six officers in crisp dark uniforms with their red flashing lights.

The police fanned out, beginning their slow walk through the forest, flashlights probing, looking for any sign of a young girl.

In the eerie light, the woods looked unreal, the trees like props on a movie set.

They parked and Sara got out. A tall uniformed man came over to them. "You're Mrs. Drury? I'm Sergeant Winthrop, LAPD."

"Has there been any sign of her?" Sara asked.

"Not yet, ma'am."

"We'd like to go into the woods, too," Sara said. "To search."

"No problem," the sergeant said, "just so long as you don't interfere with the officers."

As if being summoned by a voice, Sara started walking along one of the trails that would lead her into the dark woods.

LAURA

She remembered something she wished had stayed forgotten.

In science class, she'd learned that in a small, closed place, when the oxygen was used up, the person suffocated and died.

She was using up all her oxygen.

There couldn't be much left. This was such a tiny place; she was wrapped in so tight, with so much heavy weight on her. She couldn't move any part of her body.

Suffocation. And death.

Mommy. Please. Can't you hear me?

Just darkness, deeper than any night she'd known.

S A R A She was just starting down the gully, trying to keep her footing on the rough slanting earth, when she sensed somebody behind her, and then saw the arrow of a flashlight beam.

"I thought I'd help you."

She couldn't believe it. David Lenihan, the man from Washington.

"What are you doing?"

"I want to find your daughter. It matters to me, Mrs. Drury. Believe it or not."

"You're a strange man, Mr. Lenihan. I don't know whether you're good or bad."

"That's the hell of it, isn't it? I don't know, either. Let's just find your little girl."

COP The rookie's name was Runyon. Red hair. Freckles. Pug nose. Six months a cop.

Runyon flashed his light around. Ground was dry but spongy with moss. People had no respect for forest land. Busted bottles and empty cigarette packs and used rubbers and even a few pages of nudie magazines in here. Lot of twisted people in this world, who ought to be—

His light flashed over something to the right of a massive hemlock. He caught it in the beam.

He broke into a run, yelling, "Hey, over here! Over here!"

MICHAEL

Michael heard the cop just over the rise. Clutching his flashlight, he set off running into the thick undergrowth.

Pine branches slashed his face, but he didn't feel them.

Laura had been found.

He came upon several young cops standing over something white in the brush. Everything was dark except for where the beam of the cop's flashlight shone.

Something white. Still.

Michael stopped.

"Aw, shit, Runyon," said an older, heavier cop crouched in front of the rookie. "Just a friggin' sheet, all rotted. It ain't your fault."

"Well, I'm sorry anyway."

Just then Sara's scream pierced the dark woods.

SARA Laura was down there, Sara knew it. She could see the freshly turned earth.

Placing her newly borrowed flashlight beside the mound of dirt, she fell to her knees and dug with both hands.

"Hold on!" she shouted. "Hold on, Laura!"

Lenihan dropped to his knees on the other side of the makeshift grave and began to dig. And to call out to her. "We're almost there, Dulcie! Don't worry!"

Even in her frenzy, Sara realized that Dulcie must be the name of Lenihan's dead daughter.

$$M I C H A E L$$ Michael thought Sara was hurt when he first heard her scream. But when he saw her digging, he ran to her side and joined in.

A cop fell to his knees and helped. Another cop held two lights aloft and trained them on the grave.

Then, faintly, it came: a sound like bursts of a high-pitched hum.

"Laura!" Sara cried. "Laura!"

Less than two minutes later, Sara and Michael Drury held their dirty and frightened, sobbing and gasping daughter in their arms.

"The friggin' rug saved her," said the sergeant, shaking his head as tears rolled down his face. "It trapped a pocket of air and let her breathe."

S A R A The ambulance bearing Laura and Michael left for the hospital.

Sara was in the back seat of a squad car, still parked at the woods. For all the blood on Laura's arms and chest, her gunshot wound was superficial. While the extent of Laura's psychological trauma was still unknown, physically she was stable.

Sara had desperately wanted to go with the ambulance, but the white-haired detective named Robbins, seated beside her, had forced her to remain. He insisted repeatedly that she had to tell him everything, that her recollection of the details was "a matter of the greatest urgency." He wanted to know everything about the case from the time Bellamy came to the office and told her about the combination to the safe.

Rain had begun to fall, sparkling the windshield. Detective Robbins turned on the wipers.

Dazed, Sara had told Detective Robbins everything she knew.

"But you don't know what was on the tapes?"

"No. Just something worth money and lives."

A knock on the driver's window.

"Call for Detective Robbins from the commissioner," said a cop to the driver.

Robbins waved his acknowledgment. "We have a direct line in the police van over there. Excuse me for a few minutes."

Sara laid her head back against the seat.

All human noise was distant and forgotten. Just the soothing rain and the rhythm of the wipers.

Sara closed her eyes and dozed. When she opened them, Lenihan was sitting beside her.

"Hi," he said.

"Hi." She smiled. "Thanks for helping me with Laura."

"My privilege."

"I know why you helped me, Mr. Lenihan. Your daughter, I mean. I'm sorry you lost her. I also know that you're with Washington and that you want the tapes."

"All that's true."

"I know. I want you to have them. I certainly never wanted them."

Lenihan's relief was palpable. "Can I do anything for you?"

Sara smiled. For the first time in days.

"You can tell me what's on them."

"I'm afraid I can't."

Sara sat up. Pawed sleep from her face.

"There's a plane leaving in one hour and ten minutes, Mrs. Drury. In order to make it, I need to leave right now."

She took the envelope from her jacket pocket and handed it to him.

"I'm sorry about your daughter, Mr. Lenihan. I'm sure you loved her very much."

She reached across the seat and grasped his hand.

"Good-bye, Mrs. Drury. I hope things go well with the three of you." The sorrow had returned to his eyes and voice. He stuffed the tapes into the pocket of his Burberry coat. "Thanks."

He stepped into the rain and the night and was gone.

TOLSON

Tolson knocked on Edgar's door.

Edgar sat behind his desk in his private office: as usual, with his jacket on, his hair perfectly combed, as if posing for an official picture.

Clyde closed the door behind him. "Friend of mine from the LAPD called. They've got a positive ID on a body."

"Melanie?"

Clyde nodded.

"Sonofabitch."

Edgar suddenly looked old and frail. Clyde felt sad. Both of the men knew that what had been at stake here was far more important than the tapes; it was their power and their future.

"Sonofabitch." Only a whisper now.

"Why don't you have a drink, Edgar?"

"No, thanks."

"There'll be other ways to get Jack Kennedy. This is just a setback."

Edgar looked up at him. "They aren't afraid of us any more, Clyde. Not the way they used to be. Those tapes would have brought us back."

Clyde started to speak but stopped himself. Why lie any more? Edgar was right. The tapes had been vital to sustaining the kind of power—and fear—that Edgar and Clyde had for so long enjoyed.

"Well, if you're not going to have a drink, I am."

He went over to the concealed bar and poured a Scotch.

He carried the drink to the window and looked out on Washington.

"We've still got a lot of good years ahead of us, Edgar."

"No, we don't and you know it. They're going to get us soon enough. All those bastards."

Clyde looked down at Edgar. Uncomfortably, he put a hand on Edgar's shoulder.

"We'll go fishing, Edgar, and say 'fuck you' to all of them."

But Edgar was neither watching nor listening. He was somewhere else.

Clyde finished his drink, put his glass back on the bar, and left the office.

There were times when Edgar needed to be alone, and this was one of them.

Clyde would have to be strong for both of them, just as he'd been so many times over so many, many years.

LENIHAN At L.A. International Airport, David Lenihan made the call that John Fitzgerald Kennedy, thirty-fifth president of the United States, had been anxiously awaiting.

The number was private, known by only three people in the world.

"It's done," Lenihan said.

"You got them?"

"I got them."

"Oh, David . . . David. You saved our ass. Bless you, my son." He laughed. He was a charming bastard, JFK was, no doubt about it.

"I'm on my way back."

"I'll have champagne waiting."

Lenihan had wondered if he'd actually have nerve enough to say it. He hesitated and then spoke. "Jack, a little girl was almost killed because of this."

"I'm sorry, David. You know I wouldn't—"

"I'm not going to clean up any more of your messes. Do my regular job, fine. But no more of your private scrapes. You're jeopardizing the whole country. Do we understand each other, Jack?"

Lenihan had known how Jack would react. Icy silence. Nobody talked to Jack Kennedy that way.

Finally: "We'll talk when you get back."

John Fitzgerald Kennedy hung up.

For a moment, David Lenihan felt a spasm of remorse. He would never again be in Jack Kennedy's innermost circle.

But then he smiled. He didn't want to be in Jack Kennedy's innermost circle anyway.

He picked up his luggage and walked toward the gate.

S A R A

Laura yawned. "I'm kind of sleepy, Mommy."

She smiled. "I know. It's eleven-fifteen at night."

"We'll be here in the morning when you wake up," Michael said, leaning over the hospital bed and kissing Laura on the forehead.

The doctors had wrapped her shoulder wound in gauze, stitched her facial lacerations, and taped a badly gouged knee. She looked like a war veteran.

The rain streaked the window with silver drops. Outside, it was dark, but this night was not scary.

After she was asleep, Sara said, "She looks so beautiful in her bed." Tears filled her eyes and her throat got raspy. "I love her so much, Michael, I can't tell you."

He took her to him, but as she came into his arms, she knew it was gone: that brief troubled intimacy that had been theirs again over the fear of losing Laura. They were distant again.

"I'd better tell you," Michael said. "Kathryn is waiting for me downstairs."

She smiled. "I figured that."

"I'm sorry."

"No reason to be," Sara said, feeling lonelier than she could ever remember. "You've got your life now, and I've got mine."

He left, and Sara sat alone by her daughter's bedside.

Suddenly, Jeff appeared in the doorway. He came into the room and sat down.

346   E. J. GORMAN

"I saw Michael leave. Can I sit here awhile?"

"Sure."

For a while they sat and said nothing. She was comfortable enough with Jeff not to talk. Then Sara slept. For the first time in years—in decades, it seemed—her sleep was dreamless and profound. She knew now that everything would work out. There would still be pain and doubt and memories, but she was free now of Michael's shadow. Free.

She slept.

And in the morning when she awoke, she saw Jeff coming through the door with orange juice for Laura and coffee for Sara.

Excerpt from Marilyn Monroe's personal tapes

I remember the first time I ever went into a movie theater to see myself on the screen. It was a wonderful experience for me because I realized that I didn't have to be Norma Jean any more—so unhappy and insecure and afraid. Now I could be Marilyn Monroe, who looked so radiant and happy and content, and nobody would ever know that I was really still Norma Jean. As time went on, I started seeing Marilyn as somebody separate from me—like an older sister who lived an exotic life in Europe or somewhere romantic, somebody that Norma Jean aspired to be someday. That's what I'd do when I got very depressed sometimes, I'd disguise myself and slip into a theater and watch myself be transformed into somebody who was fifteen feet tall and was the happiest person on earth.

In writing this novel, the following books were used as principal reference material:

J. Edgar Hoover, The Man and the Secrets. Curt Gentry. Norton, 1991

Inside Hoover's FBI. Neil J. Welch and David W. Marston, Doubleday, 1984

With Kennedy. Pierre Salinger. Doubleday, 1966

Little Man, Meyer Lansky and the Gangster Life. Robert Lacey. Little Brown, 1991

My Twelve Years with John F. Kennedy. Evelyn Lincoln. David McKay, 1965

Kennedy and Johnson. Evelyn Lincoln. Holt, Rinehart, Winston, 1968

The Texas Connection. Craig I. Zirbel. Warner Books, 1991

Goddess, The Secret Lives of Marilyn Monroe. Anthony Summers. MacMillan, 1986

Norma Jean, My Secret Life with Marilyn Monroe. Ted Jordan. William Morrow, 1989

The Marilyn Scandal. Sandra Shevey. William Morrow, 1988

Donovan of Oss. Corey Ford. Little Brown, 1970

City of Nets. Otto Freidrich. Harper and Row, 1986

Marilyn and Me. Susan Strasberg. Warner Books, 1992

Hedda and Louella. George Eels. Putnam, 1972

The Secret and Confidential Life of J. Edgar Hoover. Anthony Summers. Putnam, 1992

Life with Rose Kennedy. Barbara Gibson. Warner Books, 1986

Architectural Digest Celebrity Homes. Viking Press, 1977

J. Edgar Hoover: The Man in His Time. Ralph de Toledano. Arlington House, 1973

The Kennedy Years. Viking Press-*The New York Times,* 1964

Marilyn's Men. Jane Ellen Wayne. St. Martin's Press, 1992

Marilyn: Her Life from A to Z. Randall Riese and Neal Hitchens. Corydon, Weed, 1987

Marilyn: Norma Jean. Text by Gloria Steinem, photographs by George Barris. Henry Holt, 1986

I would also like to acknowledge the work of Sue Grover, who spent many hours in the Los Angeles Public Library finding information on the L.A. of the early sixties; the staff of the Cedar Rapids Public Library, who put up with months of my daily requests; Don Cole, who helped me with details of 1950s Omaha; Natalie Kleis of the Cedar Rapids Fire Department, who helped me understand burns and the process of suffocation; Dr. Tracy Knight, for his help with all the psychiatric portions of this book; Matthew Bialer for one supremely important suggestion; and my wonderful wife Carol, whose suggestions and encouragement kept me going through the ten months of writing.